Revenge

Other Victor McCain Thrillers

The Hand of God

The Watchers

The Speaker

Revenge

A Victor McCain Thriller
By
Tony Acree

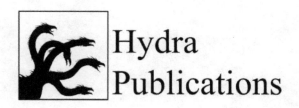

Hydra
Publications

Printed in the United States of America

ISBN-13: 978-1-942212-31-7

Cover by Karri Klawiter

Hydra Publications
Goshen, KY 40026

www.hydrapublications.com

Dedication

In memory of:

Hugh Blair
Sarah McNeal Few
Jim Fulks
Dick Root

CHAPTER ONE

Ruth Anne was going to die before the day was over. Kurt was sure of it. For about the millionth time, he fingered the ring in his pocket and daydreamed about the moment he would go down on one knee, say the magic words, and then slip the ring on her finger.

She'd been after him for months now about getting married and he knew she would keel over from excitement when he proposed. You could hardly find a space in their home which didn't have a *Brides* magazine somewhere within reach. He would sit down at his computer only to find an open browser windows featuring sites where you register for wedding gifts. Ruth Anne could be as subtle as a sledgehammer.

Kurt knew he should have proposed sooner, but he wasn't sure he had it in him. After all, less than a year ago if he so much as looked at a woman, he'd break out in a sweat. If one spoke to him, he'd break out into hives. He still walked around with Benadryl in his pocket—just in case. Being with Ruth Anne had changed his life and made him feel more confident, like a real man. But the "old Kurt" still hid behind a wall deep inside him ready to pop out at the first sign of anxiety.

He thought about how they'd met in Hawaii: she was possessed by a fallen angel who was controlling her body, and had buried him alive to try to pull information from him, and then attempted to drown him when he wouldn't talk...how many couples claimed to start out a relationship like that? Not even Romeo and Juliet compared to their story.

Victor and Samantha came close, but they were no longer a couple, not since Vic shot her and then helped to kill her dad. Kind of a downer when it came to relationships. What kind of card do you buy for that? Hallmark claimed to have a card for all occasions, but Kurt doubted any cards covered blowing someone up—in sympathy.

But they'd be different. Once the bad angel was forced to leave Ruth Anne's body, they had bonded over the shared experience. One of the Watchers also killed her mom and brother, leaving her with no family. Now he was all she had left. Maybe one day they'd have kids. He swallowed hard and forced the thought away. One step at a time, Hot Shot.

The hair dryer shut off in the bathroom. He pulled his hand out of his pocket to stop playing with the ring and forced himself to look casual. He went back to work on a new "worm" he planned on inserting into the system of the Church of the Light Reclaimed, a group of nut-bag Satanists with whom Victor and the rest of the gang were at war. His job, along with a group of other hackers, was to disrupt their operations and make it harder for them to survive in cyberspace.

Ruth Anne stuck her head into the room. Her long blonde hair gleamed and fell about her shoulders. She came in, sat on his lap, wrapped her arms around his neck and kissed him. A former University of Kentucky cheerleader, she had the kind of body that made men drool. Dressed in a nice shirt and jeans, she was headed to work at the local Barnes and Noble store. She smelled of strawberry shampoo.

She broke the kiss first and asked, "What do you have planned for the rest of the day?"

"You're lookin' at it. Lots of Diet Dr. Pepper, a little Fireball Whisky and a whole lot of kickin' Satanist ass. Well, at least in cyberspace. I keep hoping Vic will let me in on another mission, but he says I have to finish more training before he'll let me join them. Kind of ticks me off."

She ruffled his light brown surfer boy hair and laughed. "Baby, Vic loves you like a brother and only wants to see to it you stay alive. And I, for one, love him for it."

For the past couple of months, Kurt had started taking Tae Kwon Do with Winston at Hwang's Martial Arts, along with weapons training at a shooting range. He knew he needed the training, but he itched for action. His brief taste of being on the front lines during a trip to Wisconsin where he took out a Black Hat hacker dude had him hooked.

"I know he does. But it's hard waiting. I want in and not just here," he said pointing at his computer.

"Your time is coming, big boy." She paused a beat, then asked, "Hey, since you're not going anywhere, can I drive the Mustang?"

The Mustang was another change in his lifestyle since meeting Ruth Anne. Previously, he drove a minivan, but when they got together, she refused to date a man driving one. She said it was totally uncool.

So one day he and Vic went car shopping and found a white Mustang with a blue stripe down the middle. He almost wrecked it the first time he took it out for a spin and really put his foot to the accelerator—the rear end fishtailing back and forth across the road. But he had to admit, he and Ruth Anne rocked in the vehicle when they were out on the town.

"Only if you promise not to dent it."

"You know I won't."

"So says the woman who backed her car into the basketball goal at the end of a friend's driveway, then scratched the side of her car pulling out of the garage: three times."

She slapped him playfully. "All right, smart ass. I'll be careful. Besides, you left your car out in the driveway, so I won't have to worry about the garage."

She kissed him one more time, then stood up and left the room. He watched her walk out, amazed at how lucky his life was. A few minutes later, he heard the front door open and then close. When the Mustang fired up and pulled out of the driveway, he thanked the good Lord above he didn't hear any crashes.

He'd already made reservations at seven p.m. for Ruth's Chris Steak House, Ruth Anne's favorite restaurant. He planned to go over later in the morning to drop off the ring with the maître d to get things ready. During dessert, the server would bring out cheesecake with the ring placed on top. Then he'd drop to one knee and ask her to spend the rest of her life with him.

He hoped.

The thought of proposing made his skin start to itch. He closed his eyes and practiced some deep breathing techniques, trying to bring his body under control.

Might be a good idea to have some of his Benadryl on hand, just in case.

CHAPTER TWO

I really hate the cold, especially when I have people following me who want to kill me. Over the summer, I royally pissed off Alex Dabney, the owner of Dabney Industrial Tech, and one of America's largest weapons manufacturers when I promised to hunt him down and kill him. Did I mention he also has a fallen angel riding shotgun in his brain telling him what to do and providing him with knowledge only the Divine know? Yeah. Makes a difference and it put a real damper on our relationship.

Dabney and I ran into each other in Philadelphia at a Democratic fundraiser. I was there trying to stop a madman from blowing up the President and Vice President of the United States when Dabney was there and I found out Gadriel, a fallen bad-ass angel, had taken possession of him. Because I needed to deal with the bomb, I couldn't afford to throw down with him in a public place until a later time. We both threatened to kill each other and we both meant it.

A few days after that encounter, he put out a contract to have me killed. A cool ten million dollars. Admittedly, I found the amount flattering, but when you're a billionaire, ten million dollars is a drop in the bucket.

I was working to find him first, but he caught a private jet out of the country to some exotic destination unknown. If I had to guess, he'd stay in hiding until someone got lucky and took me out. The problem for me was now there were those out there trying to collect on the paycheck of a lifetime—like the two bozos following me today.

I was trying to do a little Christmas shopping. That's when I picked up the tail while strolling the aisles at Target. I made them while looking at the holiday sales on TVs. The men couldn't have been more obvious trying *not* to be obvious, watching me while they pretended to shop the Christmas CD end cap. I'm sorry, but when you pretend to be engrossed in a Slim Whitman Christmas CD then I know you're up to no good.

When I got back to my red '69 Chevelle, I thought about trying to lose them, but then changed my mind. I needed some extra work to keep me sharp for when the time came to take out a bad guy with some brains. I'm the Hand of God, God's bounty hunter. It's my job to end the lives of some of the more evil things Satan lets loose on mankind.

Doing that means I often have to kill people. Demons and other monsters, too. But killing people is something I'm good at. I got my start with Special Forces killing Al Qaeda and Taliban goons for Uncle Sam. When I got State-side, I went to work collecting bounties. Now I do the same thing, but when I find my mark, I take them out: permanently. The people I track down face the punishment of God, not the judicial system.

I drove slow enough for the two of them to race to their car, a lime green Toyota Corolla, and fall in behind me. The car's color made keeping track of the car incredibly easy. Hell, I'd bet the farm the thing would practically glow in the dark. I made my way out of town and headed south on I-65, the Corolla hanging a few cars behind me.

I took the exit for Bernheim Forest, made my way into the park, pulled into a lot and then turned off the car. I got out of the Chevelle and walked quickly down a path into the forest. Using my superior peripheral vision, I could see the Corolla come to a stop a few spots down from mine. It was hard to miss. We were the only two cars in the lot.

The temperature hung in the low forties with a breeze kicking up around twenty miles an hour and the air felt raw and cold. I stuck my hands deep in the pockets of my black bomber jacket to keep them warm. I felt a twinge of excitement when I heard two car doors close. Seems the two men were going to join me on my walk. Sweet.

You'd think at some point they would wonder why I would go for a walk on a cold, windy day in a forest miles from the city with no one else around. I'm guessing they thought this was the perfect spot to shoot someone and stash the body.

They were right.

The forest, comprised mainly of oak and hickory with a good dose of firs, crowded each side of the path. It wound in and around different hills and ridges, hugging the edge of a deep ravine. I'd visited the forest and walked its many paths quite a bit during autumn, trying to keep in good shape and using it as a place to get away from everything and everyone—to be alone with my thoughts.

I heard them on the gravel behind me and when the path made a sharp turn down and behind a taller than average hill, blocking me temporarily from their sight, I took off at a jog. I hopped off the path, circling around the hill, and then climbing it from the other side. Having secured the high ground, I flopped onto my stomach and waited.

It wasn't long before Tweedledum and Tweedledummer came into view. The men looked Asian and were of average height. They both sported scruffy beards, knit caps and big down jackets, one a bright green, the other a bright yellow. The thing that interested me most, however, were the guns each carried out and ready. If I had doubts about their intentions before, I didn't now.

I let them wander a ways down the path, then scurried down the hill and fell in behind them. They walked another twenty yards or so before they realized they were being followed. The problem for them? My gun was up and pointed at them, while theirs were still down at their sides.

"Do what I tell you to do, and maybe you boys will live to see another day," I said. "Do...you...speak...English?"

I felt relaxed and ready, having been in this situation more than anyone should ever be. But these were the situations I lived for, the dangerous ones. My adrenaline kicked up a few degrees, my senses keying in on everything around me.

They glanced at each other for a second and then Green Jacket said, "Yeah, dumbass, we speak English."

"Sorry, I didn't want to take a chance there would be anything lost in translation. I want the two of you to slowly put your guns on the ground, then take a step back. Do it now, please."

Yellow Jacket found his tongue. To his partner he said, "You know how we were talking about how we would split up the money? There is no way he can shoot both of us before one of us shoots him. If we both go at the same time, we can let him decide who keeps the money. More fun that way."

"What do you mean I can't shoot both of you? I can squeeze this trigger quicker than you can bring your arms up."

"Nah, man. I don't think so. I watched this show the other night on how Oswald couldn't have shot Kennedy because of how long it takes to pull the trigger. He never could have gotten the shots off in time. Same for you. You won't have time."

I almost shook my head to make sure I heard what I thought I heard. "I guess that proves you're no rocket scientist. Oswald shot a rifle with a bolt action. This is a Glock 20. But hey, whatever floats your boat or sinks your ship."

The two men looked at each other one final time, shrugged and raised their guns at the same time. I shot them both before they could even raise their guns level, although Yellow Jacket did squeeze off a round which missed me by about two miles, but at least he gave it the good old college try.

I advanced on the two men, making sure they were dead, before I holstered my gun. I caught one in the perfect center of his chest, the other a bit higher. Still, not bad shooting.

I grabbed both men by their jackets and pulled them over to the ravine. Then I picked up each one and tossed them down the embankment, watching each bounce out of sight.

With that finished, I went back to the trail and spent some time covering the evidence of the attack and picked up the shell casings, dropping them in my pocket.

I walked to my car without further incident, hopped in the Chevelle, pointed the car towards Louisville, and hit the gas. With any luck, I wouldn't be late for my date.

*****

Using high-powered binoculars, he watched the bounty hunter slip into his car and leave. He waited twenty minutes to make sure he wasn't going to return, then started his own car and drove into the parking lot, taking the spot next to the rental used by the would be assassins he hired from California.

He got out, unfolded his tall frame and stretched, before heading down the path the other three had taken. He buttoned up his great coat, and slipped on a pair of fur-lined gloves, while his eyes scanned the path, watching for where the confrontation happened.

A black man in his early thirties, he was tall and solid, yet moved with the grace of a much smaller man. His brown eyes finally picked up a spot where he thought it most likely his two hired gunmen met their death. He walked to the edge of the ravine and could see twenty feet down where something had rolled through the grass before disappearing from view.

Satisfied, he retraced his steps and left. He had set the two men after the bounty hunter to watch how he reacted. He found it interesting the man handled it the way he did, leading the two men to a more than adequate kill zone, then taking them out.

There had been no real risk of the two killing McCain, but if the two hired guns had managed to eliminate the bounty hunter, then he would have killed them and claimed the contract. At least now he knew more about the man he hunted than he did before. He would spend several more days watching him, learning his habits, before acting. Killing him would be a rewarding challenge.

Adding a Hand of God to his list of kills would make the name Black Ice even more famous among the assassin elite. He might even retire. Ten million dollars would be a great way to cap a profitable career. And mounting the head of Victor McCain to his wall? Priceless.

CHAPTER THREE

I walked into Molly Malone's in a better mood than I'd been in for months. Killing people shouldn't make me so happy, but in this case, it did. It's not like the two men weren't asking for it. They planned to kill me and dump my body, so they deserved me killing them and dumping *their* bodies. What made me really happy was how well the plan worked. Nothing like when a plan comes together.

Molly's is an Irish pub where I enjoy eating most of my meals. The food is good, the service excellent and the main feature, a bar, fills up most of first floor. Good food and booze, what a winning combination—though I now kept the booze part of the equation to a more manageable level. Over the summer I thought I'd find the answers to all my problems in the bottom of a bottle and it nearly got me and others killed.

I made it to my usual booth to find a woman already sitting there. Detective Linda Coffey sat in my spot where she could watch all three doors to Molly's, keeping an eye on everyone who entered the restaurant. This forced me to take the seat across from her, which didn't fill me with joy as now I had my back to the room. As I sat down, I could feel the twitch start between my shoulder blades. In my mind I brought up the image of Wild Bill Hickok facing away from the door when Jack McCall shot him in the back while he held aces and eights.

Coffey, dressed in a light blue suit and white shirt, which brought out the green in her eyes, tucked a lock of shoulder length brown hair behind one ear as I sat down.

The Guinness on the table in front of her let me know she was off duty. I waved to the waitress, pointed to the Guinness, and she brought one for me. She'd waited for me to show before ordering and I got the usual, shepherd's pie, while she went for the fish and chips.

The waitress left to place the orders and I looked into the eyes of the woman who wanted to send my brother to the gas chamber for murder, which would be a neat trick since my brother was dead. Well, used to be dead, but was now once again among the living. Kind of. It's complicated.

Michael Christopher "Mikey" McCain is my older brother and one of the most evil people to have ever lived. I became the Hand of God when the previous Hand, Dominic Montoya, was shot and killed by Mikey and one of his henchmen and I did nothing to stop it from happening. The only way to save my own soul was to become the new Hand of God, hunt down Mikey and kill him, which I did the previous winter at my father's old hunting cabin in Eastern Kentucky. I strangled him and then tossed his body into a deep sinkhole. As far as the world knew, Mikey ceased to exist on that day.

The cops already had a warrant out for his arrest over several dead bodies that were found in one of his warehouses which burned to the ground. True, I'm the one who burned the warehouse down and killed most of the people there, but considering Mikey was in the process of creating a highly contagious bird flu that would kill thousands of children, I didn't lose any sleep over the situation.

But now it appeared Mikey had returned as one of Satan's twelve Infernal Lords. There are twelve Infernal Lords at any one time running around the planet. When one dies, another person serving eternal damnation in Hell gets another chance among the living to cause chaos and death. I recently killed one of the twelve named Muramasa, an insane former samurai, opening up a spot for Mikey.

In August, I returned home to find Coffey and her prickly partner, Detective Sam Wallace, at my mother's house, investigating the murder of two of Mikey's former security guards only days before. To say I was shocked would be an understatement.

The two guards used to work at the warehouse and I bet Mikey blamed them for not stopping me from crashing their party. It would be the kind of douche bag thing he would do.

To make sure Mikey had returned, Winston and I drove out to check the sinkhole. When we got there we found only dirt and debris at the bottom. No Mikey. The only explanation was Mikey now had what he'd always craved: power and near immortality as an Infernal Lord—along with a healthy dose of hatred for Yours Truly.

I expected Mikey to come for me, at some point, but I wasn't able to find a trace of him in the months since the murders at the warehouse. And neither had Coffey or her partner. Nor had he taken a shot at taking me out. It bugged me to no end. Perhaps Mikey felt the best way to survive being an Infernal Lord was to stay as far away from me as possible, considering I'd killed one and helped kill another. But knowing Mikey, I doubted that was the case. He would come after me with "when" the only real question.

Coffey and I started to meet for lunch on a regular basis to discuss the case. She didn't know I needed to find him even more than she did. We enjoyed talking together, and the more we met, the less we talked about Mikey.

She had no idea what I really did with my time, thinking I was still a bounty hunter. Many times I considered telling her the truth, but something made me stop. Coffey was all business: a no nonsense, by the book cop who lived to put the bad guys away. I got the feeling she wouldn't approve of my extra-curricular activities of killing people for a living, even if they were evil. I thought of the two men now rotting at the bottom of a ravine in Bernheim Forest. If she knew, it would be her job to put me away for life. And I had no doubt she'd do it.

She leaned in and looked at me closely, laughter in her eyes. "What's the matter, tough guy? Afraid I can't handle watching your back?"

"You know what it's like to not be able to see what's coming. And for all I know you can't even get the gun you carry on your hip out of its holster. Ever drawn down on anyone? Or is the gun only for show?"

I barely finished the sentence before I found her gun pointed at my nose. I didn't even see her hand move and found myself holding perfectly still, despite the fact I saw her finger resting along the side of the gun and not on the trigger.

"Fast enough for you?"

I tried to think of something smart ass to say, but only got out, "Uh-huh." Victor McCain, man of action and few words.

She laughed and returned the gun to her hip. I glanced around Molly's and noticed a couple watching us, their eyes wide. I pointed at Coffey and said, "She's practicing to play Annie Oakley in a remake of *Annie Get Your Gun*."

They smiled weakly and did their best to pretend to ignore us which made me laugh.

Coffey shook her head. "You seem to be in a really good mood.

What have you been doing? Win the lottery?"

"Don't I wish. No, I went Christmas shopping and I actually enjoyed it. The man you see before you is now filled with the holiday spirit."

"Bah humbug. You're full of it, that's for sure, but it's not Christmas cheer. No man enjoys Christmas shopping." She took a sip of her Guinness. "But since you brought it up, what'd you buy me?"

"Who said I was getting you anything? If you want the truth, I was trying to find something for Wallace, but couldn't find a copy of *How the Grinch Stole Christmas.*"

She tilted her bottle towards me and we clinked in salute to the season. "You know he hates it when we see each other. He believes you had a hand in helping your brother disappear, since being a bounty hunter you would know all the tricks."

"Which is why Wallace needs to pull his head out of his ass and look elsewhere. You have my word, if I knew where Mikey was I'd tell you. My brother and I were never close and I owe him nothing. If the evidence says Mikey is a murderer, then I want him behind bars. But I have to tell you, I still don't see how Mikey could have snapped their necks. You've seen the pictures of my brother. He wouldn't be able to snap a pencil in two, let alone someone's neck."

She nodded in understanding, but said, "Yet fingerprints don't lie. Plus, the DNA evidence we found on the bodies also point straight to your brother. He's our killer. I only wish we knew where he was hiding."

"If I had to guess? Mikey's on a beach somewhere in South America using bad pickup lines on any woman with a pulse."

"Speaking of which, how come you've never used one on me?"

The sudden change in the conversation caught me off guard and I paused before answering. The waitress showed up with our food and it gave me an extra minute to think about how to respond.

To be honest, I wasn't sure why not. There was no doubt we'd been getting closer over the last month. She was attractive, fun to be around, and could watch my back if things got out of hand. On the other side of the coin, being near me guaranteed to put her in danger and sooner rather than later. I remembered watching the Spider-Man movie where Peter Parker broke it off with Mary Jane just to keep her safe and I thought, *"What a wuss."* Now I knew exactly what the man had been thinking.

Samantha, the woman I still considered the love of my life, ended up being shot by me, and that might not have been the worst thing she suffered through due to our relationship. If Coffey and I started to date, what would that mean for her? Could I keep her safe? I knew the answer was a big ole "hell no."

Over the summer I'd also had a brief fling with a woman named Elizabeth Bathory. Then I found out she was an Infernal Lord, formerly known as the Countess of Blood, which kind of took the wind out of that one. Some people claim their love life has gone to Hell. Me? I'd slept with someone from Hell. My love life is very strange.

When the waitress left, I decided telling her the truth might still be a bad idea. I decided to punt. "Well," I said, "it's because you're a cop on Mikey's case. I figured you weren't allowed to go out with a person involved in a murder investigation, even if I had nothing to do with what happened."

"You'd be right, normally. I'm not supposed to get involved with possible suspects or witnesses. But you're neither. You've come up clean. You were on the east coast when the murders happened and we've spoken to enough people to corroborate your statement that you and your brother were not close. In my mind, you're out of it. And believe me, if Wallace could find even a hint you're dirty on this, he'd be all over you."

"Good to know, because I didn't. And having Wallace all over me brings up a mental image I'd as soon forget."

We both ate a bit of our food when she said, "Let's say for fun, we'd never met before today. And let's say it's late on a Friday night and things are hopping here at Molly's. You walk in and see me standing at the bar. What's your line?"

I washed down some shepherd's pie with a swig of Guinness before answering. "Right. It would be something like this: I'd walk over and say, 'my buddies bet me that I wouldn't be able to start a conversation with the most beautiful girl in the bar. Wanna buy some drinks with their money?'"

She wiggled a hand back and forth. "Not bad. The answer is, 'Yes I would.' Considering it's Friday, how about tonight, at nine p.m. I'll be standing right there." She pointed to a spot near the end of the bar. "I'll wait to see if you come in and offer up your line. But don't wait too long. If I someone makes a better offer, I might take it."

"Story of my life. Always coming in second. Nine p.m.? I'll be here."

We spent the rest of the late lunch talking about the things a new couple talk about. All the while, I kept thinking to myself, "A date with a cop who's tracking down my brother for murder. What could go wrong?"

CHAPTER FOUR

Kurt tossed the empty Diet Dr. Pepper can into the trash can in the corner of the room and raised hands in triumph for making the long distance shot. Still the Man.

His iPhone beeped to remind him it was five past four in the afternoon and he needed to go take a shower. Ruth Anne would be walking in the door any minute and he wanted to be ready.

He spent the time in the shower rehearsing his proposal. He'd written a full page of ideas he wanted to try, then narrowed them down to a few words and then wrote a bullet point outline of the five major things he wanted to remember to say to her when he went down on one knee.

The big problem turned out he could only remember about two when his nerves kicked in and he broke out into a sweat. In the end, he decided to wing it. At the worst he would stick with the "will you marry me" line.

He finished his shower, toweled off and brushed his teeth twice, capping it off with a full ten minutes of gargling with mouthwash. He breathed into his hand and had to admit to himself, he smelled pretty damn good.

He got dressed and walked out to the living room, expecting to see Ruth Anne on the couch watching *Dr. Phil*. but she wasn't there. He pulled out his phone and checked the time, seeing it was now almost five o'clock. Ruth Anne should have been home almost an hour ago.

He glanced out in the driveway, but no car. He sat down in front of his computer and tried to do a bit more work, but he couldn't concentrate and his code more resembled alphabet soup than it did workable hacker code.

When the time hit five-thirty with no Ruth Anne, he called her phone, but it went straight to voicemail. He left her a message to call him as soon as possible. He wanted her to have time to freshen up before they left. Sometimes she could take forever to put herself together.

At a quarter to six, his nervousness changed to panic. He didn't want to be late and lose his reservation. He thumbed through his contacts until he found the number for Barnes and Noble and hit dial

"Thanks for calling Barnes and Noble, this is Marty, how can I help you?"

"Hey, Marty. This is Kurt Pervis, Ruth Anne's boyfriend. Is she still there?"

Marty managed the Barnes and Nobel and had been the one to hire Ruth Anne. "Sorry, Kurt, but she's not here. She didn't show up today. I tried calling her to see if she was sick, but she never answered or returned my phone calls."

Fear flooded Kurt's body and he jumped up and walked quickly to the front door. "Marty, Ruth Anne left for work around nine this morning. Oh, God. I hope she didn't have an accident."

"Ah, man. That's not good. Keep me posted on what you learn, okay?"

"I will Marty, 'cause something's not right."

Kurt hung up the phone, shrugged into his winter coat and went outside. They lived on a quiet street in Goshen, a small river town about twenty minutes from Louisville. He walked to the end of their driveway, searching up and down the street. Nothing.

He went inside the house and tried calling her again, but it still went to voicemail. Kurt practically ran to his computers, sat hurriedly in the chair and pulled up the site for Find My iPhone. He typed in her Apple ID and password, then hit enter. He waited impatiently, drumming his fingers on the desk top. Finally, the website told him her phone was offline and couldn't be found.

Swearing, he rested his head in his hands, then another thought struck him. Worried his car might be stolen, Kurt paid to have a LoJack System installed.

He forced himself to calm down and to think of the name of the right website. Once he did, his fingers flew across the keyboard, typing in the address, then his screen name and password. A moment later a map of Louisville appeared with a little blue dot showing him the location of his car.

The dot sat still, meaning at least the car was not in motion. But where the dot sat, confused Kurt. It showed his car sat in one of the long term parking lots at the airport.

Fear gripped him and his hands began to shake. All thoughts of marriage faded, Kurt hit the speed dial on his phone. Ruth Anne was gone.

*****

I'd almost made it to the Derby Mission when my phone buzzed in my pocket. I fished it out and, seeing Kurt's name, answered.

"What's up? Decided to—"

"Vic, she's gone. I can't find her anywhere."

Kurt sounded more panicked than I'd ever heard him before. "Slow down there, Kurt. Do you mean Ruth Anne?"

He filled me in on Ruth Anne not showing up for work, and then not coming home.

"Doesn't she have an iPhone? Did you try the Find My iPhone app?" I asked.

"Come on, man. That's the first thing I did. And it's not showing up. It says her phone is offline. When you call her number, it goes straight to voice mail. But that's not what scares me, Vick. I have a LoJack System on my car. It says the car's at the airport. I told her she should have had that chip put under her skin. What are we gonna do?"

Kurt, Winston and I'd gotten a GPS chip inserted under the skin at the back of our head, under the hairline. We did this in order to track each other in the event we were ever kidnapped again like Kurt was in Hawaii. Not just anyone could track us: you had to know the right website, sign on name and passwords.

Kurt tried to convince Ruth Anne to do the same, but she refused. She'd read somewhere when she was younger the verse in Revelations about how the coming of the Antichrist would lead to every person carrying the mark of the beast and the article said it would likely be a chip inserted into the skin. It had always freaked her out and no matter how hard Kurt tried to convince her, she refused to have the procedure.

"You can't beat yourself up about that, man. She made the choice herself. Listen, I'll swing by and pick you up. I should be there in about fifteen minutes. Did you call any of her friends to see if they might know where she'd run off to?"

"Dude, ever since that thing with the fallen angel, she's only hung out with us. She won't even shake hands with a stranger. She always tells them she's a germaphobe, but really she's a demonaphobe."

There was brief pause. "Ah, hell. Vic? Do you think the demon came back and has control of her again?"

"I don't think so, Kurt. Brother Joshua said it would take years for the demons to return, if at all. Besides, you said Ruth Anne has become a true believer, so there's no place for them to return."

I became a mini expert on the workings of demon possession when the Watchers made a grand return by possessing the souls of non-believers in God. If they tried to possess someone full of the faith, nothing can happen. Only empty vessels in the soul department can be snatched.

"Sit tight, Kurt. I'm on my way."

I pushed the speed limit racing to Kurt's house. On the way, I called Winston Reynolds and told him to watch his ass in case someone was targeting us and to be ready later. I had a bad feeling about this.

Reynolds had worked for a rival bounty hunter murdered by the Church of the Light Reclaimed. He joined me to exact revenge on the people responsible, which included my brother Mikey. Now he acted as my good right hand when it came to carrying the fight to the enemy.

When I swung into the driveway, I found Kurt waiting outside holding his laptop. He hopped in on the passenger side, opened back up his computer and checked the location of the car: still at the airport.

We didn't talk on the drive to the Southside of the city. The Louisville International Airport is located right off I-65, a few miles south of downtown. We made our way around the airport loop and into the long term parking area. It took about five minutes, but we found Kurt's car parked in the open air lot.

Kurt jumped out of the car before I came to a full stop and ran to the Mustang, despite my shouts for him to wait. I jammed the car in park and got out.

He hit the key-fob to unlock the car and threw the door open, searching inside for Ruth Anne. I jogged up and looked over his shoulder and I could see she wasn't in the car.

He started to jump in when I grabbed him and spun him around. He tried to break free and cocked his fist to hit me when common sense returned and he lowered his hand.

"Vic, she's gone. Why won't you let me search the car?"

"Listen, Kurt, we don't know what's happened yet. There could be evidence in there that you could ruin by blundering around. Let me have a look."

He nodded a yes. "Good man, Kurt. Now, do me a favor and

fetch me a pair of latex gloves from the glove box in the Chevelle."

He did as I asked and I leaned in for a look around, trying not to touch anything. I don't know why, but I knew this wasn't right and I didn't want to screw things up.

Kurt handed me the gloves and I slid them on and I got to work.

"The first thing that strikes me as odd, is where the seat is positioned."

"What do you mean?" Kurt asked.

"I've seen Ruth Anne in this car and the first thing she does is move the car seat all the way forward. She's what, five foot one? Look where the seat is positioned. It's not all the way forward, but it's not back very far. You or I would have to move the seat almost all the way back to get into the car. So whoever drove it to the airport wasn't very tall, but taller than Ruth Anne."

I leaned into the car, making sure not to touch the wheel or the shifter. I found no purse and cell phone. And there was something else very odd: a brief whiff of a smell and not a good one. I couldn't place it, but my first impression was rotten meat.

Then I noticed it, down between the seat and the console: a small dot of dark on the gray interior. I pulled out my phone and turned on the flashlight app and shined it down on the spot. It looked like a drop of blood.

I got out of the car and shut the door, pulling off my gloves. I don't know what expression I had on my face, but Kurt went perfectly still.

"What did you find?" he asked, his voice devoid of emotion.

"Trouble."

CHAPTER FIVE

"Maybe she needed time away. She wouldn't be the first woman to have cold feet when it came time to get serious in a relationship." Detective Coffey sat sideways in the front seat of the Mustang, wearing her own pair of gloves. I called her when my alarm level tripped into overdrive.

Kurt spun around in a circle, the frustration easy to see. "She didn't leave town. She didn't run away. We were very happy. I planned to propose to her tonight. She didn't leave me. I know she didn't."

Coffey got out of the car. "Still, even if you're right, they won't file a missing person report for twenty-four hours." She stared at me. "Convince me she didn't decide to take a hike."

I pointed through the driver side window at the steering wheel. "That's what convinced me."

"What about it?"

"Kurt likes to eat Three Musketeer Bars and he got chocolate on the steering wheel. I've been after him for days to get it cleaned up, but he ignored me. The wheel is now sparkling clean. Someone wiped it down. I think they were wiping away their prints. If I'm right, and you throw in the blood spot, I think that points to foul play. If she was headed somewhere like on a cruise she wouldn't care about her fingerprints."

Coffey thought for a few beats, then went to her car and got a bag from the trunk. She removed a small kit from the bag and proceeded to dust the steering wheel and shifter for prints. After a few minutes she pursed her lips, then put her gear away and got out of the car.

"Fine, you've convinced me. There's not a single print on the steering wheel or the shifter. I can't work it because I'm homicide, but I'll contact a friend and call him out here to start working the case."

She pulled a phone from her pocket and stepped away a few feet. Kurt moved next to me and we both leaned against the Mustang. "What do you think?"

"I don't yet. I think it's clear someone took her but not much else."

"It has to be Mikey. Has to be."

"Let's not jump to conclusions. We don't know it's him. Yes, the person driving was small, but there may have been several guys who grabbed her and then one of them, a short guy, drove the car out here. We need more evidence."

"Let me show you something." He walked over to my car and got his laptop, opening it. "The LoJack software lets me track where the car's been. She left this morning and drove to work, then the car went straight from there to the airport."

"Does it show you how long it was at each spot?"

He shook his head. "Nah, just where it went."

I checked the time on my phone. "It's closing in on nine p.m. Let me meet with Winston and we'll go over to Barnes and Noble and see if they have outside cameras watching the parking lot. Maybe we can have a look at what happened."

"I'm coming with you." He slammed closed the lid of the laptop and tossed it on the seat of my Chevelle. His eyes were wide, his breathing quick and a small line of sweat formed on his forehead.

"No, you're not. You're going to stay here with Detective Coffey and wait for the other detective to arrive. Then you're going to go home. If someone took her, they may call you with demands. You need to be ready in case they do."

"Man, I need to help you. I have to be in on this."

"And you will be. But first things first. Let me do my job and you do what I asked you to do. It's why you called me, right?"

He didn't like it, but he nodded his head in agreement. Coffey finished her call and joined us. "Detective Ware is on his way. I gave him the low down on what we know so far, which isn't much." She put her phone away. "Tell me, Kurt. Why would someone want to kidnap Ruth Anne? Does she have any enemies? Are either of you worth a lot of money? Why do you think someone took her?"

Kurt glanced at me quickly, then looked at the ground. "I don't know, detective. Ruth Anne makes friends with everyone. And I'm not worth much. I do freelance computer work. It pays all right, but it's not like I'm living the high life."

His glance at me wasn't lost on her. "Don't jack me around, Kurt." She pointed a finger at me. "You either, Vic. You guys know something you're not telling me. Now's not the time to lie to me. You guys called me, remember?"

She was right, and using the line I'd just given Kurt drove the point home. I was asking her to do a job with only half the information. But I wasn't actually lying either. I didn't know who took Ruth Anne and because of what I did, the list of potential suspects was large. I wanted to tell her the truth, but I once again stopped short of spilling my guts.

"Look, the list of bad guys I've hunted is a long one and I've used Kurt to help me track some of them down. I'll go through my list and see who might be out of prison and in town wanting to cause Kurt or me trouble."

I could tell she didn't believe me, but she dropped it. "I guess meeting at Molly's is out?"

"Yeah. Sorry. I need to get working on this myself. If this isn't a crime of opportunity and someone is doing this to hurt us, then I want to be proactive. Know what I mean?"

"I do." She took me by the arm and led me away from Kurt. In a low tone, she said, "I don't know why you're lying to me, but I believe you have your reasons. I have only one question for you and I want the truth: does this have anything to do with your brother? You've said several times you and your brother weren't close. Would he have any reason to go after Kurt or Ruth Anne to hurt you?"

I watched a plane taking off, a UPS cargo plane. They call them brown tails because the tail of the aircraft is brown with the UPS logo on it. I wish I could hop a ride on one of those planes out of town to avoid her questions.

I finally looked her in the eyes. "I honestly don't know. I really don't. Mikey has always resented me, from the time we were kids. But I don't see where kidnapping Ruth Anne gains him anything."

She watched, mulling over my response and trying to decide whether I was telling the truth or lying my ass off. "Fine, but if you're dicking me around on this, Vic, I'll come down on you hard."

I raised my hands in surrender. "No worries. If it's Mikey, I want him caught." We walked over to Kurt and I asked Detective Coffey, "I need to get moving, you don't need me any longer, do you?"

"No. I'll wait here with Kurt until Ware arrives."

I placed my hand on Kurt's shoulder. "Don't worry, man. We're going to find her. You have my word. Come hell or high water, we'll do what it takes. She's one of us. You hear me?"

He didn't answer, only gave me a small nod, not meeting my eyes. I gave Coffey a fist bump, got into my Chevelle and left the airport. I pulled my phone out of my pocket and hit the speed dial number for Winston.

"What's the word?" he asked.

I filled him in on the latest. "I'm headed your way. I want to go check out the camera situation over at the bookstore. Pick you up in ten?"

"I'll be ready," and he hung up.

I hit the ramp to I-65 South and floored it.

If someone with the Church of the Light Reclaimed took Ruth Anne, and my gut told me they did, then things were coming to a boil. The only question was, who would end up in the pot?

CHAPTER SIX

Winston hung up the phone and turned off the TV. He stood, stretched and thought about Ruth Anne and Kurt. The girl couldn't catch a break. Spent last winter with a demon running loose in her brain, only to be kidnapped before the next Christmas rolled around. Victor didn't come out and say it, but he could tell he thought Mikey or the Church was involved.

He longed for the good ole days when someone who became dead actually stayed that way. They were living in one messed up world. It didn't really matter. They killed the man once, they'd do it again.

He opened the door to his hall closet and was about to reach for his coat when he stopped. He quietly shut the door and listened. He thought he heard something strange and out of place, but he couldn't be sure. He walked softly to the front door and glanced out the window. The driveway was empty and there were no cars parked on the street.

He almost chocked it up to his imagination, but then he heard another sound: a thump, coming from one of the bedrooms. Turning off the light in the living room, he picked up his gun from the coffee table and thumbed off the safety.

He eased slowly down the hallway in the dark, his gun held in a two-handed grip in front of him. He knew every inch of his house and didn't need the lights to guide his way. He paused at the bathroom, but didn't sense anything wrong, and continued to his bedroom.

Looking into the room, he saw one of the panes of glass in the window next to his bed had been knocked out. That must have been the sound he heard. The porch lamp at the next door neighbor's house provide enough light to cast his room in shadows. The curtain moved gently with the breeze, but he could tell the window was not open.

He edged into the room and began to make his way around the

bed to the window when another sound made him freeze. It was a sound he'd heard once before, many years ago on a farm his uncle used to own in Tennessee: the sound of a rattlesnake—at least one, and likely two, were heard in the darkness.

He moved his head very slowly, trying to see them on the floor of his bedroom, but no luck. They had to be under the bed right next to his foot. Now he knew what the thump was that he heard. It was someone dropping rattlesnakes into his room through the broken window. Sons of bitches.

On that summer day in Tennessee, his uncle had sent him to the barn for a bale of hay to spread over some grass seed they'd thrown down in the yard. He made it a few feet inside the door when the snake sent up his warning rattle a few inches behind his right heel.

His uncle, standing a few feet away, heard the familiar sound and told him to stand very still while he got his shotgun out of the truck. He told him to not move even his head to look for the snake. While his uncle was gone, those were the longest two minutes of his life. Big dogs? Spiders? Satanists? No problem. Snakes scared the crap out of him.

This time he held the gun in his hand, but couldn't see the snakes from his current angle and he didn't dare to bend over to try to find them. He swiveled his head and checked the bed cover to make sure no one had thrown one on top of the bed, but it was empty. He worked hard to try to slow his breathing and heart rate, worried the snakes could sense his fear and strike.

Winston closed his eyes and said a silent prayer and then, while trying to keep the lower part of his legs from moving, he bent at the knees, crouched a few inches and leapt onto the bed.

He felt something strike the side of his boot, an inch or two from the top, but it did no damage, thanks to the leather. He thanked God for keeping him safe, so far, and for a great pair of Red Wing boots. He reached over to turn on the light next to his bed to look for the snakes, but then stopped. He glanced out the window trying to see if the person who dropped in the rattlers was still there, waiting for him. If he turned on the light he'd be a sitting duck with no way to make it to the door without risking being attacked by the snakes.

He took the phone out of his pocket and turned it on, then quickly dimmed the brightness to almost nothing, along with the audio on his phone. He snagged a pillow and placed it between the phone and the window and called Victor.

"Man, I'm almost there. What's up?"

Winston leaned over and placed his lips near the phone and gave Vic a quick account of the break in and the snakes. "Vic, I need you to check out my yard first and make sure there's no one out there, then come in here and kill these snakes."

"Winston, I hate snakes. You're telling me a former NFL linebacker can't handle a couple of little snakes?"

"Man, quit yanking my chain and hustle on in here and help a brother out. From the sounds of things, they ain't small."

*****

I parked down the street from Winston's house, got out of the car and cut behind his neighbor's house, scanning his yard looking for any sense of danger, but I saw nothing out of the ordinary. My breath floated in front of me in small puffs, the night dropping down below freezing.

Houses up and down the street were decorated with Christmas lights, people getting lost in the season. One of Winston's neighbors had his house decorated to look like a Gingerbread House. Absolutely stunning.

I slid my gun from its holster and put it in the pocket of my leather bomber jacket, keeping a finger on the trigger while I crossed into Winston's yard. I made it almost to the bedroom window when I stopped, the hair on the back of neck standing on end. I still couldn't see anyone, but I had the weirdest sensation someone was watching me.

There were no other houses behind Winston's, with his yard running to the edge of a wooded area. Behind the tree line, a creek ran the length of the subdivision.

I stopped next to his window and in a low voice said, "Keep the light off. I don't see anyone, but something's not right. I think someone's watching from the tree line and I'm going to check it out."

"Man, you shouldn't be doing that alone. Come in and wipe out these snakes first and we can both go."

"They might be gone by then. Hang on. I won't be gone long."

I didn't wait for him to say anything else, but walked cautiously towards the trees, my gun now out and by my side. Someone, or something, was out there watching and waiting. I could feel it. I'd gotten the feeling more than once on mountain trails in the dark in Afghanistan where the Taliban would set up ambushes for my Army unit, hoping to take us out in the dark. Often I'd been right and we'd turn the tables and wipe the sick sons of bitches out, and I knew I was right this time.

I stopped at the edge of the woods, listening. I heard nothing but the sound of an occasional car passing by on the road in front of Winston's home. From the woods, near silence. It seemed the whole woods, the animals and even the wind, had paused to see what was going to happen next.

The feeling of malice hit me like a physical force and it made my skin crawl. Every fiber of my body wanted me to turn around and run the other direction, to the safety of the known and to the light. It royally pissed me off. For as long as I could remember, when someone tried to push me around, to intimidate me, to scare me, I always reacted by moving forward instead of retreating—usually with incredible violence. I didn't like being scared and it made me want to go all Punisher on someone.

With a snarl I marched right into the woods. I didn't try to be quiet. If there was something out there, it already knew I was here and I'd be damned if I was going to act like I cared. I moved straight ahead towards the creek, steady but alert. After about twenty yards, the light from Winston's neighborhood started to fade and I considered using the flashlight I had tucked into my inner coat pocket, but left it there, allowing my eyes to adjust to the darkness instead.

I've always possessed great night vision and I stopped short of the creek, the water bubbling by me. I turned around in place slowly, trying to see into the darker shadows, searching for something which didn't fit.

The feeling of being watched increased and I'd had enough. "You know, only pussies hide in the dark."

That got a reaction.

Something on the other side of the creek moved quickly in my direction and it smashed through trees and underbrush right towards me, but then stopped short of showing itself.

I kept the gun at my side and waited. One minute. Two. Then three. Nothing. "Come on, asshole. Here I am. Step on out and let's settle this. Or are you worried I might kick your ass back to Hell?"

I didn't know if it was Mikey, but if it was, I knew how to push his buttons. He hated being called a pussy. I didn't call him by name because if it wasn't him? Well, I didn't want to look like a dork. Either way, it seemed I'd yanked its chain hard enough.

I started to open my mouth and pile on when I sensed something flying in the air towards me. I tensed, but the object came up short, and rolled to a stop at my feet. Then whatever was out there, moved away from me, fast, and deeper into the woods.

I listened for a few more minutes, but I knew I was now alone. With the sense of malice gone, I reached into my coat pocket and pulled out my flashlight, switched it on and pointed it at my feet.

Bloody hell.

I felt bile rise up in my throat and anger exploded inside me. The head of a woman with blonde hair lay at my feet, resting on one cheek. The thought it might be Ruth Anne scared the hell out of me. I used the toe of my boot and rolled it over so I could see her face. I let out a small sigh of relief when I saw it wasn't her, but my insides twisted at the loss of life.

She looked young, perhaps in her twenties, her eyes open and staring at me. I knew I would have many sleepless nights ahead with those eyes haunting me.

I doubted her death had been an easy one. It appeared her head had been ripped from its body, the stump of the neck was ragged and uneven. It would take incredible strength to do this to a person. I wasn't strong enough to do it and I doubted many people alive could accomplish such a feat. But I'd run up against undead people who could do this without breaking a sweat: Infernal Lords—Mikey.

I tried hard to keep from jumping to conclusions. If it turned out to be one of the twelve Infernal Lords loose on the planet, it didn't have to be Mikey. It could be any of them. But I knew better. It was Mikey.

I turned off the flashlight letting the night once again swallow me up. It matched the darkness I felt settle at the bottom of my soul.

I often wondered why I kept on fighting as the Hand of God. What was the point? Every time I killed some form of evil, another one seemed to be right behind it. But this time I knew what had to be done. Mikey needed to be stopped. And soon. It needed to be me to avenge this poor woman and all the others my brother had murdered. And even if it turned out not to be him, it made little difference.

I stood there, bowed my head and I made a promise to the dead woman to not let her murderer go unanswered and to seek revenge on the monsters who did this to her.

And I made a promise to my brother, too. Be ready Mikey. You think you're the one with the upper hand, with the super powers, and the immortality? In the end, you'll be one more dead prick rotting in Hell. This time, permanently.

CHAPTER SEVEN

I made my way back to Winston's house and used a key he gave me to let myself in. I went to his garage first, grabbed a rake hanging on a peg, and then stopped in the kitchen and selected the largest knife he had in the knife drawer. Armed and ready, I carefully made my way to his bedroom, flipping on lights and watching for snakes.

I edged into his bedroom slowly and hit the wall switch, turning on the overhead light. Winston sat on the bed, his legs crossed at the ankles, but as far away from the edges as he could manage.

I used the rake to lift the bed skirt, with a rattle going up immediately. I used the rake to drag out one of the snakes and then pinned it to the floor while I used the knife to cut off its head. I repeated the process with the other snake, finally freeing my friend from his temporary bed prison once no other snakes were found in the bedroom or rest of the house.

I then told him what happened out in the woods and after cleaning up the snakes, together we retraced my steps to where the head had been tossed across the creek and now rested among a pile of fallen leaves.

When Winston saw the face, he let out a low moan and walked away a few paces, his hands covering his face. He dropped them and in the glow of the flashlight, I almost didn't recognize him, his face was so contorted with anger and rage.

From the time we'd met, he'd always been the calm one, the voice of reason when I wanted to go all Hulk on people and let my anger loose on anyone or anything in my path. When I doubted why I got out of bed each day, he would be the one with words which would keep me going. In all the time I'd known him, he never once lost his temper. Not once.

Until now. He looked into the night and screamed, "You son of a bitch. I swear to God I will find you and rip your heart out with my bare hands."

"Ah, man. You know her, don't you?"

He turned to me, tears streaming down his face. "She was my neighbor. Her name is Ashley Truman. Or was. She worked at Audubon Hospital in the emergency room. Vic, she was only twenty-four years old. I talked to her this afternoon, out in the backyard. Whoever did this must have seen us talking. Man, if she's dead because of me..."

He let the thought trail off and bowed his head, shaking it from side to side. I went to him and placed my hand on his shoulder. "You know as well as I do that you didn't kill this woman. Some sick asshole did. And you and I will find who did this and avenge her. You hear me?"

"Yeah. I hear you."

He took a moment and gathered himself, then asked, "What do we do about this? Do we go to her place and see if her body is there? Or do you think she's still out here somewhere?" he asked gesturing to the woods around us.

"Right now, we have Ruth Anne to think about. We can't do anything for Truman. We need to try and see if we can find out who took Ruth Anne and that means going to Barnes and Noble and seeing if they have security cameras. If we call the cops, we'll spend the rest of the night making statements and answering questions."

He pointed to the head. "You want to leave her out here? Like this? Man, I can't do that. What if a coyote or other animal finds her? No, no, no. I can't. I can't, Vic."

I stared at my friend and realized he was right. Innocent bystanders were now becoming targets. Leaving the two would be assassins in a ravine to rot until they were found I could justify. The family of Truman deserved better than never knowing what happened to their loved one, even for a day.

For the second time that evening, I took out my phone to call Detective Coffey. I knew before I dialed, she would be less than thrilled to hear from me. Turned out I was right.

*****

I watched from the window in Winston's kitchen as the crime scene techs carried their lights and gear into the woods to start processing the area around the dead girl's head. Detective Coffey sat with Winston at his dining room table going over his story for the third time.

Leaning against the kitchen counter, her partner, Detective Sam Wallace, continued to chime in and pepper Winston with questions about his relationship with the dead woman. In his late forties, he wore a rumpled brown suit with a gut which made the buttons on his shirt look like they might fly off and shoot across the room. Graying hair cut short to the skull made him look older by a good ten years.

He asked Winston, "When you talked to her this afternoon, what did you talk about?"

"What the hell difference does it make what we talked about? Neighbor shit. You know, the weather, the Christmas lights on the house on the other side of mine."

Wallace either didn't catch the growing anger in Winston's voice or didn't care. My bet was didn't care.

"How would you characterize your relationship with the deceased?"

"Man, I already told you, we didn't have a relationship. We were neighbors. That was it. Nothing else."

Wallace snickered. "Maybe that was the problem. You wanted more and she turned you down. You end up pissed off. It's understandable. One thing leads to another and things spiral out of control. I can see how—"

Winston exploded out of his chair and if I had been a hair slower in muscling between the two, he might have decked Wallace then and there.

Wallace grinned and continued, "See, just like that. Is that what happened next door? You're a real brick, Reynolds. You might be strong enough to yank the poor girls head off."

Coffey stood. "Come on, Sam. Ease up."

I got Winston to return to his seat, then turned on Wallace. At six foot six inches, I had a good six inches on the cop, and I used my bulk to crowd him against the kitchen sink.

"You know what, asshole? You don't like me? I understand that. But when you start in on my friends the way you're doing I may kick your ass myself. And don't think your partner here will be able to stop me."

I thought for a minute he might spit in my face, his own rage now flowing to the top, turning his neck and face a deep red, but he stopped short of actually doing it.

"Back off, McCain, or I'll come down on you so hard you won't know what hit you."

I leaned in close and whispered in his ear so only he could hear me. "You're out of your league, dick wad. If you make me come for you, they'll never find the body."

He tried hard to keep up the tough guy image in front of his partner, to stand there and not show fear. Yet I could see it in his eyes, trying to stay hidden and not succeeding. Breaking eye contact he slid by me and tried to regain some of the machismo he'd lost by bumping me hard with his shoulder.

He stopped at the kitchen door, turned and said, "I'm going to find your brother and when I connect him to you and you're convicted, I'll make sure I'm there to see you gasp for your last breath when they gas your ass."

He stormed out. Coffey shot me a helpless look and followed him. For the time being Winston and I were left alone, neither one of us talking. My friend sat in his chair, and stared at nothing, and I could only imagine the thoughts slamming around inside his head.

We'd seen more than a few horrors over the last year or so, but the brutal murder of Truman tore him up inside. Murdered because she lived next door to the wrong guy. I knew the only way to even begin to make things better would be to hunt down and kill the ones responsible. But speaking from experience, it didn't help much.

Detective Coffey stuck her head around the door frame and waved for me to follow her outside. I nodded and fell in behind her, stopping to squeeze Winston's shoulder.

I pulled the door closed behind me and joined Coffey on the front porch. A few neighbors stood outside in pajamas and coats, watching the flashing of the cop blue lights, a stark contrast to the multi-colored Christmas lights strung around Winston's shrubs and front door. Wallace fired up his unmarked and tore out of the driveway.

We watched until his tail lights disappeared in the night. "How's he holding up?" Coffey asked, her hands stuffed deep into the pockets of her coat.

"He'll be okay, but this is not the kind of thing you get over easily."

She nodded. "You know this from experience, I take it?"

"Yes. I can't begin to tell you how many people I shot and killed while fighting in the deserts, mountains and towns over in the Middle East. And how many good friends I lost. At some point, you become numb to the carnage, but it never leaves you."

"I can only imagine. I have two cousins with the Marines, and they've both done multiple tours over there. They won't talk about it. I know one of them is seeing a therapist. He sometimes wakes up in the middle of the night and hits his wife. She has to sleep in another room, for now, until he can control his nightmares. They don't know if he'll ever sleep peacefully again."

I didn't respond, knowing many of the guys I served with who told similar stories. But not me. I slept like a baby every night and I used to worry what peaceful slumbers said about my own soul. Then I realized it didn't matter. I am who I am and I would have to live with myself.

Coffey craned her neck and stared up at the clear night sky, stars twinkling from high above. "You know, it's nights like this that make me wish I'd never given up smoking."

"I hear ya. It makes me want to find a bottle of Fireball and hole up somewhere. But that's not an option for people like us, is it?"

"No, it's not." She took a deep breath and let it out, slow and long. "Someone is targeting your crew, Vic. I could chalk Ruth Anne Gardner's kidnapping to a random act of violence. But now the neighbor of one of your other friends is murdered and the head thrown at your feet? They have to be connected."

Once again, I went quiet. I agreed with her, but what could I say? "Yes, Detective Coffey, I believe one of the many Satanists I've pissed off is now trying to take us all down," I said to myself. But not quite the thing you want to say aloud—if you want others think you're a sane and rational human being.

When I didn't respond, she continued. "I do have a question for you. You said you've continued to work as a bounty hunter, but there is no record of you bringing in a bounty for payment in more than a year. Wallace ran your sheet. How've you been paying the bills?"

"You been checking up on me, Detective?" The chill in my voice matched the chill in the air. I stuffed my own hands in the pockets of my bomber jacket, more so she couldn't see me clenching and unclenching them than to keep them warm.

"Like I said, Wallace ran your bounty sheet. He made sure to shove it under my nose months ago and I let it slide. It was none of my business, or his, for that matter. Now it is. This is going to put your life under a microscope. Wallace is going to tear your life, and the life of your friends, apart. Best to start with me. Let me help you out here."

I strode off the porch and walked slowly into the yard a few paces and then turned to face her. "I do work for the Derby Mission. I sold my condo and most of my possessions and moved into a room there at the mission, stashing the money in the bank. For the mission, I do background checks, make sure there are no bad guys hiding out there, that kind of thing."

She raised an eyebrow. "Victor McCain living and working at a homeless shelter? You never told me this. You said you were working as a bounty hunter and Reynolds and Pervis help out. When Wallace pulls Reynolds bounty sheet, is he going to find out there aren't any bounties on his sheet either? And Wallace will check. You can count on it."

She had me by the short hairs and I wasn't sure what to do about it. One of the advantages of being the Hand of God is never being arrested by the cops. Supposedly. And while I'd not done anything illegal in the cases she and Wallace were involved in, it didn't mean having them sticking their noses into my business wouldn't be a real pain in the ass.

"Check all you want. Wallace is a prick and is looking for any excuse to jack us up. I just didn't think I'd hear it from you, too."

I brushed by her and headed inside. I didn't make it two strides before she snagged my arm, spun me around and poked a gloved finger into my chest. "Don't pull that bullshit with me. I could have made an issue of these things months ago, and didn't. I trust you. But when you hide things from me, it makes it harder. And you're not telling me everything. Don't insult my intelligence again with the 'I don't know" crap.'"

Once again, she nailed it and I fought to regain my composure. She'd cut me a lot of slack and when I asked her for help, I did so while tying one hand behind her back by not sharing my suspicions about Mikey or about the other supernatural whackos I dealt with on a regular basis. And both times I'd called her, she came. No questions asked. She deserved better.

"Look. You're right. I'm not giving you the whole story." She started to interrupt me when I held up my hand, stopping her. "And I will. Soon. But not before I work out some things. It's complicated, okay? Give me a bit more time and I'll lay it all out for you. Once I know for sure what it is I'll explain."

Happy is not the word I would use to describe the look she shot me, but she grudgingly agreed. "Fine. I'll give you the time you're asking for. But don't wait too long, Vic. The wolves are at the door and they're after your ass."

"Story of my life, sister. Story of my life."

CHAPTER EIGHT

A few minutes later, Coffey's phone went off, playing the theme from *The Rockford Files*, an old private dick TV show my dad watched. She answered it, listened for a few seconds, then thanked the person on the other end and hung up.

"They found Truman's body not far from the creek. There's evidence of a violent sexual assault. Whoever did this is one sick son of a bitch."

"Ah, man. I need to go tell Winston."

I made it to the door before Coffey called out my name. I paused with my hand on the knob. "Yeah?"

"Watch your back, Vic. If I was a betting woman, I'd say someone's trying to punish you. When they're done going after those around you, they *will* come for you."

Not much I could say to that nugget of home-spun detective wisdom, so I headed into the warmth of the house, finding Winston sitting in the same chair, still staring off into space. When I told him about the cops finding Truman's body, a slight nod of the head was the only sign that he heard me. Then he bowed his head and said the Lord's Prayer.

The techs would be out in the woods for most of the night and there was no point in waiting for them to finish. Winston and I followed Coffey to the Homicide Unit on West Jefferson downtown, where we both made video and written statements. When I asked where Wallace went she told me he was out running down a couple of leads, but wouldn't say what. They finally cut us loose around two in the morning.

We walked in silence to the Chevelle. Once we were both in the car with the heater cranked up, I asked, "Do you want me to take you home, so you can try and snag some rest?"

"You really think I'm going to be able to sleep? Nah, man. Let's go over and see if they got anything on the security cameras at the bookstore. The quicker we can gain a line on who's doing this, the quicker we can put them in the ground."

I couldn't agree more, but deep down I was worried. I'd seen more than one guy pushed over the edge by death and destruction and I could sense something different in my friend. If we could find and take out the murderer maybe he would feel better, but I doubted it.

Admittedly, the same could not be said for me. I remember something said by the greatest fighter in the history of boxing, Muhammad Ali. "I'm a fighter. I believe in an eye-for-an-eye business. I'm not a cheek turner. I got no respect for a man who won't hit back. You kill my dog, you better hide your cat."

I like hitting back. I like stomping the bad guys into the dirt. I know it doesn't do much for the whole "save your soul" thing, but it's what makes me good at what I do. So sue me if I enjoy it.

Winston, on the other hand, despite his tough exterior and the work we do, has always remained more pure. I've always considered Winston the counterweight of goodness to my darker tendencies. He's my moral compass. The man sitting next to me now, however, radiated the same desire for mayhem as I felt and it bothered me. If Winston lost his moral compass, who would keep me in check?

I cruised into the parking lot of the shopping center and stopped in front of the Barnes and Noble. All the stores had long since closed and we were the only car in sight. We had not been there long when an older man in a golf cart covered in plastic appeared from behind the building and puttered up to my window, unzipped his door and stepped out.

In his mid-sixties with Mark Twain hair and mustache, a wad of chewing tobacco tucked in one cheek, he rapped on my window with a gnarled knuckle and motioned for me to lower it down.

When I complied he said, "Listen, fellas, you can't be parkin' here now that the stores are closed. So I'm a gonna need you to crank her back up and head on out."

"Actually," I replied, "we're here to see you."

"The hell you say." He spit a stream of tobacco juice on the ground. "You can tell my ex she ain't gettin' another dime out of me. I done about as much as I plan to do where that witch is concerned."

"No worries, old timer. Your ex didn't send us. We're here about something else."

I explained to him about Ruth Anne's abduction and our theory she was taken from here in the parking lot. He rubbed a finger along his mustache from side to side, thinking.

"I didn't hear nothin' about no abduction, but then again, I don't hear much working on this shift. Bounty hunters, huh? Why don't you fellas follow me? We can go to the office and see what the video feed shows. Hell, that's how I knew you were here. I don't like being out in the cold unless I have to. Messes with my arthritis somethin' fierce. I watch the monitors and then head out when the kids come in here joy riding."

He climbed inside his plastic cocoon and took off and we followed him around to the rear of the complex. We met him at a dull gray metal door where he selected one of several dozen keys that dangled from his belt. They all looked the same to me, but he knew which one he needed and the three of us were inside in short order.

We wound our way around several desks into a room not much bigger than a large walk in closet. A row of monitors filled one wall showing different views of the complex.

He plopped down into a worn swivel chair and asked, "When did you say you thought this woman was snatched?"

"Between nine-thirty and ten this morning in front of the Barnes and Noble."

His fingers tapped a few keys and a second later we were watching the parking lot in front of the bookstore. He tapped a few more keys and the black and white video started to move at a faster pace. At nine-forty, the Mustang eased into a parking spot a good distance from the store.

"That's her. Can you back it up and slow it down?"

"You betcha." He paused the video, reversed it a few seconds and then it started up again in normal speed. Winston and I leaned in close over Mark Twain's shoulders. We once again watched Ruth Anne pull into the parking spot. The driver side faced away from us but we could see the top of her head when she opened the door and looked like she was leaning across the seat to pick up something, perhaps her purse.

Ruth Anne made it halfway out of the Mustang when a white panel van shot into view and pulled in next to her. The side door slid open, and a man jumped out and tried to grab her arm. Ruth Anne slapped his arm to the side, dove into the car and tried to slam her door closed, but the man followed, using his shoulder to keep it open. We watched the scene play out silently on the monitor.

The quality of the video made it hard to see what exactly

happened in the car, but Ruth Anne's head was slammed forward into the dash several times. Then the man got out of the Mustang and glanced around to see if anyone noticed what had taken place. Evidently satisfied no one did, he reached into the car and yanked Ruth Anne out by the collar of her coat and into the van. He was gone for a minute, then he got out again, pulled the door shut and slapped the side of the van twice. The van took off. The man got into the Mustang and then drove out of the parking lot.

The security guard let out a low whistle. "I'll be damned. That guy pounded the crap out of that little girl and somebody on the morning shift missed it."

Winston leaned over the keyboard controls, reversed the video and then froze it on the man's face. It was a clear view.

Winston straightened and anger made the veins in his neck pulse as he fought for control. "Well, now we know," he said.

"Yep. We do," I replied.

Despite the distance and the poor quality of the video, Mikey McCain's smiling mug stared directly into the camera. There was no attempt to hide who he was.

Winston must have been having similar thoughts. "Why go to the trouble to wipe down the car at the airport, when he didn't try to hide his face here?"

"Because he knew we would find the video first. He wanted us to know it was him, but not the cops."

Mark Twain turned in his chair to look at us. "You know this asshole?"

"Afraid so," I replied. "Listen, Pops, we need you to keep this to yourself. Can you do that?"

"Not likely. I ain't risking my job for you guys. I need to call the cops and report it. That little girl's done been kidnapped." He shot another stream of juice into a garbage can next to his desk and worked the chaw of tobacco harder.

I got out my wallet. "Yes, she has. And my friend and I are going to find her and get her back. But what we need is time. If you call the cops, they will be all over this video and I can't have that." I fingered out a couple of hundreds and held them out. "I'm not asking you lie to anyone. If the cops show up and ask to see the video, then show them. All I'm asking is you don't call them. Let them come to you."

The man licked his lips a couple of times. "You two ain't some kind of drug dealers are you? I don't want to be involved in drug shit. If this is a personal beef, I'd just as soon you fellas leave me out of it."

"No. I'm a bounty hunter and this guy," I said, pointing at the screen, "is mad at me for catching him once before. I thought he was out of the picture, but looks like he's not. The woman is the girlfriend of a good friend of mine. It's up to me to make this right."

The guard never took his eyes off the money. "And when you find him, what are you going to do to him?"

I offered him the money without replying. The man wiped his hands on his pants a couple of times, then snatched the money from my fingers and tucked it into his shirt pocket.

"Fine. I won't call the cops. But I won't lie for you, ya hear me?"

"Loud and clear. Thanks for helping us out."

Winston and I both shook the man's hand, then left the same way we came in. Once we were both in the Chevelle, Winston asked, "Think he'll keep quiet?"

I started the car and dropped it into gear. Leaving the shopping center. "Considering he took the money, yeah, I think he will. But I wouldn't want to bet the farm on it. Let's head over to Kurt's and see if he can track down the license plate number."

*****

Kurt met us at the door, having seen us pull in the driveway despite the hour. Where Winston and I were dragging butt, Kurt was wired. We followed him to his computer room and found out why: his usual Diet Dr. Peppers had been replaced by several cans of Monster Energy drinks. His eyes were open wide and if he blinked once a minute, I would have been surprised.

"Any word from L.M.P.D. on the kidnapping?" I asked.

"Not yet. They were going to pull the airport video surveillance tape, but they won't have any word for me until tomorrow. I got the 'these things take time' line."

"I've got a plate number I need you to run."

"How does the van tie in?" he asked, He sat at the keyboard, fingers paused waiting for me to give him the license plate number, which I did. Some years before Kurt hacked into the DMV and set up a backdoor which allowed him access to the system any time he needed it. Now he did.

"Run the plate first."

He navigated to the proper screen, typed in the number and chewed on a thumbnail while he waited. In short order, the information on the plate came up. The van, owned by a man named Daniel Jenkins, had been reported stolen two days before.

Another quick search and we learned the cops recovered the van earlier tonight. They found it abandoned at the Oxmoor Mall. The van now sat at the impound lot waiting for the owner to claim it.

Winston let out an exasperated sigh. "Right, so they cut the van loose. Any way you can track the van using traffic cameras?"

Kurt shook his head. "Not likely, considering how many white vans there are in town, but I'll give it a shot. Where've you guys been? Did you have any luck with the Barnes and Noble video? Is that where the van comes in?"

I glanced at Winston before answering. My fellow bounty hunter and friend closed his eyes and bowed his head, and I wondered if he was praying. "Yeah, we have news, and you're not going to like it."

I gave Kurt the rundown of the events at Winston's house and the murder of Ashley Truman. I could see the muscles in Kurt's neck working and his left eyebrow began to twitch.

"And the video at the store?"

"It was Mikey. He had help, but it was him. No doubt about it."

I told him what we'd seen on the video. Kurt tilted his head towards the ceiling, his hands on the top of his head, his lips pursed, then his hands were once again flying across his keyboard. Not exactly the reaction I'd expected.

"Uh, Kurt, are you okay?"

"Yeah. Great. Fine. Peachy. Wonderful. Fuckin' thrilled."

Winston shrugged his shoulders and I did the same. Kurt glanced at us and said, "What?"

"Well, I thought, well, you know. That you would be more upset."

"Dude, I'm more pissed than you can ever imagine. But now we have a lead. When we didn't know for sure who it was who took Ruth Anne, we were dead in the water. Now we know it's Mikey. And he has help. That means they need a place to stay. With what went down at Winston's house, I'm guessing they're close. And they'll need money. Money means the Church. I'll blow through every account they have and see if I can find him that way."

"Then we'll leave you to it. Winston and I need to find some sleep. And you need to do the same thing. You're no good to us if you burn out in a day."

He shot me a middle finger and, Lord help me, it made me laugh. Winston joined in and a second later, so did Kurt.

When the laughter died down, Kurt, his face a mask of determination, said, "We're going to find your brother and then I'm going to kill him. And this time he'll stay dead."

"Amen," agreed Winston.

No backing down with my friends. "Amen and damnation. Time to go all Revelations on his ass. Mikey's going down."

They nodded in agreement. With nothing else to say, Winston and I left. Mikey'd thrown down the gauntlet. Now I planned to pick it up and bash his head in with it.

CHAPTER NINE

We decided Winston should bunk at the Mission for the night, what with all the cops and techs at his place he might never get any sleep. I edged into my parking space next to the mission's beat up old van and we made our way inside. I had my own room down the hall by the maintenance closet and Winston found a spot in the men's dorm.

I made arrangements to meet Winston in the cafeteria around ten a.m., allowing both of us at least a few hours of sleep, and he took off for the dorm.

I glanced down the hall to Brother Joshua's office and had to admit some surprise to see a closed door and the lights off. I couldn't remember the last time I'd come into the mission and not found him there, no matter the hour.

J, as I called him, is the man who tells me who to track down and who to whack. I'm Tony Stark to his Nick Fury, though J doesn't wear an eye patch. Truth is, I don't know much about him. I couldn't tell you of which faith he belongs. I don't know anything about his family. And when it comes to basketball, I don't know if he's a fan of the Dirty Bird Cardinals or the team anointed by God: the Kentucky Wildcats. One tidbit of information I do know is, from time to time, his body is commandeered by the archangel, Uriel. I've learned to tell when Uriel is making an appearance because the feeling of power goes up by a factor of about a gabillion.

It is said Uriel is one of the few angels who talks to God directly and is the one appointed to guard the Gates of Hell, keeping the bad guys from busting out once their ticket is punched for basement storage. I believe he is the one who tips off Brother Joshua on who has been naughty enough for me to track down and eliminate.

The previous winter I watched him kick a fallen angel to oblivion in a matter of seconds. The same type of exorcism by a priest can take days. When an archangel tells you to hop out of someone's body, you go.

Tonight, it seemed, both man and angel were taking a break. I dragged my sorry ass to my room, kicked off my boots and sat on the edge of the bed. I tried to think of what I needed to do next, but my brain refused to work. I couldn't remember the last time I felt this tired. I set the alarm clock for nine-thirty. I considered getting undressed, but decided I didn't care enough to do so. I turned off the light and fell instantly to sleep.

*****

I awoke a couple of minutes before the alarm went off and felt pretty decent, all things considered. I hit the shower, got dressed and headed to the mess hall where I found Winston at a table in the corner talking to a couple of the homeless guys. Whenever I ate at the mission, the homeless men and women gave me a wide berth, only sitting at my table if they didn't have any other choice.

With Winston, they were totally different. They were drawn to him like a bear to honey. He would tell them stories of his days playing football at the University of Louisville and for the Jets in the NFL, and they hung on to every word. The men and women who came in contact with him would leave feeling much better about themselves than when they sat down.

This morning the tables had turned. I watched them while I slid my tray down the serving line, receiving a generous portion of eggs and bacon. Today, the men and women sitting with him did the talking, while Winston sat silent, listening. One guy patted him on the shoulder, offering some words of sympathy.

I poured a cup of coffee, added it to my tray and joined them. When I sat down, all the other people mumbled something, got up and left the two of us alone.

"Must be my aftershave," I said.

"Man, considering you've been wearing the beard now for months, I think it's more likely your looks run 'em off."

"Chicks dig the beard, didn't you know that?"

He shot a skeptical look in my direction, but kept quiet. I dove into the food. One thing I can say for the Derby Mission, they feed everyone they take care of very well.

We ate in silence for the rest of the meal. After sopping up the last of the egg with a bite of biscuit and popping it in my mouth, I stood and took my tray and dishes to the cleanup window. Winston did the same and then fell in behind me when I went in search of my boss.

This time the door to J's office stood open and I rapped on the frame before entering. A black man of middle years, he sat behind a large green metal desk donated by the Army Reserve Center. I think the chairs were thrown in on the same deal: they were also army green and not overly comfortable.

Winston and I dropped into two of them and waited for J to finish reading something on his desk computer. When finished, he pushed his reading glasses up onto the top of his head and sat back in his chair and waited for us to start.

"Mikey's in town and on the attack."

"Tell me."

And I did. When I finished, Brother Joshua said to Winston, "I'm sorry about the loss of your friend. I will say prayers for her family and friends, and for you as well."

Winston only nodded, his expression neutral. The nod had been the only movement since sitting down. He didn't join in or add anything to my telling of the facts, he only stared at J and waited.

"Do you believe Ruth Anne is still alive?"

"I do. If she wasn't, I'd think Mikey would have put her on display somewhere by now. My guess, he's saving her for some kind of end game. But who really knows, J. I mean, he's frickin' nuts."

"It goes without saying, you, Winston and Kurt need to be extra careful. He will undoubtedly be looking for other opportunities to create pain and suffering where you three are concerned. Keep me in the loop on any new developments."

He pulled his glasses down into place and returned to reading, signaling our meeting was now over. Ever the conversationalist.

We left and stopped briefly in the front lobby of the mission. The cold weather drove most of the homeless in the city indoors to any warm spot they could find and they sat around the lobby, talking, reading or staring off into space.

"Why don't you go snag your coat and meet me out by the Chevelle? We might as well head over to Kurt's to see if he's found anything yet and formalize a battle plan."

Again, only a nod and he walked off not saying a word. I watched him walk away and tried to gauge his inner mood from his body language, but other than the silence, he acted the same. True, the constant smile had yet to reappear. I would need to keep a close eye on my friend.

I pushed the mission door open and stepped into a crisp Kentucky morning. The door closed behind me and I glanced at the wreath hanging on the door. Despite the despair and want which accompany many of the homeless in town, the mission managed to lift up the spirits of the men and women who stepped inside for a meal or a safe place to sleep.

My job description included doing my best to keep evil from their door. Nights like the last one proved I might never be out of work.

I walked over to the Chevelle and leaned on the trunk while I waited for Winston. My eyes traveled up and down the street and at the warehouses on the other side. Instead of wreaths, many sported For Sale signs with a number to call, if interested.

This early on a Saturday morning, the street was empty save a battered old sedan at the end of the block. The glare from the sun prevented me from seeing who sat inside, but I could see the figure of someone behind the wheel. Exhaust fumes plumed out behind the car in the cold air. Small puffs of white occasionally rose from the driver's side window, lowered down enough for someone to blow out cigarette smoke.

In most places I wouldn't give the car much thought, but in this part of town, and at this time of the morning, a car parked up the street made me curious. I pushed away from the Chevelle and started to walk in the car's direction. I didn't make it more than a few strides when the blue lights in the grill came on and then off. A police car, unmarked. Wallace.

I flipped him the bird and retraced my steps to the Chevelle, as Winston came outside. He saw the car and raised an eyebrow, but I shook it off and got in the car. A second later he did the same.

"Company?" he asked.

"Wallace. I have a sneaking suspicion we may have a babysitter for the rest of the day, but screw him. I can lose him anytime I want. Let him tag along if he likes."

I put the car in reverse, backed into the street, rolled down the window and flipped him off again as I roared on by.

I watched the cop car in my rearview mirror, fully expecting the blue lights to come on again and for the asshole to pull me over, but Wallace didn't move. To hell with him. Wallace ranked low on the totem pole of things I needed to worry about. I hoped.

CHAPTER TEN

Wallace watched McCain and Reynolds turn right and then disappear from view a few blocks from the mission. He tried hard to keep the rage building inside him in check and not boil over and lead him to do something he'd regret. He took a few more puffs on his Marlboro and the more he thought about it, regret was the wrong word. He'd love to jack up McCain and his posse, even if it meant breaking the law—he just didn't want to get caught doing it. He could retire any time he wanted and losing his pension this close to the end would really piss him off, especially for a dirt bag like McCain.

He knew deep down the bounty hunter was dirty. He could feel it. The problem was proving it. And with Coffey wrapped around his finger and running to him every time McCain called like a love sick puppy it only made him more determined to bust him.

He had to be dirty. Over a year with no discernible income meant either family money or something illegal. He had dug deep into McCain's finances and talked to family friends and knew there was no family money to speak of. His brother, Michael, the murderer, managed to build up a small fortune, but almost all of his wealth was paper and went up in smoke when the warehouse went up in flames.

He warned Coffey about becoming more involved with the bounty hunter, knowing she'd regret it the second the truth came to light. He laid out his evidence to her in a heated discussion the other night at Coopers, a cop bar down on Frankfort Avenue, only to have her rebuff him, telling him she was sure there was a reasonable explanation for the lack of a money trail. The night ended with her storming out and him drinking more Jack D than he should have.

He knew, in his gut, McCain was dirty and connected to his

brother and he'd find the connection and bury him with it. Wallace took one last puff on the stub of his cigarette and flicked it out the window, then he rolled it up.

He began to put the car in drive, when he stopped, his hand on the gear shift. From the doorway of the building across from the mission, a figure leaned into view and glanced up and down the street before disappearing back into the building.

"Holy shit," Wallace whispered, "it's Michael McCain." He threw the car into park and thought about calling Coffey for backup, but quickly discarded the idea. He'd bust Michael McCain and if he was alone, he'd beat the shit out of the little prick until he gave up his brother. McCain might file a complaint of police brutality, but it would be his word against a decorated cop who claimed McCain resisted arrest. It wouldn't be the first time he'd beaten information from a scumbag, but it would be the most enjoyable.

Wallace got out, locked the car and then walked quickly down the block to where he saw McCain disappear. A large sign with the name Volkov Reality and a phone number hung on the wall next to the door. He'd heard whispers about the Russian immigrant turned American capitalist, and none of them good.

"Damn community slowly going to hell with all the foreigners flooding the city," Wallace thought to himself. He'd been called a bigot on more than one occasion. Screw them, too.

All you needed to do was to look around neighborhoods like this one to see the American dream slowly becoming a thing of the past. It made him damn glad he never had kids.

He slid his gun out of the holster under his arm and slowly turned the knob on the door, finding it unlocked. Wallace cracked the door an inch, then pushed it open with his foot. After the door swung enough to allow him to enter the building, he caught it with his heel and quietly closed the door behind him.

Several large windows covered with grime, allowed diffuse light to illuminate the inside of the building. Dust covered every surface, including the floor and he could see a spot where McCain must have stood by one of the windows. A pane of glass had been rubbed clean enough to give anyone standing there a view of the mission across the street.

The tracks led away deeper into the gloom until they disappeared behind a sheet of dirty opaque plastic which covered the entrance to the rest of the building.

Wallace moved cautiously to the plastic and pulled it back with his free hand. The light failed to reach this far into the building, but he could see well enough to pick out several rows of some kind of manufacturing equipment, most of which were rusted all to hell. Yet another nail in the coffin of the good ole U.S. of A. There was a time when Americans made what they used. Not anymore. They would rather buy cheap pieces of crap made overseas than keep the jobs here.

The air carried a musty, metallic smell and he fought the urge to sneeze. Wallace pushed aside the plastic and moved deeper into the building, searching for McCain. He could no longer see the footprints on the ground and he stopped, once again listening.

"Looking for me, Detective Wallace?"

Wallace spun around to find Michael McCain standing a few feet behind him holding a piece of rebar about three feet long. He held it casually, resting it on one shoulder, like a hitter on deck waiting for his chance to bat.

The detective found he could agree with Victor McCain on one thing: his brother didn't look strong enough to bend a straw, let alone someone's neck. If he was five foot six, it would be a stretch. He wore a blue Oxford button down, khaki pants and loafers. Looking at him you'd think he planned a trip to Land's End.

Wallace pointed his gun at the other man's head. "Here's what's going to happen. I'm going to tell you to put the rod down, but I want you to ignore me so I can blow your damned head off."

"Come now, detective. Really? And here we've just met. I think you'd really like me if you give me the chance. I'm one of your biggest fans."

Wallace felt the hair all over his body stand on end. After years of walking a beat in some of the rougher neighborhoods in Louisville and then almost twenty as a detective he knew when his life might be on the line and his intuition practically screamed at him to run. He tried hard to find some moisture in his mouth, fighting an instant cotton mouth.

"Last time I'm going to tell you. Drop the steel and drop to your knees. Now!"

McCain stepped closer and began to tap the rebar on his shoulder. "Can't do, detective. These are new pants and I don't want to get them dirty."

"Have it your way, asshole. I warned you."

Wallace pulled the trigger over and over, until the slide locked to the rear, the clip empty, the sound deafening in the confined space.

Wallace could feel his heart trying to beat its way out of his chest, his breath coming in great heaves, as fear made him take a step back.

McCain's face contorted in rage and he turned it towards the ceiling and screamed. Bullet holes riddled his shirt and he now held the rebar straight out to his side. When the screaming stopped he returned his gaze to Wallace, the pleasant banter over.

"Are you through, old man? I told you these clothes were brand new and now you've ruined my shirt. That really ticks me off."

Wallace was stunned while his brain tried hard to comprehend what his eyes were telling him. "You should be dead. How are you still standing?"

"Well, see, that's the thing. I'm already dead. My brother killed me. Look, I can see you don't understand and it's a long story. I'll fill you in later, but right now—"

McCain swung the rebar one handed in a quick, tight arc and caught Wallace on the wrist which shattered and forced him to drop his gun. In the same fluid motion, McCain reversed the arc, using a violent backhand to smash it on the detective's right knee, where the joint exploded into fragments on impact. Wallace lost his balance and toppled backwards, while pain like he'd never imagined flooded his body.

"If I was honest though," McCain continued while walking around Wallace, the rebar now a walking stick, "in the long run, Victor did me a favor killing me."

"You crazy, son-of-a-bitch, so help me God I'm going to—"

McCain snarled, raised the rebar and brought it down on Wallace's other knee with such force it was as if his knee ceased to exist, the rebar nearly decapitating the leg at the knee.

Wallace screamed, the pain all he could think about while he writhed on the cold concrete floor. It seemed to take forever, but the pain began to fade to a dull ache and he knew he was going into shock while his body rebelled at the horrific damage it suffered at the hands of a madman.

McCain squatted next to Wallace and tossed the rebar away into the distance, the metal bouncing off the forgotten equipment.

"I'd appreciate you not mentioning God in my presence, if you don't mind." He paused, seeming to think about something, then he snapped his fingers. "You know, detective, what I think you need is some fresh air. You've spent so much time in the city, I think the change will do you good. What do you say? You up for a road trip?"

Wallace barely listened while tears welled in his eyes. He didn't want to die, but knew he was as good as dead. "Go screw yourself," was all Wallace could manage to say and closed his eyes, willing the darkness to come.

Just before his wish was granted and the darkness overtook him, he heard McCain say, "Screwing with the McCain boys will be the death of you, detective. Oh, yes it will."

CHAPTER ELEVEN

Kurt opened the front door before Winston and I could even knock. The hacker took a moment to scan the street before retreating a step and allowing us to enter.

He shut the doors and stepped by us, walking down the hallway to his computer room. Winston and I both noticed the gun tucked into the back of his jeans.

"Kurt, make sure you don't shoot your ass off with that lead slinger. Literally," I said. "Any word from the cops?"

He removed the gun from his pants and set it next to his computer, then he sat down in his office chair and Winston and I took a seat on a couch, the only other furniture in the room.

"Nothing. I called them several times this morning, but Detective Ware keeps saying these things take time. And then he pressed me about what I may be keeping from him which might have put her in danger. Seems he and Wallace have been sharing information. They wanted to know how I managed to buy this house and the car."

"What did you tell them?"

"I told them I consulted quite a bit and I gave them the name of the shell company I created to pay myself from the stolen Church money, Cable System Consultants, so it looks legit. But Ware's been digging and he's having trouble finding out anything about the company. Well, big ole duh. It doesn't exist. I know he thinks it's a front and he's right, but he thinks it's drug-related and that we might be laundering money. What a dork."

"To hell with'em," Winston said. "Let'em dig. They ain't going to find nothin' they can use against us, so Ware can just suck a big one. You find anything out there in cyberspace we can use?"

Kurt swiveled around to his computer keyboard and hit a few keys, bringing the monitor to life. I could see what looked like a list of names with several columns next to each name.

"This is a list of all the Church people we know about. We try and keep track of them by using the GPS in their phones." He struck a few more keys and the list got smaller. "Out of the known members, almost two dozen of them dropped off the grid. They turned off the GPS on their phones and went dark."

"When did this happen?" I asked.

"Three days ago. And they're completely off grid. They aren't using any of their credit cards, debit cards, or Starbucks cards. Any cell phone they own hasn't moved in days. So I think they're all using new burners. As far as the world is concerned, they no longer exist."

Winston shook his head. "Good to know, but how is this going to help us? Man, we need something we can use to flush these guys out."

Kurt raised his hands up. "Hold on, hold on." He once again turned to the keyboard, fingers on the keys and pointed to the screen, which showed a single name.

"Elwyn Garey. He's known to work for the Church as a wheelman. The dude has a long rap sheet, car theft, illegal street racing, among other things. Garey's cell phone hit on the grid last night. He lives in San Francisco, but when I pinged his phone overnight, the return came off a tower over near Churchill Downs, somewhere between the track and Frayser Elementary School. The GPS on the phone has been turned off, which means I can't hone in on his exact location and that's the closest I can come to finding the phone through his cell phone carrier."

I ran a hand through my beard, thinking. "That's a pretty good-sized area to search. Don't get me wrong, it helps, but we need more."

"Dude, I can give you more. Do you know how the phone companies identify your phone?"

"Phone number. Easy one," said Winston.

Kurt smiled for the first time since Ruth Anne's kidnapping. "Close, but not quite. And cell companies don't call it a phone number. They call it a mobile subscriber integrated digital network number. Then they use that to create an international mobile subscriber identity. That's what they use to actually track your billing. And then they use that to create an international mobile station equipment number. That's the phone's serial number. You can find out yours by dialing *#06#. Pulls it right up."

Winston snorted. "How the hell you ain't cross-eyed is beyond me."

Kurt ignored him. "And once I have the serial number, I can find him using a StingRay."

He waited for us to respond, but I looked at Winston and we both shrugged our shoulders. "I'm assuming you're going to tell us what that is?"

"You, the mighty bounty hunter, doesn't know what a StingRay is?"

"Kurt, I always track down guys the old fashioned way. Talk to their friends and family, drop by their old haunts, and beat the crap out of a few people, if needed. We call that grunt work."

"Right on, brother. We are some bad MoFos," said Winston and then he offered me a fist and I bumped mine to his.

"Dinosaurs. How you ever found anyone before I came along, is beyond me. A StingRay is a rogue cell tower and they are about the size of a large suitcase. Vic, if you can borrow the van from the mission, I can sit in back and then we can drive the van around the part of town where we think he's hiding out. When the StingRay is in range of his phone, it will ping the StingRay instead of the real cell tower. Then we drive around and I can put us within ten yards of the phone," he hesitated before continuing. "There's only one catch."

I raised an eyebrow and waited.

"To buy the one we need will cost me around seventy-grand. I know a guy where I can pick one up today, but I'll have to wire the money to him this morning."

I let out a low whistle. "That's a hunk of change, no doubt. But Kurt, I don't care if we spend every penny we have in the bank. If you think it will help us find Ruth Anne, then spend it."

Early in my fight with the Church of the Light Reclaimed, the scumbag nut-jobs who worship Satan, I stole around $30,000,000 from them. Well, truth be told, Samantha stole the money, but then gave it to me. I now use the money to take the fight to them. Poetic justice.

I could see the relief in my friend's body language. "Cool, dude. I'll call the guy. But I might need one of you to go with me. It's not exactly in the best part of town."

"I'll go and keep him out of trouble," offered Winston. He paused. "You know, Vic, you often talk how you love the fact this job gives you a chance to beat the shit out of people, how it helps you alleviate some of your aggression because the people you pound on deserve it. Right now, I need someone to pound on. What do you say,

Kurt? Want to go piss off some people?"

He picked up his phone and started to punch in the numbers. "Let's order the Stingray first, then hell yeah."

"Lord help me. I've created two monsters."

"You didn't create us, Vic," Kurt said, with the phone to his ear, "the monsters did."

CHAPTER TWELVE

Wallace jolted awake when the van came to an abrupt stop. Pain from nearly every part of his body slammed into his brain, his nervous system screaming for relief. He was lying in the rear of an old van, with no windows in back. He started to try to roll over when the doors flew open and Michael McCain stood there, smiling.

McCain grabbed his coat by the collar and pulled him roughly from the vehicle. Wallace didn't think he could feel any more pain, but he was wrong. When his legs hit the ground, he screamed in new agony from two shattered knee caps.

McCain hauled him across a gravel road, one handed, with no more effort than he would if he was carrying a bag of feathers. They reached a black ranch rail fence, McCain switched his grip, picked him up and tossed him over the top rail. Wallace landed face down in a foul smelling mud and promptly vomited his breakfast from the stench and the pain.

It took a Herculean effort, but he finally managed to roll over onto his back and used his one good hand to scrape the mud from his face. He watched McCain leap like an acrobat from the ground to the top rail, where he sat and rested his hands on his knees, perfectly balanced.

"I have to hand it to you, detective. Most men with two busted knees and a fractured wrist wouldn't have survived the ride out here to the farm. I mean, look at your wrist? It's pointed in the other direction. Hell, that's hard for even me to look at. And I apologize for crushing your one knee like that. I let my anger get the best of me. Forgive me?"

All Wallace could do was moan. The mud made him feel even colder and his teeth began to chatter. He used his one good hand to try and push himself away, but it was no use, and he gave up the effort.

"You really had a hard on for my brother, didn't you?"

"You t-t-t-wo are m-m-m-urderers. I hope you b-b-b-urn in Hell."

"Been there done that, detective. And you're right. We *are* both murderers. But for opposite teams. He's working for the side who is going down. I serve the Lord of Light, Lucifer. The Light of the Morning. There's a war going on, detective, and you managed to end up between us and that's a bad place wind up. And I couldn't have you arresting my brother, now could I? I want him free as a bird so I can make him suffer. Little by little, I'm going to destroy anything he's ever loved."

"You're insane."

Wallace closed his eyes and fought not to throw up again. The smell. God, the smell. He tried to place it, knowing he should recognize the smell, but his brain refused to work.

McCain snapped his fingers several times. "Stay with me detective. We're almost done."

McCain let out a high-pitched whistle and Wallace opened his eyes. The bluest sky he'd ever seen greeted his gaze, a few small white clouds drifted overhead. He was near death, his teeth no longer chattered and he couldn't feel his body.

"How's Reynolds holding up? You should have heard his neighbor scream before I popped off her head. I have more plans for ole Winston."

Wallace closed his eyes again, and he thought of the things he'd said to Winston Reynolds, not sure whether he'd killed his neighbor, but wishing he had because of his relationship with Victor McCain. Seems he'd been wrong about Reynolds.

"You're a real piece of shit, you know that asshole?"

"Oh, no doubt. But then again, people have told me that for years. Well, I've enjoyed our little chat, detective. I really have. And I hope you're getting some benefit from the fresh country air." McCain wrinkled his nose. "Okay, not that fresh right here. Have you ever been on a pig farm, detective?"

The memory came to Wallace from when he'd been a young man. His family went on a vacation to visit his grandmother at her horse farm, but on the trip they'd passed a pig farm. His father explained that the farmers would take a huge fifty-gallon barrel into the city and stop by all the restaurants, picking up their scrap food and tossing it into the barrel. Then when they came home, they'd tip the barrel over and spill the slop into troughs for the pigs to eat.

He'd nearly gotten sick from the smell and had rolled his window up as quickly as he could, his father laughing from the front seat. He now knew he was lying in a pig pen.

He turned his head and saw a man in overalls on the other side of the pen pull up a large door and lock it into place. Three large sows waddled quickly out into the light.

McCain pointed. "The one on the left is Mavis. The one in the middle is Mildred. The one on the right, the really big one is Myrtle. Damn if she isn't always hungry. The other two come in around six hundred pounds, but ole Myrtle is closing in on eight hundred. Did you know pigs will eat damn near anything?"

He whistled again and the pigs came jogging in their direction. Wallace felt panic explode in his chest and he tried again to push himself away from the pigs with his hand, but only moved a few inches. He looked to McCain.

"Please, don't do this. Don't let me die this way, I beg you."

"Are you kidding? I hear they eat everything, clothes and all. The Church of the Light Reclaimed has been using this farm for years, but I've never seen Myrtle in action. She's a legend. I wouldn't miss this for anything. I wonder how long it will take them to eat you. I'm guessing about a half hour. What do you think?"

The pigs snorted when they came to a stop. Wallace raised his hand to try and hit them and scare them away, but the big one, Myrtle snagged his hand in its mouth and bit down hard.

Wallace began to scream and then the other two dove in and began to rip him to pieces, their teeth cutting through his clothes and into his skin like they were eating butter.

In the last seconds of his life, all the pain ceased. He was vaguely aware of the pigs pulling him this way and that while they tore him apart. He felt like he was floating above the scene, watching as if it was happening to someone else. He had read of people who survived near death experiences describing the same kind of feelings and he found it a curious thing. His out-of-body-self turned away from the carnage below and looked to the heavens and the bright blue sky until his vision began to fade and he died with the sounds of Myrtle's snorting chasing him into the darkness.

CHAPTER THIRTEEN

Kurt made his arrangements and the two of us wired the money. Only Kurt knows all the account numbers while I know only the passwords. It takes the two of us, together, to complete a transaction and move large sums of money. That way, should the Church lay their hands on one us they still can't access their money.

A few minutes after the money transferred, his phone beeped with a text message. An address, nothing more. Kurt picked up his gun, slipped it into a holster and clipped it on his belt in the small of his back. Winston and I followed him to the front door where he snatched his coat off a rack and we left, with Kurt stretching out on the rear seat of the Chevelle.

I drove to the mission and went inside to pick up the keys. When I came out, Winston and Kurt were leaning against the van, an old white Ford Econoline. The seats were easy to remove if we wanted to haul things and right now there were two rows of faded blue bench seats. It looked like it had been beat all to Hell and back, but it ran like a top.

I tossed Winston the keys and he snagged them out of the air and unlocked the van. Kurt walked to the other side and got in while Winston slid behind the wheel. He got the van started and rolled down the window.

"So you aren't going with us?" he asked.

"I have a few things I'm kicking around in my brain that might help us. You two go run down the fake cell tower thingamabob and call me when you're ready to rock and roll. I'll join you when you're ready to go."

"I heard that. Stay alive and watch your ass, old man."

"And you kids be in by midnight."

He laughed, rolled up the window and left. I glanced up the

street and noticed Wallace's car sat in the same spot. I decided I'd had enough of him for one morning and walked up to confront him. I didn't have to walk far before I could tell the car was empty. I glanced inside to make sure he hadn't fallen asleep or keeled over from a heart attack, but he wasn't there.

I took a look around and decided to check inside the mission. Perhaps he went to roust the folks at the Derby City Mission about Winston and me.

Another blank. A quick search of the mission showed no signs of Wallace and no one had seen a cop come in asking questions. When I went outside to the Chevelle, still no Wallace, though the car remained. I thought about texting Coffey to see if she might have picked him up and then just as quickly changed my mind. What did it matter?

I hopped behind the wheel, fired up the Chevelle and turned up the heat. I turned on the radio and dialed in to the all-Christmas-all-the-time station. Vince Vance and the Valiants were belting out "All I Want for Christmas is You."

It made me think of the women in my life: Detective Coffey, Samantha Tyler and Elizabeth Bathory. Three very different women in their own right, but all very strong-willed. I had to accept that Samantha and I were not going to be a "thing." And while I had to admit, Elizabeth Bathory had been a thrill ride, it was not a relationship built to last. Hand of Gods and Infernal Lords were not exactly friends, let alone lovers. After all, I'm supposed to eliminate them on the spot.

Detective Coffey, to me, seemed the most grounded of the three women. She knew who she was and what she wanted. A talented detective, she worked to make a difference and I could tell I'd begun to have more serious thoughts about her. But nothing could happen between us until I found Mikey and put him in the ground.

Mikey had upped the stakes, taking Ruth Anne and murdering Ashley Truman. Winston, Kurt and I were running around trying to find him and we were exposed. We needed help. In fact, what we needed was a tank. And I knew right where to find one.

*****

Black Ice sat in the bagel shop across the street from Molly Malone's, enjoying a large cup of steaming hot coffee and a plain bagel, with Philadelphia Cream Cheese. His laptop sat open before him to a Microsoft 365 account with an active document. If anyone glanced over his shoulder, they'd find a novel titled "The Letter." If asked, and so far no one had, it was about a man who opens the wrong letter by mistake and is drawn into a world of intrigue, murder and assassinations. Hey, what do all the great writing gurus say: write what you know?

He had considered writing a novel before and when he collected the cool ten mill for killing Victor McCain, he might actually do it; after all, everyone else was. For now, it gave him a cover for always being in the same seat at the bagel shop.

He decided it was time to take out McCain and he'd rather do it here—near the bounty hunter's favorite hangout—where he'd be most likely off his guard.

After following him the last few days, there was little doubt in his mind that there was another player involved. He'd followed McCain and the man known as Kurt Pervis to the airport the day before and then pulled some strings at the police department to learn Pervis' girlfriend had gone missing.

He also watched through binoculars when McCain went into the woods behind Winston Reynolds house, and later watched the cops haul a body-laden gurney out of the same woods. He'd dropped the tail when they ended up down at police headquarters.

He planned to sit in the bagel shop for a day or two and see if McCain came to Molly's for lunch. And when he did, he hoped the Hand of God enjoyed every bite because it would be his last.

*****

I parked the Chevelle in an open spot next to about a dozen cars and a dusky gray Harley Fat Bob outside the Riverside Inn. A tired single story wooden building that sat close to the bank of the mighty Ohio River, Riverside Inn had been many things over the years. Originally it was a mom and pop operation serving classic American fare. My dad used to brag about the fish sandwiches which he claimed were as big as your hand. And my Pops had one hell of a big hand. When the owners died, their children didn't want the restaurant and they sold it to a guy who tried to turn it into an upscale steak place only to find out the clientele in the area liked their food cheap and quick. When it folded, a man named Arvel Jarrett bought the place, ripped out all the fancy trim work, built a bar large enough for dozens of people to pull up a stool and slam down a few brewskies. The food wasn't half bad either.

And he needed the space because Arvel had a lot of friends. And they all rode motorcycles. And sold drugs. And ran prostitutes. And anything else illegal which would turn a profit. Arvel's old man, Alvin, founded the Tyranny Rides Motorcycle Club in Louisville in the 1960's.

It didn't take long for Alvin and the boys to force out chapters of rival gangs. They lived by a simple rule: do what we tell you to do or you die. Straightforward and effective. When Alvin went over the rainbow to see Dorothy and Toto, his son seized command. They called Riverside home and I knew I'd find them here and, voila, there they were.

I needed to talk to one of their members, Cletus "The Tank" Bone. Tank matched the name, coming in around six foot three and weighing somewhere north of three hundred pounds and with arms the size of a mid-size car.

I'd tracked him down my very first year as a bounty hunter. No one else would take the bounty and the bondsman offered me double to bring him in. Being a greenhorn I jumped at the chance having no idea what I was signed up for.

I caught him screwing some poor girl in a flophouse downtown. When I kicked in the door and found him on top of the woman, it reminded me of an old rhyme I'd heard back in my grade school days. "Fatty and Skinny went to bed, and when Fatty rolled over, Skinny was dead." How the poor woman managed to survive is beyond me. And the thought of a bunch of little Tanks running around was a scary thought.

The room was on the second floor and before it was all said and done, we brawled our way outside where I ended up throwing Tank off the balcony and onto a Mini Cooper in the driveway—okay, fine. I didn't *throw* Tank anywhere. But I did shove him hard and he fell backwards against the wooden railing, which never even slowed him down. The fall totaled the car and knocked Tank out cold. His buddies busted his balls for months afterwards about how a Mini Cooper took out the Tank. Hilarious.

I knew Tank was inside because the Fat Bob was his bike. There were very few bikes which could haul his fat ass around and still keep air in the tires. Tank rode the damn thing all winter long. I guess when you have as much natural insulation as he does, you don't feel the cold like the rest of us mortals.

Before I got out of the car and walked to the door, I removed my gun from its holster and slipped it into the pocket of my bomber jacket. I knew they'd have a look out and I'd rather not advertise the gun until I needed it, but wanted it quicker than a holster pull.

I yanked the handle of the door and pulled it open and went

inside, allowing the door to close behind me. I knew I'd stepped into a nest of rattlers more dangerous than the ones I'd killed in Winston's bedroom.

Several dozen men, most still wearing their Tyranny Ride jackets, hung out in the room. Most were drinking, despite the mid-morning hour. Budweiser was the drink of choice, but I noticed the occasional glass of the hard stuff. Truth is, I was surprised any of them were already awake. They were late night kind of guys, not early risers.

The bar took up the center of the room, with an open door behind it leading to the kitchen. Most of the tables for eating were on the left side of the bar and most of the bikers were lounged around different tables, talking and drinking. A woman worked behind the bar, setting up for the lunch crowd. Black hair pulled into a ponytail, she wiped down the bar with a white towel.

A couple of pool tables filled the right side of the room and there were two men engaged in a game, with a large stack of cash on one rail. Tank Bone leaned against the wall, his head bopping to music only he heard in his head.

Every man stopped what they were doing when I walked into the bar. Everyone but Tank. Tank bellowed something that might have been a swear word, launched himself from the wall, reversed the pool cue in his hand and came at me, ready to beat me to a pulp with his stick.

All the other men had come to their feet, not knowing who I was, but ready to watch Tank beat the ever lovin' crap out of me. I let him move close enough to start his swing, removed the gun from my pocket and pointed it about an inch from his nose. He froze, the cue held high in mid-swing.

His rusty brown hair was cut short, his beard making up for the lack of hair by falling half-way down his chest. If Hell had a Santa Claus, he would look just like Tank.

He wore a black leather vest over a white T-shirt, faded jeans and black shit kicker boots. The man's eyes were a brown so dark they looked almost black. Right now they were focused on the dangerous end of my Glock.

The other men in the bar stopped what they were doing, a couple with hands behind their backs gripping their own weapons, waiting to see what happened next.

"Now, now, Cletus, is that any way to greet your old friend, Vic?"

Through clenched teeth he said, "We ain't no friends. And don't call me Cletus. It's Tank, asshole. And you got some mighty huge cajones coming into our place like this with a gun. I don't think you're gonna leave here under your own power, McCain. You shoot me and my brothers will eat you alive."

"You still mad over that damn Mini Cooper? Come on, Cletus, you know that wasn't personal. I don't want to shoot you. I came here to offer you and the boys a job. Why don't you put down your pool cue and I'll put up my gun and you and I can sit down and talk in a civilized manner. I'll even use small words so you can keep up."

His eyes narrowed to small slits and I could see him thinking hard. I could almost smell the smoke from his brain going into overload. Tank wasn't known for being a bright man, but he wasn't quite stupid either. He lowered his hands to his side, one holding the cue which he tapped against his leg, the other clenched, ready to jump into battle.

"All right. I've lowered my stick. Now lower your gun, asshole."

"How about you tell your boys to relax first. I'll watch you finish your pool game and we can talk business. Deal?"

He thought for another minute and then gave the others a curt nod. Hands were removed from behind backs and they all returned to their tables and stools, not exactly relaxing, but willing to wait for new orders. The woman behind the bar tried hard not to laugh, but was losing the battle.

I shoved my gun into the pocket of my jacket and followed Tank over to the table. He walked to the far end and bent over the felt, the pool cue now being used for its intended purpose. With an angry motion, he pistoned the stick back and then forward and sent the cue ball screaming down the table, practically crushing a striped ball into the corner pocket.

I sat down on a stool with my back to the wall where I could see the rest of the bikers. Tank's opponent was a ratty looking guy wearing a bandana over his hair, black thick framed glasses and an Adam's apple that kept bobbing up and down. It was almost hypnotic. He stood near me and I could smell stale cigarette smoke and booze rolling off the man.

Tank moved around the table, sizing up his next shot. "You said you wanted to talk business, so talk."

"What, not even going to offer me a beer? Come on Cletus, where's your manners?"

He shook his head a few times, a low growl escaping his throat. "You call me Cletus one more time and gun or no, I'm going to ram this stick so far up your ass you won't be able to bend over for a week. Ya hear me?"

I laughed and he barked for the woman to bring me a beer. She brought me a Budweiser in an ice cold bottle and I gave her my best Brad Pitt smile. With Tank glaring at her, she tried hard not return the smile, but I swear I saw the corners of her mouth turn up before she returned to the bar. Good to know I still got it. I held the beer in my left hand, my right still in my pocket on the grip of my gun.

Tank missed a shot, swore a blue streak and moved to stand beside me while the other man took his turn. At least this time Tank held the stick planted on the ground and resting against his ample stomach. A truce of sorts. "Now you got your beer, so talk."

"I need some quick muscle. I've got a couple of guys who need protected and I want the kind of men who aren't queasy about kicking some ass if the shit hits the fan. Naturally, I thought of the Tyrants. Kind of like what the Hells Angels did for the Rolling Stones during that one tour of theirs."

He scratched his beard, once again lost in thought. "We ain't exactly babysitters, McCain. What kind of trouble are you into? How dangerous are we talking here?"

"I won't lie to you, the group I'm up against have already killed at least one woman and kidnapped another. I suspect they've killed several others. These guys don't play around."

Adam's apple sank a shot and needed to sink one more and he'd be down to the eight ball. Tank still had three balls to go. It didn't look good for the old Tankster.

"How much is the Fuzz involved? We don't need any trouble with the Law."

Another ball went into a side pocket and Adam's apple lined up the final shot to win the game.

"Not on the radar," I lied. "But I don't want you to start any trouble, only handle it if it shows up. Self-defense. I've got connections on the force, so I can help smooth over anything that might happen."

"How many men we talkin'? And how much you willin' to pay?"

"Eight ball in the far corner pocket," Adam's apple called. He struck the cue ball with the end of his stick, sending it down the length of the table and into the eight ball, knocking it down to win the game with a soft click of the balls. He smiled at Tank, pocketed the money, laid the stick on the table and ambled off.

Pissed, Tank tossed his stick on the table and yelled to the bartender to bring him another beer.

"I figure four guys, two for each of my men." I named a price.

The woman brought Tank his beer and I noticed she didn't smile at him like she did me. I think Tank noticed, too. She slinked off and he followed her with a hard stare.

He drained half the beer in one pull and wiped his mouth with the back of one meaty hand. "Fine. We'll do it. But on two conditions."

"I'm all ears. Let me hear 'em."

"You'll pay double the rate you quoted. No negotiation. Double or we're not interested."

Considering I lowballed the offer, I had no problems with the money and said so. "And condition number two?"

He turned to face me, the snarl in place. "You quit calling me fucking Cletus."

I raised my eyes to the Heavens, pretending to consider his request with great care. Finally, I removed my gun hand from my pocket and extended it, showing my faith in his word. "Tank, you got a deal."

We shook and the deal was struck. We spent the next hour or so laying out how things would work with his men pairing up and doing twelve hour shifts. He brought over eight guys and filled them in on what I needed. I agreed to bring by the cash later in the day to pay the bikers for the first week.

I gave them Kurt and Winston's addresses and the first shift left to go sit on the houses. There would be no more rattlesnakes arriving in the middle of the night with the Tyranny Rides Motorcycle Club around.

I left the Riverside Inn feeling better about things. I wanted to have some beef between Winston and Kurt and the things which go bump in the night. If one of the Tyranny bikers died fighting Mikey and his thugs, I wouldn't lose any sleep over it. They were thugs in their own right and chose the life they led. And they were hardened men, used to violence and death.

I know it was only my imagination, but when I walked to the car, the morning seemed brighter, my mood much improved. I glanced at my phone to check the time and decided lunch would be a good idea. My stomach growled at the thought and I felt a hankering for some shepherd's pie and a glass of Guinness.

I got in the Chevelle and started the engine. I texted Winston and asked how things were going. A few second later, he responded with, "Okay." I sent a final text letting them know I was heading to Molly Malone's and for them to join me for lunch when they were done.

With the arrangements made, I tossed the phone on the seat and pulled on to River Road. I cruised to Zorn Avenue, the Ohio flowing by on my right, the skyline of Louisville ahead of me. Elvis sang "Santa Bring My Baby Back to Me" on the Christmas station and I sang along, tapping my fingers on the steering wheel to the beat.

I may have just made a deal with the devil for protection, but at least I could still carry a tune. Take that, holiday season.

CHAPTER FOURTEEN

Black Ice watched the red Chevelle cruise past the bagel shop and park on the next block. With smooth, unhurried motions, he lowered the lid on his laptop, unplugged the cord and slipped both into a satchel on the seat next to him.

He stood and slipped the strap of the satchel over one shoulder and took his time heading to the door, dropping the empty coffee cup in the trash. He timed it so he and McCain would pass each other near the mouth of the alley which split this block and the next. He would let McCain walk by him, pull the Browning .22 from the secret pocket inside the regular pocket in his coat and put a bullet into his head from behind his left ear. The round would traverse the length of his brain to the far side of the skull and rebound, all the kinetic energy staying inside the head. McCain would be dead before he hit the ground.

Black Ice slowed his breathing and worked to keep the adrenaline at bay. McCain was out of his car and walking briskly up the sidewalk, his gate easy and unconcerned. He whistled a Christmas song which sounded familiar, but not one he could have named. He timed it perfect, with McCain now only ten yards away staring at his phone, reading something.

Game time.

*****

The parking lot at Molly's was packed and I parked down the block. I love my Chevelle and I'd rather walk a bit than take a chance of some yahoo opening up the door on a jacked up truck too wide and scratching my baby.

I hopped out and headed to the restaurant. My phone buzzed and

I slid it out of my pocket and glanced at the screen. Winston and Kurt were on their way with the Stingray in tow. Sweet. I slowed crossing the alley before Molly's, not wanting a car flying by taking me out. That would be my luck, fighting demons, Infernal Lords and mobsters without dying, only to end up struck and killed by some teenager driving too fast down an alley while I looked down reading a text.

A tall black man reached the other side of the alley at the same time. He wore a black cashmere coat with a satchel bag slung over one shoulder and also glanced to make sure there was no traffic. I loved the coat, though it fit him better than it ever would me. Some coats are made for men who have a trimmer figure. I would stick with my bomber jacket. Better to not covet thy neighbor's coat.

*****

Black Ice moved his hand a mere two inches deeper into his pocket, his fingers curling around the grip of the Browning. The alley was empty and he imagined the unfolding scene in his head: pull, turn, point, shoot, jog down the alley, disappear and then count his money.

*****

The man and I were nearly abreast of each other and we made eye contact. I offered up a short nod of greeting and he nodded in return. Something about the man tickled the back of my mind, but I had no clue why. It made me slip my hand inside my pocket and grip my gun.

"Hey, stop right there. Don't move."

I pulled up and turned towards Detective Coffey who slammed the door of her unmarked as she got out of the car and jogged across the street towards me. I could see the eyes of the man in the cashmere coat narrow ever so slightly as he strode past me. He turned and walked down the alley and I watched him while the tickle became almost unbearable. I didn't ponder about it any longer as an angry Louisville Metro Police Detective stalked up to me looking for blood.

"What did you do? What the hell did you do?" Coffey nearly spat the words at me.

She was madder than a hornet. Normally when I make a woman this mad I have a good idea what I did to piss her off. But I didn't have a frickin' clue what had sent Coffey off the deep end. I noticed she held her right hand down near her hip where she kept her gun, her body angled slightly so she'd be able to draw down on me. Not a good sign.

"Woman, how about you cool your jets a bit? What do you mean, 'what have I done?' If you're angry I haven't donated to the policeman's toy drive this year, well, sorry sister, but money ain't actually growing on trees."

She closed the distance between us and poked me in the chest with her off hand while she spoke. The other stayed near her gun.

"Where's Wallace? Don't bullshit me, Vic. What did you do to him?"

"Wallace? I didn't do anything to him. What's happened?"

"I think you know and you're going to tell me the truth if I have to beat it out of you."

I could feel my own anger bubbling up to match hers. So much for Christmas cheer. "The last time I saw Wallace he was sitting in his car outside the Derby Mission early this morning. When Winston and I left, he was still sitting there. Where he went from there I don't know or care. What's the matter, you lose him? Why don't you check the nearest buffet and I bet you find him."

She stared at me for a moment or two longer, then spun on her heels, walked a few feet, then spun back. "He didn't report in this morning. I tried to call him a couple of times, but no answer. We tracked down his car this morning and we found it where you said, near the mission. We canvassed the area, but no one has seen him."

"Maybe he had car trouble and called a cab. Hell, I don't know. But I didn't have anything to do with it."

"Listen, Vic, a lot of guys heard about the two of you at Reynold's house, arguing. There are members of the force who are thinking you may have made him disappear. I have to know you didn't."

I could see pain mixed with the anger, doubt swirling with the fear. She wanted to trust me, but knew what it would mean if I had taken out Wallace. "Look, Linda, I didn't do anything to the man. I think the mission has cameras out front. Go by there and check them out. You'll see Winston and me leaving early this morning. The worst thing I did to Wallace is flip him off. He flicked his blue lights at us and we left. Later in the morning when I got back, the car was still there, but no Wallace. I did walk up to the car to tell him to go screw himself, but the car was empty. If anything happened to him, it's not me. You have my word."

"You better hope you didn't. You hear me?"

She didn't wait for a response, but walked angrily to her car, got in and left, never giving me a second glance. I watched her car turn onto

Shelbyville Road and disappear. Merry frickin' Christmas.

I stood still, thinking hard about Wallace. Ruth Anne snatched, Winston's neighbor murdered, snakes in the bedroom, now Wallace going AWOL. I could be certain the first three were Mikey. Maybe he was involved in also making Wallace disappear. I thought about Coffey running around with no clue about the menace oozing in and around my life and now hers. The time to tell her the truth had come and Lord's will be done.

I pushed my way into Molly's, the man in black forgotten.

*****

Black Ice opened the door to his blue Nissan Pathfinder, tossed the satchel on the passenger seat, folded himself behind the wheel and started the engine. He sat there thinking about the randomness of life. When the female cop showed up he aborted the kill. Maybe he could have taken out both of them before she could have gotten off a shot, but he'd seen her speed when she met McCain for lunch one day earlier in the week and it wasn't worth the risk.

He did regret he would no longer be able to shoot McCain up close. The bounty hunter seemed to sense something when they walked by each other, slipping his hand into this pocket where the assassin could make out the faintest outline of a gun. No, he would not risk another up close encounter. He would have to use a long rifle. Not nearly as pleasing as an up close kill, but in the end it came down to getting the job done. Thanks to his scouting of the area, he knew the perfect spot to set up. Fate may have bought the Hand of God a few more hours but it would be a short reprieve.

Death had come to town and he wouldn't leave without company.

CHAPTER FIFTEEN

Winston and Kurt found their way into Molly's and we made battle plans over shepherd's pie, fish and chips and several rounds of Guinness for Winston and I and a seemingly bottomless glass of ice tea for Kurt.

I filled them in on the disappearance of Wallace and they both came to the same conclusion I did: Mikey.

"Think your brother is keeping them alive someplace?" Winston asked.

"Who the hell knows? Ruth Anne has value, but Wallace? He doesn't mean anything to us, unless he's keeping him to have some leverage on Coffey, but I don't see it."

Kurt heaped a few more packets of Splenda into his glass and stirred it with a spoon. "Not to change the subject, but on the way here Winston and I gave the Stingray a try. Winston has an AT&T phone like Garey and when Winston called me, his phone hit the Stingray and the phone's location came up on the tracking radar. Worked like a charm."

I spooned the last of my shepherd's pie out of the bowl and stuffed it in my mouth, enjoying the last bite. "Meaning, you're confident you can we find Garey?"

"No doubt. We can start this afternoon," the hacker replied.

"You two can start this afternoon, but you won't be alone."

I told them of my visit to the Tyranny Rides Motorcycle Club and the men waiting at their houses. "I want you to go over to Winston's and pick up the two guys there. The four of you should still fit in the van with the cell phone gadget."

Winston drained the last of his Guinness. "You really think it's wise bringing the Tyranny gang in on this? Yeah, they're bad MoFos, I understand that, but they're one small step from being the type of guys we go after. This could come back and bite us in the ass."

"I hear ya, but do you want to spend the entire time running around looking over your shoulder? We need help and we need it now. These guys don't mind busting a few heads. When Mikey comes for us, I want him to have to work for it."

Winston didn't push the point, but I could tell he wasn't happy with me, but tough. "I'll head to the mission and obtain the cash I need from the stash in my room and then go pay Tank. You guys pick up the meatheads and then start cruising the area over by Churchill and see if you can track this asshole down. I'll join you after I pay the bikers."

"What do you want us to do if we find him?" Kurt asked, jaw set, eyes hard. The transition from the old Kurt which started in a coffin in Hawaii to the new Kurt seemed to have been completed. The thought of going after someone a year ago would have found Kurt running for the nearest exit, but not now. Ruth Anne meant the world to him and the man sitting across from me looked plenty determined to get her back.

"Find him first, then call me and we will see."

I waved over the waitress, got the check and paid our bill. The three of us walked outside into the crisp winter air. Winston managed to find a parking spot up near the door and he got in the van and started the engine. Kurt stood next to me and I could tell he worked to find the right words.

Finally, he said, "We're going to war, aren't we Vic?"

"We've been at war, Kurt. Only difference is now the war is on our doorstep. It's up to us to kill the lot of them."

He nodded in agreement, hands stuffed into the pocket of his jeans, keeping them warm. "Do you think we'll win?"

Simple question. No fear in the words, only a frank curiosity.

"I honestly don't know. I mean, there have been Hands of God going all the way back to the time of the Watchers, at the very least. I imagine every one of them asked the same question. How many thousands of years have passed and here we are wondering the same thing. One thing I am sure of though, none of them had friends as good as mine."

His laugh was heartfelt, if tinged with a touch of bitterness. He didn't say anything else and got in the van and the two of them drove off.

I walked to the Chevelle, passing businesses decorated for the season, people doing their Christmas or Hanukkah shopping, oblivious to the danger which lurked just out of sight. I'd almost grown numb to the danger, though I did wonder how many more holiday seasons I'd see before someone took me out. It nearly happened several times in the past year. Guess I wouldn't make it to cash in those really cool AARP discounts. Bummer.

I drove to the mission with the radio off, letting my mind wander where it would. If Mikey did make a move on Wallace, he certainly wasn't slowing down at all. My mind skittered sideways to think about my mom. How could a woman give birth to two men who were so different? We were raised in the same house with the same upbringing, yet something set Mikey on a dark path of evil and destruction, while I traveled a path trying to stop people like Mikey.

These were the thoughts I tossed around when I turned onto South Jackson and slowed to a crawl, staring at the half dozen or so squad cars parked out front, their light bars adding some color to the Christmas lights on the mission.

The doors to Wallace's unmarked were thrown open and what I guessed were techs were going over the car. I could see Detective Coffey standing in a small group with two other guys wearing suits. I recognized one of them, Detective Rhett Alvey. He'd also served Uncle Sam over in the desert, but in the MPs.

I parked down at the far end of the lot, locked my gun in the center console of my car and made my way towards the gathering of detectives. They all stopped and looked my way as I approached, and not a one of them seemed happy to see me.

I stopped a few feet short. "What, no Merry Christmas? Or are you guys ordered to only offer up a happy holidays instead?"

If I thought my humor would break the tension, I was mistaken. "You think this is funny?" asked Alvey.

"Since I don't know what "this" is, I do my best to try and carry the spirit of the season in my heart and share it with any and all. Why all the long faces?"

Coffey closed her eyes, her face pale and I knew something very bad had happened.

"Time to shut your mouth, asshole. We'll be the one's asking questions." This from the other detective, a Hispanic man of average height who looked like he might be in his late twenties. He wore an olive green suit with a custom made look. He filled it out well, too, with the "I just left the gym" kind of physique.

"Asshole? Now you've gone and hurt my feelings. I don't believe we've had the pleasure." I stuck out my hand, but he didn't return the gesture, so I shrugged and stuck my hands in my coat pockets.

"Knock it off, McCain. You too, Ventura." Detective Alvey. A white man of around forty, he looked like he'd left the military only the day before. Close cropped haircut, extra polish on the shoes, blue suit immaculate and a posture ramrod straight all screamed military. Some guys were never able to leave their Army days behind.

"Sorry, Detective. No harm meant. I'm guessing you found Wallace?" I wanted to direct my questions directly to Coffey, but knew this was not the time or the place. She continued to keep quiet, her eyes closed, head down.

"I said we'd ask the questions. Where'd you go this morning?" Detective Ventura stepped closer, coming dangerously close to violating my personal space. I knew he wanted me to take a step back, but he would have to get used to disappointment.

I ignored him and looked past him to Detective Alvey. "Detective, am I under arrest?"

He waited a heartbeat or two before answering. "No. You're not, but we do have a few questions for you."

"Then you can call my lawyer. I'll give you a name as soon as I find one."

I moved to step around the three of them when Ventura grabbed my arm and yanked me to a stop. I glanced at his hand. "Detective, would you please let go of my arm, so I don't have to remove it for you?"

Ventura started to say something when Coffey yelled, "Would you two stop it?"

She glared at both of us until Ventura let go and I made an effort to relax. "Damn it to hell, Vic. Do you have to make everything so difficult?"

This time I didn't have a chance to reply before she raised a hand and cut me off. "I got a call from a number I didn't recognize about a half hour ago. It was a man's voice and he said if I wanted to know what happened to Wallace I should go to the Derby Mission and take a look in the last room at the end of the right hallway."

I felt a chill which had nothing to do with the weather. The last room at the end of the right hallway was my room. Crap.

"The guy hung up and when I called the number back, no answer. I drove straight here and got permission to look in the room from the mission director."

She paused to gather herself. "When I got to the room I found two things on the pillow on the bed. Tom's phone and a left hand, or what was left of it." Her voice choked a bit, but she continued. "I know it's his because he has a scar which runs down the side by his thumb he got working on a barbed wire fence as a kid."

"That's my bedroom. But then again, you guys already know this."

I had to wonder why I wasn't in cuffs or at least being hauled down to an interrogation room. Only a few hours ago, Coffey even accused me of doing something to Wallace, but while they were pissed, they weren't slapping the cuffs on me.

Alvey nodded. "Yeah, we know. We also know you didn't put the phone and hand there. The mission's surveillance cameras show a man entering the mission and walking down the hallway to your room carrying a small brown bag. He goes in and a minute later, comes back out and leaves the building. He's wearing a hat pulled low over his eyes and we never get a good look at his face. The call to Linda was made a few minutes after the man leaves the building. We found the bag in a garbage can in your room."

"Ah, man. In my room? You said only part of the hand. Did someone cut it off?"

Alvey shook his head. "No. The techs tell us something ate part of it. There are teeth marks. Their guess is pigs, but we won't know for sure until they run some tests."

"The question is, why you? Why put the stuff there? One of your boys doing your dirty work for you McCain?" Ventura asked.

"You got me. Crack detective work there, Slim. I paid someone to whack a cop and then place the evidence on my pillow for safekeeping. Beats the hell out of a mint."

"Dario, why don't you go check with the crime techs and see what they've found in the car." Alvey nodded over his shoulder towards the unmarked.

Ventura fumed, but did what he was told. When he was out of earshot, Alvey picked up the conversation. "You'll have to cut Ventura some slack. He partnered with Wallace when he first joined the forces as a detective. But it's the right question. Why you? Detective Coffey brought me up to speed about the likely kidnapping of one of your boys girlfriends and the murder of Winston Reynolds' neighbor. Someone has a serious hard on for you."

I dry-washed my face with one hand. "I'll tell you detective, I honestly don't know. I've pissed off so many people over the years, it could be anyone. I told Detective Coffey I'd work to try and figure out who might be in town wanting a payback. I think the same thing you do. It's someone connected with me or one of my guys, but I don't have a clue who."

At least not a clue I cared to share with Alvey. Coffey stared at me, her eyes this side of pleading. I decided I'd tell her everything. The woman deserved no less from me. But not now. Not in front of Alvey.

"I want a list of people you think would be both willing and capable of doing this and I want it by tonight. You hear me?"

I nodded my agreement and with a glance at Coffey, he left us, going inside the mission. I could see Ventura up by the car, his eyes doing their best to burn a hole right through me. I fought hard to resist the urge to do something else childish, and managed. Just.

I pitched my voice low enough for Coffey to hear me, but no one else. "Listen, I'm sorry to hear about Wallace. We had our issues, but the man was only doing his job. He didn't deserve this."

"You're right. He didn't. And you know who is doing this, don't you?" Her voice asked the question, her stare showed she knew it to be fact.

"I think so, yes. I believe I'm the target. I think someone's trying to punish me. I'm close to finding out for sure, but I need to dig a bit deeper without you guys slowing me down. I can do things you can't. You know this."

She searched my eyes for the truth. Wallace's likely death had shaken her, but the core of iron inside remained. "You're at the end of a very short rope. I'll give you until tomorrow morning. If you don't come to me with what you've got by then, I'll haul your ass in and find a reason to keep you there until you do. You have my word on it."

"Done. Meet me here in the morning. Say around nine and I'll tell you everything. You have my word. Tomorrow morning, you'll have the whole story."

Without saying another word, she turned and went to her car, got inside and drove off. I watched her go, my heart now feeling lighter with the decision to finally tell her everything. One way or another, I would know if she could take me the way I truly am, or if she would fry me. Either way, I now needed to do my best to give her something more than my suspicions.

For better or worse. The only problem, in my world, worse can be *really* bad.

CHAPTER SIXTEEN

I went inside and headed down the hallway towards my room, a hallway crowded with cops. The anger and hatred rolled off them in waves I could almost see. Hell, I didn't blame them. One of their own had most likely been murdered and somehow I was involved. I would have felt the same way.

Alvey stood in the doorway to my room. "Sorry, but you won't be able to go into your room for quite some time."

"No worries, detective. I have to fetch some old clothes out of the maintenance room."

He watched me open the door, step inside and grab a battered cardboard box filled with coats, pants and other clothing items. On one side someone had written DONATIONS ONLY. A slight odor rose from the pile of clothes and Alvey even leaned away from me when I moved past him.

I carried the box down the hall and to the laundry room. I stepped inside and closed the door behind me and began to dump the clothes into one of the washing machines. In the bottom of the box lay a filthy sweater. I picked it up and turned it inside out. Inside I had sewn a zippered pouch. I pulled the zipper to one side and took out several bundles of hundred dollar bills, then stuffed them in the inside pockets of my bomber jacket.

I re-zipped the empty pouch and tossed it into the washer with the other clothes. I added some All Laundry Detergent from the shelf over the machines, turned a few dials to start the load and shut the lid.

I walked out of the laundry and once again walked through the cop gauntlet to return the box to the maintenance room. Alvey watched me toss the box in a corner before he stopped me.

"Needing some new clothes, McCain?"

"We all pitch in around here, detective. It's a group effort." I walked a few steps more, then turned around. "I hope you find Wallace, detective. And the people who are responsible for what happened to him."

"We will. Count on it."

I left them to do their work. There was no doubt Wallace was no longer walking this Earth as a living, breathing human being. If they ever found the rest of the body, their anger would crank up another level and I knew I'd be a target of that anger. I needed to try and find my brother before they did. Most of the men and women of the LMPD were hard working people who would be out of their element in dealing with Mikey. In a direct confrontation, even more of them would end up dead and I didn't want that.

I pushed the front door open and nearly ran head on into Ventura. Well, my chest did. He stood there and blocked me, which forced me to wait. I wouldn't be the one to start a confrontation, but if the man wanted to throw down, then I'd oblige him.

"I'm going to bring you down, McCain. You hear me? You have my word."

I nodded sagely. "You know, detective, the last man who made me that promise is now missing a hand, at the very least. I'd be careful with the threats."

I edged by him in the doorway and knew the man would have loved nothing better than to pull out his service revolver and put a bullet between my shoulder blades. He wouldn't be the first.

Somehow he found the means to restrain himself and I did the same and made it to my car without issue, hopped inside and took off. I really did need to find a way to make nice with officers of the law, if for no other reason than to make it easier on Detective Coffey.

I tried to push thoughts of Wallace—and gnawed on hands— away and concentrated on the present. I needed to deliver the money to Tank, then join Kurt and Winston in the hunt for Garey. If we could find the Satanist he might lead us to my brother.

It felt good to finally have a plan. I'd spent the last few days reacting to Mikey's actions and not very well. Now we had a chance to find him and I planned to bring Hell on Earth when I did.

*****

When I arrived at the Riverside Inn I transferred the money from my jacket to a ratty gym bag I kept in the trunk. Tank Bone met me at the door to the bar, held out his hand and took the gym bag I offered him. Without a word he closed the door and I left. Well, at least this time he didn't try to brain me with a pool cue.

I texted Kurt and asked where they were hanging out and he replied, "South Central Park." I knew the park is close to Churchill Downs so I headed in their direction.

On the way I tried hard not to think about Linda, but failed. I knew the stress over Wallace was driving her nuts. Being eaten was a hard way to go, especially if he was still alive when it happened. And if Mikey was involved, I wouldn't put it past him. On my list of bad ways to die, death by pig would be somewhere near the top. I wished I could help in the search, but with all of Louisville Metro on the hunt, they didn't need me. In truth, I doubted they would find a body unless Mikey wanted them to. They could search every pig farm in a fifty mile radius and never find the right place.

Trying to figure out Mikey's end game didn't help either. Even now, after all the things Mikey had done, I found it hard to reconcile the man with the brother I knew growing up. His capacity for evil seemed to know no bounds. My parents were both good people who raised their sons the right way. So where did brother mine stray off the tracks?

Could the answer be a genetic deformity which made him susceptible to Satan's offer of power? Could his resentment of me be so great to sell your soul and turn to the dark side? I would likely never know the answer to those questions.

Going after Kurt, Winston and now likely Wallace, it seemed punishing those around me was his current goal. At some point he would turn his hate on me directly and I needed to be ready.

These thoughts banged around in my brain until I found myself pulling up next to the van in a parking lot at the basketball courts, the sun beginning its quick descent over the city. Winston and two guys I didn't know were shooting hoops, despite the chill in the air, and Kurt sat in the last row of seats in the van with a large box on the seat next to him which must be the Stingray and headphones around his neck.

I rapped my knuckles on the window. When he looked up from the screen I asked, "Anything?"

He shook his head and returned to scanning the information on his screen. I wandered over to the courts and the three men stopped, with Winston making the introductions.

"Vic, this is Jaxson Greene and Reggie Purcell. Guys, this is

Victor McCain, the boss."

We all shook hands and I liked the fact both men did so with firm grips. Greene, around thirty years old sported a black Van Dyke beard and mustache which matched his ebony skin. If Tank Bone had a mini-me it would be Purcell. Not quite as tall as Bone, but with the same expansive middle, his red beard framed a face any mother would be hard pressed to love. Both men gave off the air of hard living. Worked for me.

Each wore the Tyranny Rides jackets and do rags around their heads, Green's dark blue and Purcell's showed a Green Bay Packers logo.

"No luck I take it?" I asked.

"Not yet. We found a basketball in the back of the van and decided some fresh air would do us good. This waiting is driving me bat shit crazy."

I knew the feeling. "Let's play a little two on two. I could use the fresh air myself. I'll fill you in on what's going on while we play."

Winston and I took on the bikers and told them about the new problem with Wallace going missing and likely dead. The two bikers took the news like I'd told them tea now cost more in China. Nothing.

"They looking at us for Wallace?" Winston asked. "Ain't like we parted on friendly terms."

Purcell pump faked me into the air and then drove by me for a layup. Not bad for a man of ample size. "Nah. They know it's someone messing with me. I know it's Mikey."

Purcell tossed me the ball and I walked to the top of the key. "Winston told us about your brother, man. He's one screwed up dude."

"No doubt about it. And if you see him, there's something else you need to know. He's more dangerous than any man you've ever met. Shooting him won't stop him. If you can cut his head off, that would work. Or burn him to death. But he's stronger than both of you put together."

Greene laughed. "Ain't no man stronger than me and Reggie. We ain't worried about your brother. We kill him like we do any other son of a bitch who messes with us."

"Let me ask you something. Do you two think you could take me? One on one?"

The two men looked at each other, but said nothing. "In a one on one fight, Mikey can kick my ass. And he's half my size."

Purcell smirked but Greene seemed to think about what I said. "What's his thing, martial arts and shit?"

"Something like that. But Winston will back me up when I say, if it's you and Mikey, you go at him with everything you have. Don't underestimate him because of his size. You do, you die."

Purcell started to say something else, when the van's horn let out a short burst. Kurt sat in the driver's seat waving at us to come back.

We piled into the van and Kurt moved to the back seat. "We got him. He's on the phone. We need to hit the road fast. He's talking to his girlfriend. Let's move."

Winston drove, I sat in the passenger seat, the bikers in the next row, with Kurt in the back shouting out directions while we tried to hone in on our Satanist. We turned onto Seventh Street, a residential housing area giving way to more commercial properties.

"He's within a hundred yards to the west. Turn left here."

Winston followed the directions and we were cruising a road between a trucking company and an upholstery shop. I could see the railroad line up ahead.

"We're very close. Fifty yards. Forty. Thirty. Twenty. Ten."

Greene tapped my arm and pointed out the side window. "Dude smoking a cigarette, behind the dumpster over there. Can barely see him, but looks like he's got a phone to his ear."

Winston drove up a few buildings and turned around. "That has to be him," Kurt said. "When we drove by he got further away."

We retraced our route. "Damn it. He hung up." Kurt banged the side of the van in anger.

"Not to worry, Kurt. We got our man. There he goes, walking into that building up ahead. I think with him hanging up proves he's our boy." To Winston I said, "Drive up the street and park where we have a better look at the place."

He did as I asked and we parked in the lot of an auto body shop which was closed for the weekend. Traffic was light, with not much happening in this part of town on a Saturday night.

A sign touting Wolfaden Distillery graced the front of the building where our Satanist had disappeared. The complex consisted of three structures: a two story front which likely housed the offices of the company, a large three story building behind that one where the spirits are made and a third one story building.

A quick Google search spit out the history of Wolfaden. Founded in the upper Highlands of Scotland, they produced single malt Scotch whiskies. In the good ole U.S. of A. they listed facilities in Houston, Texas, Atlanta, Georgia and Louisville, Kentucky.

They were privately owned. I asked Kurt to start digging into their state and federal filings, to see if we could find out the people behind the business.

"What do you want to do?" Winston, normally calm, cool and collected, drummed his fingers on the steering wheel, his body tense.

"For now, we watch. We know Garey is inside, but no clue on how many others. I think we need to find a spot where we can watch the front and the back. We can use two cars to keep an eye on both sides."

"I'll wait here while you go pick up your car," Winston offered.

Greene piped in, "I'll ride along and get our car, too."

"Fine. Winston and Purcell wait here. I'll take Kurt and Greene to their cars. There's a Save a Step down the block. Drive there and you guys can drink some coffee and hang out until we return."

Winston drove down to the convenience store and he and the biker got out. I slid behind the wheel and Kurt, Greene and I drove away, with the hacker's computer open on his lap, his fingers typing away.

"Great idea on the Stingray, Kurt. Well done."

"Do you think Ruth Anne is in there?" Kurt asked the question calmly enough, but his eyes blinked rapidly, one of the signs that he's under stress.

"No way to tell. But the place is large enough to keep someone under wraps."

"Then why aren't we barging in there, kicking ass and taking names?"

"Because I want to make sure if she's in there, we bring her out alive, not to mention us. We don't know the layout of the place, or how many men, if any, are in there besides Garey. If we bust in the front door and she's in the back, they could put a bullet in her brain before we reach her. We need information. At least now we know where to find Garey. He's the linchpin we need to pull down the rest of them. We'll save her, Kurt."

"When we do go in, I go with you. No arguments. You either let me go with you or I go in alone."

"You go with us. Never any doubt about that one. When we put the bastards in the ground, you'll be there."

"Damn straight."

We drove the rest of the way in silence. I knew my friend not only wanted payback, but needed it. It would be up to me to try and keep him alive long enough to collect.

CHAPTER SEVENTEEN

Detective Linda Coffey parked in the street in front of her condo and rested her head on the steering wheel, eyes closed.

She wanted to keep helping with the search to find her partner but a wave of exhaustion racked her body. She had not been to sleep since the previous morning and her body screamed for release. She planned to sleep a few hours and then rejoin the hunt.

She hoped beyond hope he would be found alive, but knew in her heart he was already dead. They were on a recovery mission, not a rescue. The lab techs confirmed the bite marks on his hand came from pigs and large ones at that. The techs told them there would be nothing left of Wallace to find and every time she thought about it, her stomach felt like it was doing somersaults.

She opened her door and climbed out of the car, her movements slow and plodding as she walked up the sidewalk to her condo. She knew sleep would be difficult and wondered if she had any Nyquil in the house to help her drift off.

Halfway to her door she froze, instantly more alert, though she wasn't sure why. She scanned the neighborhood. She lived in Mallard Crossing, a series of townhomes and her place sat at the end of a cul de sac. She turned around, searching the other buildings and then down her street.

A block away she saw a car idling with only the parking lights on. She thought she could make out a figure behind the wheel, but it was too far away for her to see who it was. She stared right at the car for a few heartbeats, all her cop intuition screaming at her this wasn't right, even though there were dozens of cars on the street.

The person in the car could be waiting to pick up someone, or a pizza delivery driver checking on an address. But her mind itched, not this time. She continued to stare at the car, and began to think it was nothing more than paranoia setting in from fatigue when the headlights came on, and the car pulled slowly into the street, turned right and disappeared from view.

She realized her heart was pounding in her chest and she fought to regain her composure, angry at herself. Being a female police detective in a man's world meant being twice as tough as her male counterparts and she'd worked hard to earn their respect and trust. She couldn't allow herself to be spooked by shadows and parked cars.

Shaking her head, she made it to the door, keys out when she froze again. Her front door seemed damaged. When she looked closer, the door jam around the lock had been splintered. She pulled her gun, put her back to the wall and pushed the door open with the flat of her hand, the door swinging silently open, the lock broken.

She risked a quick glance inside, but saw nothing. She moved into the foyer, flipping on the lights, gun up and ready. Her townhome featured an open design and gave her a clear view from the front door to the rear patio. Nothing.

She strained with every sense to try to detect an intruder, but didn't hear a sound. But she did smell something, the barest hint of rotting meat. With slow, measured steps, she glanced down the hallway to her bedroom and the guest room. In short order, she cleared both, finding them empty of intruders.

She retraced her steps and also found the kitchen empty. Almost. In the breakfast nook, on her kitchen table, sat an envelope resting against a vase holding a single rose.

Neither had been there when she left the previous morning. Coffey holstered her gun and removed a pair of latex gloves from her pocket and snapped them on each hand. The envelope was a four by six greeting card. On the outside of the envelope someone had written: **To the bitchin hot Detective Coffey**. She felt her cheeks burn with anger.

She turned the envelope over. It was unsealed. She lifted the flap and inside was a card and three photos. The first photo showed a close up of Ruth Anne Gardner holding that day's Courier Journal under her chin, suggesting she was still alive. At least earlier today.

The other nearly made her vomit. Wallace, or what was left of him, lying in mud, being consumed by three incredibly large pigs. Rage roared in her mind and deep inside she felt a part of her break. She forced her gaze away from the horror and to the last photograph. It showed a woman she didn't know eating at an outdoor café. Beautiful with shoulder length red hair, her posture suggested she had no clue the photo was being taken. She found nothing on the photo identifying the woman.

Finally, she turned her attention to the card inside. She lifted the card from the envelope. The front showed Piglet from Winnie the Pooh with Missing You inscribed under the picture. Inside the card was a handwritten note.

> **Dear Detective Coffey,**
> **Your partner, Detective Wallace, turned out to be a fabulous dinner guest. Did you find the gift I left for you at the mission? I wanted you to have something to remember him by. And please pass along my greetings to my brother, Victor. He seems quite smitten with you. Tell him Ruth Anne is doing quite well and providing hours and hours of entertainment. And also let him know I've found his long lost love, Samantha. Has he told you about her? He shot her once. Strange way to show love, don't you think?**
> **All my love**
> **Michael McCain**
> **PS:**
> **I'll be seeing you soon.**

Detective Coffey let out a scream from the depths of her soul and slammed the card onto the table. When she found Michael McCain, she would put a bullet in his brain, rule of law be damned. No matter how long it took, she would hunt him until she found him and killed him.

She yanked her phone out of her pocket to call crime scene techs when her head snapped up. Out her kitchen window she had a clear view across her small backyard to the alley leading behind her condo. A car sat parked there, a man behind the wheel, watching her through the window.

She ran to the back door, threw it open and drew her weapon at the same time. She sprinted across the yard, gun up. Through the driver's side window Michael McCain smiled at her and then blew her a kiss. The car roared down the street and Coffey emptied her magazine, shooting into the retreating car. The rear window shattered and she felt she must have hit McCain, but the car careened around the next corner and disappeared.

Coffey turned around several times and screamed in frustration and anger. All doubt about Michael McCain being in town and involved in the events surrounding his brother vanished. McCain had now made this personal and she would return the favor.

She needed to know what Victor knew and she needed to know it now. The fatigue she felt only a few minutes ago vanished in a rush of adrenaline. The gun shots brought her neighbors to their doors, watching her. Let them watch.

She returned to her home and closed the door. She once again took out her phone to call the crime technicians and then stopped. If she called them, then it would be hours before she could slip free of the police bureaucracy to start her hunt. She put her phone away and, instead, grabbed the card and photos from the table and headed out the door to her car.

Behind the wheel, she made a decision. She removed her phone once again and called Victor.

*****

I sat in the Chevelle watching the front of the building when my phone buzzed in my pocket. I pulled it out and glanced at the screen and saw that it was Detective Coffey. I thought about ignoring it, but decided she might have news on Wallace and answered.

"We need to meet. Now."

"I'm a bit busy, Linda. Can't this wait until tomorrow? I promised you I'd talk to you then."

"No it can't wait. Meet me now or I'll put out an A.P.B. and haul you in. It's about your brother. So when I say now, I mean now."

Bloody hell. The woman sounded wired and I didn't doubt she would do what she said about the all-points bulletin.

"Look, it's almost seven. Give me a half hour and I'll meet you at Molly's. Good enough?"

"Fine. And you better show." She hung up without another word.

Life continued to get better and better.

I called Winston in the van and filled him in. "Sounds like she's got something about Mikey. I'll run over there and meet with her. Think you guys will be okay for a couple of hours?"

"Yeah, man. We're good. Kurt and Purcell can take over your spot until you return. Greene and I are engaging in brother talk. We'll keep an eye on the back."

"Separation of the races? I thought we were a more integrated society?"

"Well, you know. It is what it is. Keep us posted on what she has to say."

I assured him I would and took off. I put the car in drive and for the second time today headed to Molly's. I put in A Charlie Brown Christmas CD my mother had given me into the deck and cranked it up. This time I managed to think of nothing on my way over and even managed to improve my mood. Snoopy and me bopping down the highway. A little.

I parked near the same spot as I did for lunch and walked down to Molly's. Coffey parked her unmarked in the loading zone with her blue light on top of the car. I rapped the hood with my knuckles and she got out.

I started around her car and came up short, when I saw the look on her face. Anger and determination in equal measure sharpened her features. I'd seen that look on more than one girl I'd dated, but I got the feeling this had nothing to do with my dating prowess. Or lack thereof. In one hand she held a couple of photos and a card.

We faced each other and she said, "Inside or out? I'd rather talk out here."

"Fine with me. Photos?" I asked, pointing to her hand.

"Your brother sent them to me." She held up the first photo. "He does have Ruth Anne, but you already knew that, right?"

Bloody hell. I could see the paper she held and the date. Alive. At least she was alive. "Yes, I knew."

She whipped the next photo up for me to see. "He fed Wallace to some fucking pigs. He was alive, Vic. Alive when your brother did this."

She was shouting and on the verge of losing it while she shook the photo in my face. Looking at the picture of Wallace, I couldn't blame her.

"Care to tell me who this is?"

When she showed me the third picture, I felt my world fall away. "You say Mikey sent these to you? You're sure?"

"Oh, I'm sure. He came to my place. I almost got him, but he got away."

I didn't say anything. Couldn't say anything. Samantha. Mikey had a picture of Samantha. The length of her hair suggested it wasn't from that long ago.

"Answer me, Vic! You know her, don't you?"

I glanced at the card, wondering what my brother might have written inside. "Yeah. I know her. Her name is Samantha Tyler."

"And you shot her? You tried to kill her?"

Double bloody hell. He told her. "Is she okay? What did Mikey say about Samantha?"

"You answer my questions first. Did you shoot her?"

I needed time to think. "Listen, before I answer that question I need a drink. Let's go inside."

She knew I was stalling, but went along with it. "Fine."

She turned toward her car, fob in hand to lock it when she shouted, "Gun!"

I started to turn in the direction she was looking when things slowed down, each fraction of a second seeming to take a full minute. I registered Coffey pulling her gun in the lightning quick move of hers and started reaching for my own weapon. Then I felt her shove me and admitted a bit of surprise that she could even move me the few inches she did—considering I outweigh her nearly two to one.

And then, I felt someone punch me hard in the chest. I didn't see it, but knew it happened. I don't think even Tank Bone could hit me that hard. My hand refused to respond to my brain's demand of lifting and squeezing off a round and I think I dropped my gun onto the sidewalk. I heard the roar of Coffey's gun and subconsciously counted three shots.

The next sensation I felt was my back hitting the side wall of Molly's and then sliding down to the ground. I knew my body was trying to tell me something, but I found it hard to concentrate.

All of a sudden, all I wanted to do was to sleep and I fell over on my side. My head bounced hard on the sidewalk, but I didn't care.

Sleep. I wanted to sleep. I began to drift off and I heard Coffey yelling for someone to call an ambulance. She rolled me onto my back and began to yell at me to stay with her. "To hell with that," I thought. I to need sleep and I closed my eyes.

Sleep. And I knew I'd be sleeping a long time.

CHAPTER EIGHTEEN

Black Ice walked briskly through the neighborhood streets not far from where he'd just shot Victor McCain. The route had been mapped during the past few days, avoiding the streets with dogs outside or a lot of traffic. His Nissan was parked on a side street under a huge oak, the street devoid of any light.

He replayed the scene of the shooting in his mind's eye. Seeing McCain drive by; crossing the street and up the stairs of the office building facing Molly's; making it to the roof; retrieving his sniper rifle from behind the air conditioning unit; McCain coming to a stop by the cop car; the cop jumping out of her car; the two of them facing each other; McCain turning to face his direction; the crosshairs over the man's heart; squeezing the trigger; the cop somehow realizing he was there and shooting in his direction; McCain going down; dropping the rifle on the rooftop; running down the stairs and exiting the building into an alley, down the block and gone.

It all went well except the small bump the cop gave McCain. The round he used would penetrate any protective body armor he might have worn and right through his heart. The bump made him miss McCain's heart, though the wound should be massive enough to kill him.

Yet the situation bothered him. He had never been seen before when using the rifle, yet the cop made him. He had considered taking a shot at the cop as well, but her own return fire came uncomfortably close, despite the fact she used a handgun. She would not have seen much of his face, regardless.

Normally he would be several states away before the sun came up the next morning. Not this time. He needed confirmation that McCain was dead. He headed to his rental home to monitor the news and police bands until he was sure. People did not send out ten million dollar payments on "likely" dead.

And he admitted to himself that for the first time since his very first assassination, many years before, he felt a bit of unease. And if asked, he could not say why. Granted, the op didn't not go as planned, but that happened in his line of work.

No, this went deeper. Some part of his primal brain wanted him to leave town now, whether McCain was dead or not. Every human possesses the fight or flight reflex and his body chose flee.

He decided to ignore the feeling. In his long career, he had never left a job unfinished and this time would be no different. He would wait for confirmation of the death of Victor McCain, collect his payday and then retire with an unblemished record.

He made it to his car without incident and drove away into the night, the call to flee still strong. He turned on his police band scanner and began to listen for confirmation of the bounty hunter's death.

*****

Detective Coffey leaned against her car, hands and suit covered in Victor's blood, listening to the Chief of Detectives, Martie Kendall, ream her out. Alvey and Ventura stood a few feet away, eyes looking everywhere but at her.

"You mean to tell me, a suspected cop killer broke into your house and left evidence, then you engaged the suspect, firing your weapon in a residential neighborhood and instead of calling it in and summoning backup which might have allowed us to apprehend said suspect, you instead contacted the suspect's brother for a meeting? And then he's shot?"

"Yes sir, that's pretty much it."

Kendall fit the classic Irish cop mode. A large man with a bulbous nose covered in spider veins from too much drinking, he wore his emotions on his sleeve. Especially his anger. And right now he was pissed off beyond belief.

She knew when the call for the calvary went out, she was screwed. She had dropped the photos and card when she pulled her weapon and then forgot about them while trying to save Victor's life. A patrol car had been only a few blocks away and when the officers arrived, they found the pictures. Word quickly spread about the photo of Wallace. When the shit hit the fan, the fan pointed right at her.

"I thought—"

He cut her off before she could finish. "You didn't think. I can't decide if you're an idiot or just insane. Either way, your time as a D1 is over. The first thing you're going to do is return to headquarters and fill out your paperwork. Then you're going to turn in your gun and badge. You're suspended pending an investigation by the Public Integrity Unit. And I promise you, when the investigation is over, you'll be lucky if all you lose is your job. If I can find something to charge you with, I'll do it."

He stomped off leaving her alone with the other two detectives. "Sorry guys. I messed up. When I let Michael McCain slip away, all I wanted was to find his brother and pressure him into telling me what he knew, so I could find him. I wanted payback."

"I hear you," Alvey said, "but the chief's right. You really screwed up. I'll see what I can do, but surviving this will be difficult."

"Sam warned you about hanging out with McCain. Now he's dead and you're on your way to being busted out. Still think the guy's worth it?" Ventura asked.

"Jesus, Dario. How big of an asshole can you be?" Coffey pushed herself away from her car. She'd helped to load Victor into the ambulance. He was still alive, how she didn't know. He'd been wearing a Kevlar vest, but it had been no protection against the sniper shot.

Alvey laid a hand on her shoulder. "Linda, I know this is tough, but we need to ask: did you get a look at the shooter? Anything you can tell us which might help catch the guy?"

"Black man, I think. Dark complected, at the very least. He was sitting up on top of the office building across the street."

"We found his rifle. He left it behind. The techs say it's an L115A3 AMW, a sniper rifle used by the British. Didn't bother to take it with him. I'm guessing your return fire made him drop it and run."

"I don't think so." Coffey stared at the spot where the sniper took his shot. "I think he planned to leave it. He'd be rather conspicuous carrying it with him for any distance."

"Think it was the brother shooting at him?" Ventura asked.

"Last time I checked, Michael McCain was white. So no, I don't think it was the brother."

Ventura bristled at her comments. "I meant, do you think Michael McCain is behind the shooting, not whether or not it was actually him."

"How the hell should I know? I don't think so. It seems to me he has been torturing Victor, not going right at him. Why leave the photos and the note to contact Victor if he planned to kill him? I tell you what though, Ventura, I'll ask him before I blow his ass away."

Alvey stepped between them. "Enough. Listen, Linda, don't do something stupid. You're off the case. If you're not incredibly lucky, you'll be off the force. Do what the chief said. Go do your paperwork and then go home. Better yet, check into a hotel. The note made it clear he may come after you as well. Don't make it easy for him to find you."

"Screw that. I want him to find me. I want him to make a run at me." And she meant it. Not only would she not disappear, she would make sure she was easy to find.

"Sounds to me like you've learned nothing from the McCain boys. You're getting just what you deserve. If not for you, Sam would still be alive."

Ventura's barb stung because she thought the same thing. This case and her attraction to Victor put Wallace in the crosshairs. Michael was toying with them, torturing them. It's why she didn't think he'd shoot and kill his brother. Someone else was involved and she planned to find out who, whether they kicked her off the force or not.

"You know, Ventura, there's a reason Sam moved on to a new partner. Think about that for a while."

Coffey left them standing there, got into her car and drove away from the crime scene at Molly's. A few blocks down, on Shelbyville Road, she pulled into a Thorntons Gas Station.

First, she called the emergency room at Baptist East Hospital to learn whether Vic was still alive or not. They told her he was in emergency surgery, but knew nothing else. She hung up. Not dead yet. From her briefcase on the seat next to her, she got out her notepad and found the next number she needed. She typed it into her phone and made the call.

*****

Winston sat in the waiting room for those with friends or loved ones in the emergency room at Baptist East. Coffey had called him an hour before and he'd rushed to the hospital. It had been hard to persuade Kurt to stay on the stake out, but he finally convinced the hacker that he was the only one who could work the Stingray and to help them stay on top of Garey. He borrowed the biker's car and ignored the speed limit signs on the way to the hospital.

Winston talked to one of the EMTs who brought Victor in and

found out he'd died twice on the ride to the hospital and they had to use the defibrillator on him both times, returning his heart to beating. The prognosis was not good.

Coffey told him Victor had been shot by a sniper. Didn't sound like Mikey. But then again, the man was a nutcase, so who knew? She also told him about Mikey breaking into her house and leaving the photos and note. The fact Mikey had found Samantha was a scary thought. Even Victor didn't know where she was hiding.

Winston then called Brother Joshua to let him know about Vic and to have him check on Samantha. It was Joshua who had arranged for Samantha to disappear in the first place. He promised to check on her and then come down to the hospital.

As he sat in the waiting room, he recalled telling Kurt what Coffey had learned from the photos left at her house. Kurt nearly broke into tears when he heard Ruth Anne was still alive—at least, as of this morning. If she were being kept in the distillery, then it would be up to the two of them to bust her out.

His thoughts were interrupted when a doctor walked into the room and asked, "Victor McCain family?"

Winston stood. "He doesn't have any family in town. His mother is in Florida for the winter. I'm his best friend. How is he?"

"Hi, I'm Dr. Munson."

The two of them shook hands. A small woman in her late fifties or early sixties, she exuded the kind of confidence emergency room doctors needed to survive.

"I'm Winston. Did he make it?"

"He's out of surgery and in very critical condition. He suffered a traumatic gunshot wound to the chest. The bullet destroyed his right lung and caused massive internal bleeding and damage. I stopped the bleeding and repaired what I could. Frankly, I don't know how he managed to stay alive this long. Your friend has a strong will to live. But I must tell you, I don't think his chances are great. The next twenty-four hours will go a long way in determining what happens next."

Winston closed his eyes and said a silent prayer. When he finished, he asked, "Can I see him?"

"Certainly. Follow me."

She used a keycard to open two double doors and lead him down a hallway, beyond the nurse's station, to a curtained room. She pulled the curtain to the side and he saw his friend lying in a hospital bed. There were tubes and drip lines in and around his body, including a tracheotomy tube to help him breathe.

He glanced at the stat monitor and could see his blood pressure was low, the pulse weak. Winston new about spending time in intensive care, following a knife attack by a man possessed by a fallen angel. Now the roles were reversed.

The doctor excused herself and closed the curtain. Winston sat in a chair next to the bed and first texted Kurt giving him the update. He thumbed through his contact list to another name and following a brief hesitation, sent a second message. When finished, he put his phone away, took hold of his friend's hand and began to pray. For the first time in his life, he found it hard to do so. Over the last year, Victor often complained about the evil they fought, wondering why God didn't do more to stop the horrific things people did to each other. His response had always been *they* were God's response. It was up to them and people like them to try and keep people safe.

But now, with Ashley Truman and Detective Wallace murdered, Ruth Anne kidnapped, and Victor near death, he felt a wave of helplessness come upon him. If they were God's tools, then he wondered if they were good enough. Victor McCain, despite his misgivings, always moved forward and Winston believed in the cause. If Vic died? What then?

The phone buzzed in his pocket and after checking the number he answered.

"Sorry to hear about McCain. Any change?"

Brad Stiles, a soldier of fortune who once worked for Cyrus Tyler, sounded sincere. When Tyler died in a car explosion sending him to Hell, Stiles left the employ of the Church of the Light Reclaimed and began work with a security firm in Washington, D.C. Stiles had been the one to warn them about the contract taken out on Vic by Gadriel, a fallen angel bent on revenge.

"No. If anything, he's worse. Were you able to find out anything?"

"Possibly. If your cop friend has the weapon right, then it could be the assassin known as Black Ice. He's suspected in several other assassinations worldwide. Each time he left the weapon behind and it was always the Accuracy International L115A3 sniper rifle. A British soldier recorded the longest recorded kill at over twenty-six hundred yards. All that we know about him is he's of African descent and very deadly."

"No known photos? Is there anything you can tell me which

might identify him?"

"Sorry, Reynolds. No pics. Nothing. Only he always finishes the job. If McCain pulls through, you can bet he'll be around to finish what he started."

Winston closed his eyes and rubbed the bridge of his nose, suddenly very tired. "Well, the doc doesn't think it too likely he will, but thanks for what you've told me. I'll think of something."

A brief silence followed, then Stiles asked, "You want some help? I can bring a few guys out there."

"I appreciate the offer, the only problem is one of trust. Wasn't that long ago you were trying to bump off Vic yourself."

"Like I told your boss, that was business. I don't work for them anymore. If you're in a bind, I'd take me up on the offer."

Winston thought about it. Making the decisions always fell to Victor. Vic made the plans and he helped carry them out. He glanced at his friend in the bed and realized the decisions were now up to him.

"We have our own version of Elizabeth on the scene. Sure you want to help out?"

Stiles laughed. "Hell yes. You ever been big game hunting?"

"Nah, man. Ain't too many brothers from the hood running around shooting lions and shit."

"Then you wouldn't understand. Hunting an Infernal Lord is the top of the food chain. If you have one of them and Black Ice, you're definitely going to need my help. I'll be on the next flight out and I'll bring my four best guys. We should be there by tomorrow afternoon." Stiles ended the call and he put his phone away.

Winston didn't know how long he sat with his friend, praying, when a voice interrupted him. "Who did this to my brother?"

Michael McCain, Infernal Lord, cop killer, eternally damned. In the flesh. And Winston was unarmed.

CHAPTER NINETEEN

"Man, we need to catch some sleep."

Greene added a yawn to go with his stretch from the front seat of the van. After Winston took off for the hospital, they returned to their surveillance duty. Purcell tried to find a comfortable position in the passenger seat, but failed.

"Yeah, what he said. We agreed to be your bodyguards, but hell, we need to find some shut eye at some point."

"How about you two stop your bitchin'. I'm still here and if I can hold out, then you two can. Worst comes to worst, take turns napping. Those seats recline a bit."

Purcell turned in his seat to stare him down, but Kurt stared right back. The burly biker broke the stare off first and Kurt felt a rush of pleasure. Not long ago he would never have dared to pop off to anyone, let alone a member of the Tyranny Rides biker gang.

Right then he didn't want to sleep. Ruth Anne was still alive. His heart almost burst at the news. He knew she could die any moment at the hands of someone like Mikey McCain, but there was still a chance.

But at what cost? Vic was now lying in a hospital bed, near death. The news didn't sound good. And what did this mean for the rescue of Ruth Anne? The Hand of God was dying, Winston would be by his side until the very end. But every minute they waited could be Ruth Anne's last.

His laptop screen showed it was a bit shy of three a.m. Everything he ever read on the subject suggested the middle of the night was the best time to launch an attack. In the hours that they watched the distillery not a single individual came or went, other than Garey. Earlier they watched while all the lights came on inside the big building, then Garey slipped outside where he made another phone call to his girlfriend in California around midnight. When he was finished the call, he went back inside, turned off all the lights, and nothing since.

His research into the ownership of the distillery paid off. He dug through several layers of corporate filings to find out the original name on the incorporation papers for the Louisville distillery was none other than Preston Deveraux, former right hand man to Mikey. Vic took care of that person in Philadelphia, but it proved the Church of the Light Reclaimed was involved. Bad guys.

He also found the floor plans for the distillery filed with the planning and zoning commission. If they followed the floor plan there were several places they might have stashed Ruth Anne, depending on the level of involvement of the day to day employees at the plant. Garey took his smoke breaks on the rear loading docks. That would be the best way to break into the plant. The docks led to a room with two huge tanks, with a row of offices off this room. If Ruth Anne was here, she'd be in one of those offices.

Kurt gnawed on a fingernail and watched the clock move a minute closer to three. If they were going to move tonight, then now was the time. Without Vic or Winston here to guide him, Kurt made a command decision.

"You're both packing heat, right?"

The bikers laughed. "Packing heat? Man this ain't no TV show," Purnell said. "But yeah, we're armed. We'd be piss poor bodyguards if we weren't."

"Good. This is what we're going to do. We'll park the van a half a block down the street and approach the building from the same place we saw Garey go in and out. The dumpster will give us some cover. Once inside, we find Garey and force him to tell us where they are keeping Ruth Anne."

Greene began shaking his head before he even finished. "No way. McCain made it clear we were to keep you out of trouble. You go breaking in and you might get your ass shot off. We ain't taking the blame for you ending up dead."

"Did he tell you why we need this guy?" Kurt asked.

Neither biker responded. "Because they've kidnapped my fiancé. I think she's in there and I'm going to go save her. You guys can sit here and wait if you want, but I'm goin' in."

Kurt didn't wait for them to respond. He opened the side door, jumped out and began to walk to the distillery. He heard the van behind him, and in seconds they pulled up next to him.

Purcell rolled down his window. "Hop in. We didn't know about the fiancé part. You want to go all cowboy, then we'll go with you. Beats the shit out of waiting around doing nothing."

Kurt returned to the van and Greene drove down the street, turned around and parked a half block from the rear of the distillery. The rear docks were lit with a couple of overhead lights and they would be visible once they left the area around the dumpster.

"Give me a second. They have an alarm system, but I hacked into their computer and I can turn it off from here." Kurt typed a few keys, watched the screen for a bit longer, and then shut his laptop. "Done."

The three men got out and Greene went to the back of the van, opened the doors and rummaged around. When he shut the doors he held a tire iron in his hand. "You know, in case the door don't want to open."

"Good thinking." Kurt led the way to the dumpster. They paused, taking stock of the situation, but nothing moved. A ramp lead up to a long dock with huge roll up doors for semi-trucks. Off to one side stood a standard door.

"We go in that way," Kurt said, pointing to the door and they walked up the ramp. They made it to the door without incident and Kurt tried the knob only to find it locked.

He motioned to Greene and the biker fit the flat end of the tire iron into the door jam and leaned into the other end using his weight. The door burst open with a loud crack. They moved quickly inside and Purcell pulled the broken door closed. They found themselves in a large room filled with pallets stacked with barrels of whiskey. The only light came from outside through a row of large windows set high on one wall. Greene squinted at one barrel.

"Scotch single malt whiskey. That's what I'm talkin' about. We got to take one of these when we leave."

"Girl first. Let's keep moving."

Kurt led the way to the far door and found it unlocked. "On the other side of this door is their vat room. There's also a door on the far wall that leads to the offices. Garey must be in one of them. With any luck, we'll find Ruth Anne there, too."

Kurt pulled his gun from the back of his jeans and Greene and Purcell did the same. Kurt eased the door open enough for them to slide into the room.

Years before he had taken a class on the distillery process when he and a couple of buddies thought about opening their own micro-distillery. Before them ran a row of large copper vats. Part of the structure was the fermenter where water, sugar and yeast is combined and allowed to ferment for several days. When the yeast consumed most of the sugar, what's left is called the "wash" which is moved into the still where the mixture is heated and the resulting alcohol vapor is collected in the "lyne arm" and moved to the condenser and eventually ends up in a charred oak barrel for bourbon and even older bourbon barrels for scotch.

Once again, the only light in the room came from outdoor light falling through large windows running the length of the room on two sides, casting it in heavy shadows.

"The door we want is on the other side of the room," Kurt whispered. "Follow me."

He made it halfway across the room when he thought he saw movement between two vats in his peripheral vision and spun, gun up and ready, his heart pounding. Nothing. He moved a few steps in the direction he thought he saw someone but found nothing.

Purcell let out a hiss. "There's someone in here with us. I saw someone in the shadows on this side of the room."

"Me too," Greene whispered. "Spread out and let's find this son of a bitch."

Purcell went one way, Greene the other and Kurt stayed in the middle. He made it only a couple of steps when he felt a fingernail drag across the back of his neck.

He let out a short shriek, turned and fired, the gun loud among the copper stills. But there was nothing there. He rubbed his neck with his free hand and when he looked closely, he could see red. He'd been scratched hard enough to draw blood.

Before he could think of what to do, gunfire erupted on both sides, Greene and Purcell cutting loose. Kurt dove to the ground worried they might shoot him by accident. He could hear Purcell screaming in agony.

Kurt felt something land on his legs, claws digging into his legs. He turned over to find a dark shadow clinging to him. He shot several times into the black mass, but it had no effect. What looked like hands, formed of dark fog with long raven black nails, dug into his blue jeans and into his skin. Pain erupted in his legs and Kurt began to scream.

CHAPTER TWENTY

Winston stood and glanced quickly around the small room trying to find a weapon, and came up empty. Michael McCain pulled the curtain closed, cutting them off from other prying eyes.

"Take another step and I'll kill you."

Mikey laughed and waved him off. "You and I both know I could break your neck and drink a beer at the same time without even trying. Save it, Reynolds. If I wanted you or Victor dead, you'd already be that way. What I want to know is who did it?" He asked the question while jerking a thumb at his brother.

Winston knew what Mikey said was true. Didn't mean he would go down without a fight. "Why do you care?"

Mikey pulled up the other chair in the room and sat near Victor's bed. He lifted his feet and rested them on the end of the bed, crossed at the ankles and laced his fingers behind his head, relaxed.

"Oh sit down, Reynolds. Do you really want to start a fight here in the emergency room? Think about how many other nurses I could kill before I left. One dead nurse on your conscience should be quite enough, don't you think?"

"I think I'll keep standing."

"No. You'll sit. And if you don't, the next nurse who comes to check on my dear brother will die. You have my word on it. I'll pull her head off like the last one and toss it at you like a football. You had several interceptions as a linebacker. Think you could catch a head?"

Despite the relaxed easy going demeanor, Winston knew he mean it. He dragged his chair to the foot of the bed giving him a quick shot at Mikey should it come to a fight and sat down.

"Good boy. See, you can be trained. Now, to answer your question, Victor does not have permission to die until I give him permission. I'm not done with my brother. Or you. I want my brother to live a long and healthy life, knowing I will kill anything he ever loves."

"Including your mother? You'd kill her?" Winston kept listening for the nurse, afraid of what Mikey would do.

"Hell no. Mom's off limits. What do you think I am, a monster?"

"Yeah. You're a monster all right. And for what you did to Ashley Truman, I'm going to slay your ass."

"Tsk, tsk. Such anger. But back to the original question: who did this?"

"Like I would tell you, even if I knew."

Mikey dropped his feet to the ground and leaned forward, resting his elbows on his knees, hands clasped between his legs. "You know, this is really tiring. So I'll say this only one more time. You sit still and answer my questions, or I'll kill everyone on this ward before I leave. Everyone. And you know I can do it."

Winston ground his teeth, then answered. "I don't know and that's the truth. One of your fallen angel buddies put out a contract on Victor after what went down in Philadelphia. People been trying to collect. Seems someone is about to collect the fee. Might be a bad MoFo named Black Ice."

"Ah. Gadriel. Figures. He's been warned, but believes he's untouchable. I may have to educate him on how that's not true." He stared at his brother, a silent witness to their conversation. "Will he make it?"

"Doc says it's not looking good. Too much damage. I'd be surprised if he makes it through the night."

"You know, if you're willing to deal, I can save him."

Winston's eyes narrowed. "What kind of deal?"

"See, I have this friend. If you're willing to trade...I don't know...your soul for instance, he can come by and bippity boppity boo, Victor will be up and around in no time."

Winston felt his blood run cold. "Not going to happen. Not today, not ever."

"What? Your soul's not worth your friend's life? What kind of friend are you?"

Winston turned to stare at Victor, watching him fight to stay alive, knowing he would not live to see the morning. "Go to Hell, Mikey."

The Infernal Lord stood. "Too bad. Know this, Reynolds, the instant my brother leaves this mortal coil, you and his other lackeys are dead. You only stay alive if he does."

"You're a little man who wishes he was a big man. You think you're a bad MoFo, but you're still little. You best be looking over your shoulder. When I'm done here, I'm going to hunt you down and send you back to Hell. No redo's this time, Mikey."

Mikey, unphased by Winston's threat, winked and without another word, left. Winston parted the curtain and watched him walk down the hallway and out the double doors. With Mikey gone he returned his chair next to the bed, again took Victor's hand, and began to pray.

CHAPTER TWENTY-ONE

Kurt needed to see what the hell was attacking him and fumbled the iPhone out of his pocket, swiped on the screen and hit the flashlight app. A bright pinpoint of light struck the shadow and it immediately fled behind one of the huge copper vats. Gasping, Kurt lunged to his feet, desperate to find a way out, swinging his phone around wildly trying to light the whole room. Intense pain flooded him from the scratches on his legs, but he did his best to ignore it.

"Help me."

Kurt spun around and brought his light up and nearly dropped it. Reggie Purcell stood before him, clothes shredded and nearly all the skin on his face stripped away, blood covering his features like a red mask of death. Several shadows draped over his body fled when the light fell upon Purcell. The big man managed to stumble a step and then fell into his arms, taking them both to the ground.

With superhuman effort, he pushed the heavy biker off and jumped to his feet. Fear swept through him and he started to run to the door when an arm swept out to grab his ankle and he tripped. Fingers he could barely see tried to rip the phone from his hand, forcing him to drop the gun, but he held onto his phone for dear life. He swung the phone around and around him, trying to think.

Light. He needed light. The floor plans showed a light switch next to the doors leading to the offices. He once again sprang to his feet and bolted, this time in the other direction, swinging his phone around like a lighthouse. Taloned hands made of darkness plucked at him, but he made it to the door, found the bank of light switches and flipped them all up.

Instantly large halogen lights came to life overhead, illuminating the huge room. All shadows disappeared, and though he couldn't be sure,

Kurt thought he heard wailing. He ran quickly to retrieve his gun on the floor and to check on Purcell. Dead. Grizzly bear-sized talon marks covered his body.

He went in search of Greene and found him curled up in the far corner, his clothes in tatters and his face completely missing. Kurt stuck out his hand and leaned against the wall, sucking in huge gulps of air trying not to throw up.

Dead. Because of him. They told him not to come inside on his own, but he didn't listen. Both were tough guys and they didn't hesitate to come with him, to watch his back, only to die in the dark by creatures they had no chance to kill.

When he finally managed to calm his stomach he made a beeline for the door to the offices. Despite it all, he needed to save Ruth Anne, or the deaths of Greene and Purcell were pointless. He ripped the door open and stepped into a long hallway with offices down one side. At the third door down on the right a thin line of light shown from under the door.

He crept down the hallway quietly, though he figured it didn't matter, not with all the gunfire in the shadow fight. When he reached the door he considered his options. Bust in? Knock? He tried to think of what Vic would do. Try not to get shot was the first order of business.

In the end, he decided, "Screw it." He threw the door open and followed it in, gun up and ready to blow somebody's head off.

Bottles of scotch and bourbon filled shelves set against mahogany paneled walls. A large cherry oak desk occupied most of the room. Behind it stood Elwyn Garey, a large Magnum .357 clasped in two trembling hands and pointed, more or less, in Kurt's direction.

"You put your gun down, you hear me?' Garey practically shouted the command.

Kurt took another step. "Elwyn, put your gun on the desk or I'll shoot you where you stand, then catch the next flight to California and do the same thing to your girlfriend, Ellen."

Garey dropped the gun to his side and his lower lip began to tremble. A thin man with a large mop top of blonde hair, Garey sported the well-tanned look of a California guy.

Kurt pointed his gun directly at Garey's forehead. "I said, put the gun on the desk. I won't ask again."

Unlike Garey, Kurt's hand held rock steady and he meant what he said to the Satanist. He watched the other man closely and if he even moved an inch to raise his own weapon, Kurt would blow him away with no hesitation. He knew Victor never felt any remorse for killing the men and women in his battles with followers of Hell and Vic often wondered what that said about him. Kurt now knew what he meant. He knew, or at least he hoped, if needed, he would not lose a wink of sleep over shooting Garey or any other member of the Church of the Light Reclaimed.

Garey laid the Magnum on the desk and raised both hands in the air, his lip still trembling. "Come on man, don't shoot me. I don't even know how to use the damn thing, anyways."

"It's easy, you point and shoot which is what I'm gonna do if you don't tell me where you're keeping Ruth Anne."

"I don't know a thing about that, Mister."

"Really?"

Kurt moved the gun slightly to the left and pulled the trigger. A large bottle of Scotch exploded, along with the mirror behind it, sending shards of glass into Garey.

"Holy shit, man. Don't shoot! Don't shoot!"

"Dude, the next one won't miss. You have my word on it. Now, where is she?"

Garey glanced quickly at one of the walls of booze and then away. "If I tell you, then they'll kill me. Or worse."

Kurt walked quickly around the desk and pressed the muzzle of his gun against Garey's temple. "Won't be an issue for you, Elwyn. All I have to do is squeeze a bit with my finger and you won't have to worry about this world any longer. Instead, you'll have to find out what Hell has waiting for you."

Large tears began to fall down Garey's cheeks. "There's a secret panel in the wall there." He pointed in the direction he glanced at before. "But we can't open it. Only the boss can open it. There's a digital keypad in the wall and if you type in the wrong combination more than a couple of times it blows the whole damn place up."

"Is she down there?"

Kurt thought about Ruth Anne only being a few feet away but not able to reach her.

He nodded. "I think so. And she's not the only thing, either."

"What do you mean, not the only 'thing'?"

"They bought this company earlier in the year because they learned the original owners put the building on top of a burial site used for the criminally insane. He won't tell us what, but the boss says the girl has company."

Kurt felt his heartbeat pick up despite his efforts to keep it under control. "Ruth Anne. Why do they have Ruth Anne down there?"

"I'm really sorry, mister. But whatever is going on down there, they need a sacrifice. I think the boss plans on it being her."

Kurt felt his whole world fall away. "The boss. You mean Michael McCain?"

"I don't know a Michael McCain. They call him Belial. And, mister, you don't want no part of him."

"Yeah, yeah, yeah. That's Mikey. I plan to send him back to Hell."

Mikey used the name Belial in his dealings with the Church of the Light Reclaimed. Belial was the name used by one of the four kings of Hell.

Kurt picked up the Magnum and slid the gun into a jacket pocket. "Open the wall. I want to see the keypad."

Garey moved to the wall and pulled the third bottle of scotch from the left and a section of the wall moved out about three feet into the room, revealing an alcove behind it and a single door with a keypad about chest high.

Kurt knew the keypad would have, at a minimum, a four digit pin and likely one six digit or more in length, leading to millions of combinations. There was no way for him to hack into the keypad. These type of locks were self-contained. Screw it up and Ruth Anne would be dead.

Seeing what he needed to see, he motioned for Garey to close the secret entrance. When he finished he turned to face Kurt. "What are you going to do with me?"

"You got a bag here?"

"Yeah, behind the desk."

Keeping his gun trained on Garey, Kurt found the bag, lifted it to the desk and zipped it open. He rummaged around inside until he found what he hoped: a pair of handcuffs.

"Let's go," Kurt said, waving the gun for Garey to go out in front of him.

They left the office and Kurt nodded to the main plant area. Garey opened the door and led Kurt into the large room with the fermentation tanks. Kurt took Garey by the elbow and moved him over to a large tank with a huge copper pipe running down one side.

"Put your arms through the opening."

Garey did as he was instructed and Kurt slapped on the handcuffs, first on one wrist, then the other. He stepped away from the

Satanist and walked towards the offices. When he got to the door he turned to look at Garey. The man's brows pulled down and then shot up, in realization.

"No!"

Kurt turned off the lights and shut the door.

CHAPTER TWENTY-TWO

Winston dreamed. He was lying on a wooden floor, the slats old and rough, in a room covered in moldy wallpaper. He guessed it was nighttime, with light from a crescent moon coming through a dirty window behind him. From his vantage point on the floor he could see a battered door a few feet away. Something waited behind the door and he knew it wanted him. He tried to sit up, but couldn't move. His body refused to answer his commands, even to lift a single finger. He tried to scream for help, but his throat felt raw and he produced only a whisper.

With a rising panic, he stared at the door, waiting for what lay on the other side. The knob began to slowly turn and Winston began to whimper. He now knew what came for him and it was Death.

He shot awake when he heard a voice call his name. Brother Joshua stood at the foot of the bed and Winston stood to face the other man. Joshua moved by him to place his hand on Victor's forehead and bowed his head in silent prayer, finishing with a soft "Amen."

"You sure took your sweet time getting here," Winston said, unable to keep the bitterness out of his voice.

"I'm sorry, Winston. There were things which I needed to take care of before I could come down to the hospital. It didn't stop me from praying for Victor. How is he?"

Winston gazed at his friend before answering. "He'll be one of the dead soon. The docs don't think he will make it till morning."

Joshua nodded, but said nothing else. To Winston, the man seemed as unflappable as ever. And it ticked him off.

"Summon him," Winston demanded.

"Summon who?"

"You know who. Summon him. I want to talk to him. Right now. Summon him."

Joshua tilted his head slightly to the side. "It doesn't work that way. He comes to me when he needs me. I don't summon him."

Winston balled his fists at his side and worked to keep his temper in check. "You're the man he uses to manage the Hands of God. So you close them eyes of yours and pray real hard and I know he will come. Go on, do it."

Joshua stood still for several heartbeats, considering the request, then moved to the other side of the bed, his hands resting loosely on the bed rail. Then he lowered his eyes and stood that way for a few seconds and then reopened them and when he did, they were no longer alone.

Archangel Uriel, keeper of the gates of Hell, and one of only a few angels allowed in the presence of God, according to some, looked back from Joshua's eyes. Winston could feel the hair stand on end all over his body and felt dazed by the power of the angel.

He wanted to drop to his knees and beg forgiveness for having summoned Uriel to this room, for even daring to have the gall to do so. But lowering his own eyes, they fell upon Victor in his hospital bed and found himself remaining upright, defiant.

"You summoned me? Why?"

It was Joshua's voice but it carried a timber no mortal could ever hope to match. Vic talked often about what it felt like in the presence of the divine and now he knew what he meant.

"I want you to heal him. You can do that, right?"

"I am sorry, but I don't interfere with the course of a man's life. He will either live or die on his own accord."

"That's a load of crap." Winston knew he should speak with more reverence, but couldn't help himself. "You don't interfere? Every time you tell Joshua who you want Victor to hunt down and deliver to Hell on your behalf, you interfere. And you've done so ever since Adam and Eve got tossed out of the Garden for biting a piece of forbidden fruit. Don't interfere? Bull."

Joshua's facial expression never changed, but Winston could feel the angel's anger, like standing too close to a high power line makes your skin tingle. "It is not done."

Winston stepped up and gripped the bed rail on his side, hard enough he felt he could break it in half, the unconscious body of Victor McCain lying between them. Bad-ass angel or not, he wouldn't back down.

"Yes it is. And you can. We need him. His brother is running around the city murdering people and he's lying in this bed because he was doing your dirty work. Don't feed me this crap 'it's not done'."

"Victor made his choice and knew the dangers involved in taking up the mantle of the Hand of God. He accepted this would one day be his likely fate."

"But it doesn't have to end this way. Not now. Not this night. He's fighting for you. Doesn't that mean anything to you?"

Joshua/Uriel's brow furrowed a fraction of an inch. "It is not done."

"So help me, if you say that one more time, you're going to have to pry my ass off you."

Winston closed his eyes and prayed for calm. The irony of the situation was not lost on him. When he once again looked at the angel, he asked, "Has it ever been done?"

"No. No one has ever asked."

"Has God forbidden you to help?"

Winston waited for the answer, knowing without knowing how, this was the question which mattered.

"No."

Simple answer, profound consequences.

"Then I'm asking. I'm begging you, help him."

Uriel moved to stand closer to the head of the bed, his fingers brushing Victor's brow, brushing back a lock of hair. Then with a fluid motion he grasped the trach tube and pulled it out. Immediately alarm bells rang out from the monitors around the room and Victor stopped breathing.

Winston felt horror and lunged at the angel at the same time a nurse threw the curtain to the side and began to enter the room. Uriel threw up a hand and everything stopped, frozen in time. The curtain hung suspended in midair, the nurse with one foot off the ground. Winston came up short of actually grabbing the angel and stood, stunned. He could see into the emergency room and no one moved.

"What have you done?"

Uriel dropped the trach tube onto the bed. "Do you understand the magnitude of what you are asking me to do?"

"Is this a trick question? What I want you do is save his life."

"His life is not what is at stake. Each man and woman is here for only a finite amount of time. What is important is what happens when you leave this world behind."

"You mean his soul. Victor became the Hand of God to reclaim his soul, to make it to Heaven. You're asking me about his soul."

Uriel said nothing.

"If he died right now, would he make it?"

"I will answer you, but you won't remember the answer when this conversation is over. I want you to understand the magnitude of what you ask of me. Yes. He would be granted eternal salvation. But it is a close thing. If I do as you ask and return him to this world, there is no guarantee it will remain so. He will face many trials and tribulations from this point forward. The faith he carries now is new and fragile. Man is granted free will and things can change. Victor may change. And if he loses the faith, then the outcome will be different."

"You're telling me this because?"

"I want you to know the full cost of what you ask. You will have to live with the decision. You risk much. Eternal damnation versus eternal salvation."

"We need him. I need him. God help me, but I can't do this alone. I'll dedicate my life to helping him. To try and keep him on the righteous path."

"The men and women of Earth have a saying: the road to Hell is paved with good intentions. No matter what you do, it will be Victor who decides his faith and his fate, not you. But so be it."

Uriel placed a hand on either side of Vic's face and turned it towards him. He then gently kissed Victor on the forehead and said a few words in a language Winston could not understand, yet he could feel the power.

Victor's eyes flew open, a look of intense sadness on his face and he croaked, "Father" before closing his eyes and falling into a deep sleep, his chest rising and falling on its own, no longer needing the trach tube.

The wound in his throat where the trach tube had once been vanished, the skin smooth and unbroken. When Winston looked on the bed he could see the tube itself no longer lay upon the sheet.

"I have done as you asked. It will take a day or so before he will be as he was before, but he will live. Do not summon me again."

He turned and left the room and time once again began to run its normal course. The alarms blared and the nurse returned to motion.

"What happened?"

Winston started to tell her, but stopped. He looked around the room like a man searching for his lost keys. "I'm not sure. I sat in my chair dozing and then the alarms went off."

She went to the monitors and reset them. While she did this,

Winston tried to remember what he'd been doing before she came in. He could almost remember and then the thought would disappear. He thought he dreamed about a door and he felt fear, but couldn't be sure. And for some reason, Brother Joshua was involved, but no clue as to how or why.

"No telling. The good news is, it seems your friend is doing better. All his stats are improving. That's good news."

She was right. Victor looked better. His breathing seemed normal and color had returned to his cheeks. The nurse offered a smile and then left the room, pulling the curtain behind her. Winston sat down in his chair and rested his face in his hands and thanked God for Victor improving.

The phone in his pocket buzzed and he read Kurt's name on the screen when he pulled it out and answered the call. He put the phone to his ear and listened while he watched Victor.

He listened to Kurt's news and responded, "Go to the van and drive to the convenience store. I'll be there in a bit."

He thumbed through his recent calls and tapped one of the numbers. Detective Coffey answered on the third ring. He filled her in on Vic's improvement. "Any chance you can come sit with Vic while I take care of a few things?"

"Why not. Seems my career might be over, so I might as well. I'll be there in less than half an hour.

He hung up the call and stood. He bent over and kissed Victor on the forehead and felt a feeling of Deja vu, the scene tickling something in the back of his mind. He knew deep down Vic would make a full recovery. Knew it. Yet along with the knowledge, he felt something else: fear. Something about Victor's improving condition made him worried about his friend in a way he'd never felt before.

Brushing it off he turned to collect his things so he could leave when Coffey arrived, and he noticed something on his friend's face. A single tear.

CHAPTER TWENTY-THREE

Winston sat with Kurt in the front of the van and stared out the window at the distillery, thinking about Detective Coffey. She'd been worn out and battered when she showed up to replace him, but not beaten. He could see what Vic liked about the woman. She possessed an inner strength few could match and he felt Vic was in safe hands while he dealt with current developments.

"Both of them dead? No doubt?"

Kurt paused in his typing, his fingers over his keyboard. "Dude, if you'd seen them, you wouldn't have any doubts either. Both biker guys are now on the big bike ride in the sky."

"And Garey. You're sure? Did you go check on him?"

Kurt had given him the lowdown on the shadow monsters which attacked them when they entered the distillery. While he found it hard to fathom, he long ago learned not to question the spooky things they fought in their battles against the dark forces of Satan.

Kurt resumed typing on his laptop. "Nope. I figured when the screaming stopped, so did he."

Winston wanted to berate his friend for going inside without talking to him first, but in the end, he let it go. If it had been him? He would have done the same thing. Kurt loved Ruth Anne and risked his own life to save her, continuing on after the death of the bikers. That took real guts. Who was he to tell Kurt what he could or couldn't do? If anything, Kurt seemed more assured. Gone were the days when his hands would shake from talking to a beautiful woman, or when his face would turn green from the thought of doing something dangerous.

With each new crisis, the "old Kurt" faded further and further away. Where many men would shrink when faced with the extreme horrors of their life Kurt thrived.

"Explain to me what you did next."

Kurt pointed to the screen. "When Garey told me the only way below was through the keypad, we needed a way to capture the code. I knew Mikey would never give it to us, so I came back to the van. In my laptop bag I keep a few things I might need when we're in the field and one is a micro camera. It's wireless and there's a small piece of adhesive on the back. So I put one in the upper corner of the alcove with an angle to show us a view of the keypad when Mikey next goes down. I then hooked into their WiFi system. You would need my level of skill to find it. Now I can watch the alcove from the van and when we have the code, I plan to go down there and rescue Ruth Anne."

"You know when Mikey finds the dead bodies, he's going to know we were there. We lose the element of surprise."

"Screw surprise. I want him to find the bodies. I want him to wonder if Garey might have known the code for the keypad and given it to me. For all I know, Garey may have been feeding me a line of bull when he said he didn't know the code. I want Mikey to go check on things below, see if we've been down there. That's how I'll learn the code."

"Then we're going to need backup." The van dashboard clock indicated it was just after five a.m. "For now, why don't you stretch out on the bench seat in the back of the van. I'll keep an eye on the laptop while you catch an hour or two of sleep. I'll wake you and you can relieve me. Then later in the morning, we can arrange for more help."

"Dude, you're so old school. I've got a motion sensor on the feed and I set it to sound an alarm on the laptop and wake us up if someone enters the room. We can both catch a few hours of sleep. We don't even have to be here. We can head to my house and sleep in a bed."

"Done. But you live too far away. We'll stay at my place. We can pick my car up when we come back." He put the van in gear and pulled out onto the quiet street.

"Uh, don't you have a problem with snakes?"

"Not anymore. Snakes are all dead. Besides, if you're a bad enough MoFo to handle a shadow monster, you can kick the crap out of a rattlesnake. Did you learn anything about the place there before the bourbon folks moved in?"

"Yeah, a bit. The Ives Home for the Criminally Insane opened in the mid-eighteen hundreds. They tried all kinds of weird treatments on people. They did everything from chemically inducing seizures to electroshock to lobotomies. They would take an ice pick and then stick it into the brain through one of the patient's eye sockets, then wiggle it around. More often than not, patients died from the treatments and there was a shaft where they'd throw in the dead and then cover it up. Reports say thousands were killed and buried there. When the state got wind of their disposal methods, they shut the place down."

"Never heard of it." He'd heard of Waverly Hills, the former tuberculosis sanitarium where tens of thousands of people died and where people now came from around the country at Halloween to take tours of the building with claims of ghosts walking the halls, but Ives failed to ring any bells.

"Not a surprise. Seems Ives burned to the ground not long after the turn of the century. When it did, they flattened the place and turned it into a parking lot. It remained that way until the distillery bought the land and opened for business a few years ago."

"Makes you wonder what Mikey found down there. I guess we'll know soon enough, if your camera works the way you hope."

Kurt tilted the laptop to show Winston the screen and he could see a bird's eye view of the alcove. Kurt tapped a few keys and the camera zoomed in tight on the keypad, the glowing green numbers clear and sharp.

"Won't be a problem. When Mikey enters the code, I'll have it."

Winston was impressed. "You go, Kurt. Now all we need is the calvary. Stiles and his guys will be here by morning and I bet once I talk to Tank, we'll have a boatload of pissed off bikers willing to join in the fight."

"Or wanting our heads. Are you sure you can trust either Stiles or the bikers?"

"Hell, no. I don't trust any of them, but we need them if we're going to take on Mikey and his gang."

"And whatever's down below. Garey seemed scared shitless. If what's down below is worse than the shadow thing-a-ma-bobs, then we've got problems."

"First things first, Kurt. Don't go borrowing trouble. First we get the code. Then we kill Michael McCain, rescue your fiancé and we go all fire and brimstone on anything else."

"Cool. Fire and brimstone. Love it. Great idea. Count me in." He sat and thought for a few seconds. "Uh, Winston. How are we going to do that?"

"I'm still working on that part."

"Dude, work harder."

Winston snickered. "I'm waiting for divine inspiration to hit me. If that don't work, then I'm sure I'll think of something."

"I have faith. We're going to save Ruth Anne, wait and see. She's going to be okay."

"Damn straight."

Winston held out his fist and Kurt bumped it, first on top, then on the bottom. He wanted the hacker to have hope, to believe they could make it happen, even though he didn't share the same feeling. Kick the ass of an Infernal Lord, one of the twelve single hardest people to kill on the planet, then any of the goons he may have brought with him and finally an unknown terror buried beneath the bowls of the distillery? He knew it to likely be a suicide mission.

But he would do it all the same. If it meant his death, then he was okay with it. He knew when he signed on to help Victor his life would likely be a short one. When you do battle with the Devil, at some point, your number comes up. He only hoped when his ticket got punched, he took as many of the wicked with him as possible. And he had some thoughts on how to do just that: fire and brimstone. Fire and brimstone.

CHAPTER TWENTY-FOUR

I dreamed. At the end of a long winding country road sat a towering oak on the edge of the Ohio River. When I was a young man I'd bring a book and sit under the tree and read until the light faded and stars would blanket the sky.

In my dream, the transition from day to twilight had begun and I closed my book and leaned against the tree to watch the night close in around me. I heard footsteps and turned to find my father strolling down the road to join me.

I felt a joy in my heart, having lost my father years before to a heart attack. Vincent McCain moved with a step of a young man and with a grace which almost made me cry. My father topped out at six foot eight inches and in my memory, grace is not something you would say about him. Power and strength, but never grace.

"Mind if I sit down?"

I scooted over and gave him part of the tree. He plopped down, snatched a blade of straw grass, and stuck it in his mouth. He stretched his long legs out in front of him, and smiled.

"You know, Vic, when you used to come down here to read I wondered what the hell you were doing. Now I understand. Unlike the rest of us, you always knew how to stop and smell the roses. It's beautiful."

"Thanks, dad."

We sat for a few minutes, not talking, enjoying each other's company. A flock of geese flew low over the river and landed softly, wings extended wide as they glided to a stop on the water.

My father appeared to wait for me to do the talking. I hated to break the silence, but knew I must.

"I'm dead, aren't I?"

"Soon, son. Your time is almost up. I'm here to bring you the rest of the way. We will sit here until it's time and then I'll take you home."

I felt the tears streaming down and in the past, I would have worried about crying in front of my father, worried about him thinking me soft. Not now. These were tears of joy. I became the Hand of God to redeem my own soul, with hopes of heaven being the ultimate reward. My father being here meant I'd made it, though not without regrets.

"I'm sorry I didn't do a better job taking care of mom and Mikey when you died. I should have been more involved in my brother's life. If I had, maybe he wouldn't have turned out the putz he is now."

"There's nothing you could have done, Victor. Mikey chose his path and will pay the ultimate penalty when his time comes. And you did well by your mother. I'm very proud of you."

My father stood up. "Well, it's time, Vic." He offered me his hand. "We'd best be—"

A blast from a trumpet interrupted him and he tilted his head, brow furrowed. I jumped to my feet, a sudden fear erupting inside me.

"What is it? What's going on?"

My father closed his eyes and when he reopened them, this time I saw tears in his eyes. He placed a hand on my arm. "I'm sorry, Victor, but things have changed. You must go back. It seems your time in the mortal world is not yet finished."

"No. I don't want to go back. I want to stay with you. Please, dad, let me stay." I gripped him by both shoulders, desperate not to leave his side.

"Son, listen to me. You're needed. There are things you must do before you can return. But listen to me. Are you listening to me?"

I nodded, unable to speak. My whole body trembled.

"I want you to keep fighting, to do what is right. If you do, then when the time comes I'll be here, under this tree waiting for you. You mustn't give up. You'll continue being tested and I expect you to make it back to me. Understand?"

"Tested? I'm tired of being tested. I want this over. I want to stay with you."

My father engulfed me in a huge hug, his arms tight around me. "Victor McCain, you're *my* son. You will do what needs to be done and then return to me. Stop the whining. McCain's don't whine."

Now that's the father I respected and remembered. Tough love. I cleared my throat a couple of times and finally managed to squeak out a,

"Yes sir."

"That's more like it." He broke the embrace, took my face in his hands and then kissed me on the forehead. "Now get a move on."

He pointed up the road and I began to walk away from him and salvation. Tears tumbled down my cheeks unchecked, a nearly overwhelming sadness accompanying each step. I only made it a short distance when he called to me. I turned and saw his own tears. I couldn't remember ever seeing my father cry.

"I'm proud of you son. Don't ever forget that. You hear me?"

To hell with what others wanted. I wanted to stay. I went to move to join him, but my feet wouldn't move. I stood rooted to the spot. "Father, what's happening? I can't move. Father?"

"I love you son."

And then the darkness flooded around us. "Father? Father?"

I could no longer see him and I screamed to him one last time. "*Father*!?"

He was gone. For a second time, I'd lost him and an unbelievable sadness threatened to drown me. So close. I was so close. And then the dream ended.

*****

I opened my eyes. I could see a curtain and heard the sounds of a steady beep and hum of machines. A hospital room. Why was I in a hospital room?

"It's about time you woke your ass up."

I turned my head, the dream beginning to fade. Detective Coffey sat in a chair next to the bed, a broad smile creasing a weary face.

"Where am I?" The words came out in a scratchy croak.

She rose and covered my hand in both of hers, squeezing hard.

"Baptist East Hospital. What do you remember?"

"You yelling something, then someone hit me. That's it."

"What I yelled was 'gun' and what hit you was a large caliber round from a sniper rifle. You took one to the chest. Punched right through your vest and then out the back. A clean shot through and through. There was a lot of blood and I could have sworn you were a goner. Seems you're making a miraculous recovery."

"I feel like a giant has picked me up and thrown me down and then stomped me to a pulp. Lucky, I guess."

She bent and kissed me. This shocked the hell out of me. I must have really been near death. "I'm not sure, but I thought you were mad at me, though I don't remember why."

She straightened. "You don't remember the three photos?"

Ah, bloody hell. The photos. The memory crashed landed in my brain. "Uh, yeah. I do now."

"Who exactly is Samantha and why did you shoot her?"

Before I could explain a voice interrupted and said, "I am, and it's complicated."

Samantha Tyler let the curtain fall into place behind her and stepped to the foot of the bed. The two women stared at each other and I could feel the tension in the room ratchet up a couple thousand times over.

Double bloody hell. I might have been better off dead.

CHAPTER TWENTY-FIVE

Winston glanced into the living room where Kurt was fast asleep on the couch. The hacker slept with two pillows clutched to his chest and his blanket covering only his feet. Kurt insisted on leaving his Christmas tree on to help him fall asleep.

Winston managed a few hours of sleep after he taped a piece of cardboard over the broken window in his room and made sure the house was free of poisonous reptiles. He should have felt exhausted, but all in all, he felt better than average. Nothing like running on fumes.

Kurt's laptop sat open on the coffee table, the camera feed of the alcove showing no movement. Both slept with their guns within easy reach, but nothing happened over night.

Winston shook Kurt a couple of times. He struggled to wake up, but finally opened his eyes and yawned, still clutching both pillows. "What happened? What's wrong?"

"Not a thing, man. Here's what we're gonna do. I'm going to drive over to the Tyranny Rides hangout. Though it's early on Sunday, I bet they have someone in there. I'll tell them what went down at Wolfaden and find some muscle to help out. You keep sleeping. You're gonna need the rest when we hit 'em."

Kurt rubbed his face with both hands. "Dude, I can go with you."

"I know you can, but you're not. It's more important you get some sleep. We'll need you sharp when Mikey hits the room. Besides, nothing's going down until he does and you'll be the first person to know."

Kurt flopped down on the couch, resigned and exhausted. "Dude, you're right, I'm more than worn out. I'll call you when the alarm goes off on the camera."

"Good deal."

Winston went to his room, took a quick shower and changed clothes. When he went to leave, he found Kurt snoring softly. He pulled the blanket up to his chest and thought of turning off the tree, but decided to leave it on. He set the alarm to the house and went out to the van, his gun in the pocket of his jacket, his hand on the gun.

The street looked quiet. And normal. Up and down the street, Christmas lights twinkled in the early dawn and several yards with inflatable snowmen or Santas bobbed in the breeze. Normal everywhere, that is, except for the house next door where Ashley Truman's door was covered with police crime scene tape, her Christmas lights off. He tried to push the vision of her head out of his mind, but failed. With a heavy sigh, he unlocked the door to the van, got in and started it up.

Parked on the curb a few spots down from his house sat a Chevy Blazer with two biker guards keeping watch on his house. They'd been there when they got home, but he didn't want to deal with them until he got some sleep. Now he needed them.

He pulled even with the Blazer and rolled down his window. The driver did the same. Winston could see two men, both north of forty years old with hard stares.

"I'm Winston Reynolds. I need you to call your boss. I'm on my way over to the Riverside Inn. I need him to meet me there."

The driver let out a fake laugh. "Tank ain't gonna want to get up and be out this early. You want to wake him up, fine. You do it. But I ain't callin' him."

"If he wants to know what happened to Greene and Purcell last night, he'll drag his ass out of bed. And you're gonna call him. Once you do, continue to keep watch on the house. The guy inside is a target."

"What happened to Reggie and Jaxson?"

"Call your boss. He can tell you."

Winston drove off and rolled up the window. He knew when Tank learned what went down then things would turn rough quick. On the way over to the biker hangout, he worked on a plan he'd been kicking around in his sleep. He grabbed his phone and made a phone call.

His uncle answered on the second ring. "Aren't you up a bit early for a young man? Or are you still up from the night before? You need bail money?"

"Come on, Unc'. You know I'm a choir boy. And don't you ever sleep? You picked up awful quick."

Lewis Reynolds was his father's only sibling. After serving in both the first and second Gulf Wars, he came home disillusioned when it came to his government. He joined several militia groups around the country. He believed at some point the government would one day come to take his guns and he planned to be ready to stop them.

Being "ready" meant a concealed bunker stocked with every type of weapon you could buy legally and several you couldn't buy anywhere but on the black market. Several times his help had been instrumental in taking out those associated with the Church of the Light Reclaimed.

While Lewis didn't know all the details on what he and Victor were doing, he never asked questions when they asked for help. Family helps family.

"I keep old man time, Winston. Besides, when I served Uncle Sam, we got up before the sun. I see no reason to change things now. You, on the other hand, like the sleep of the young. If you're calling me at six forty-five in the morning, you must need help."

"Yeah. We got some things going on. Remember that night at the last cookout, when you and I were arguing about superhero movie bad guys and you told me about your favorite bad guy?"

"Yeah, I remember."

His uncle's distrust of the government meant he would never discuss something possibly illegal openly on a cell phone, only in person, so they sometimes talked in code.

"The one you liked the most, you went on a long time about how it would be possible to do what he did."

"What the hell you got goin' on, nephew?"

"You hear about that shooting last night at Molly's?"

"Yeah, what about it?"

"Someone took a shot at Victor McCain. He's in intensive care out at Baptist East. Looks like he'll make it, but it was a close thing."

"Lord Almighty. You know who did it?"

"I got some ideas. That's why I need your help. I need to deliver some payback to some bad MoFos, Unc'. And I may need to do it in a way that delivers that message to a large group of people at once, one they can't stop once it starts."

"Hmm. Well, yeah. I think I can procure what you need. It will take some time, though. You don't just become a super villain in a few hours, you hear me?"

"Yeah. I hear ya. Call me when you have something."

"I take it this means you won't be joining your aunt this morning for church?"

"I don't think so. I appreciate the help, Unc'."

"Don't you worry about it. But watch your six, nephew. You need any extra help, you call me. I still know the business end of a troublemaker."

Winston knew a troublemaker in his uncle's world meant a sawed off shotgun. "I'll keep that in mind, but doing this other thing for me will be more than enough, I promise."

They said their goodbyes and Winston put his phone away. The last thing he wanted to do was to drag family into his fight with the Church of the Light Reclaimed and their minions. Truth be told, it was his only real worry when it came to helping Vic, making his family targets. Truman's death proved the point. He would keep his uncle out of the fight.

On the river he could see a towboat pushing several barges full of coal upriver, likely to one of the power plants in Pennsylvania. Even on an early Sunday the river rats were still working. Good for them.

His phone buzzed and when he looked at the screen he didn't recognize the number. When he answered a man asked, "Is this Winston Reynolds?"

"Maybe. Who's this?"

"Tank Bone. Victor gave me your number in case of emergencies. Greene and Purcell didn't check in last night with their replacements and now the boys over at your place said you wanted me to meet you at HQ to talk about them. What the hell happened? I keep calling Victor but he won't answer his damn phone."

"That's because someone shot him last night. He's alive, but still unconscious when I left. I'll fill you in on what's going on but not on the phone, Tank. I'll be at your place in about five minutes. Meet me there."

"Already here. When the boys didn't call, we mobilized a few guys to come find your ass. Tell me, are they still alive?"

"See you in five."

Winston ended the call. He needed to make sure he kept Tank on the team. When he learned his men were dead would he blame them and become an enemy or would he want revenge on the ones who murdered his men? If he was a betting man, he'd bet on revenge. Either way, he would know in a few minutes.

He rounded a curve and hit one of the few long straight stretches on River Road when a Ford F-150 came flying up the road behind him, turned on his blinker and moved to pass. Winston glanced at the speedometer. He was doing five over the limit which meant this guy had was in a hurry.

The truck nosed past him and when it did, the truck pulled hard to the right and crashed into the van. Startled, Winston lost control of the wheel and the truck pushed the van off the side of the road.

It felt like he floated, until the van crashed down the embankment, rolled over twice and plunged into the Ohio River.

CHAPTER TWENTY-SIX

Samantha had changed in the months since I shot her. Her red hair, once short, now fell almost to her shoulders. Her clothes, from her jacket to her boots, were all black. And she just looked different. If you forced me to put it into words, she seemed older. Her innocence ripped from her, she wore a more world-weary expression. Then again, being shot by your lover and having your father killed by one of his friends would do it.

Coffey jerked a thumb at Samantha. "I'll ask you again, did you really shoot her?"

"Yes, he did. And he murdered my father. Who are you?"

Coffey let go of my hand and stiffened. "Linda Coffey. I'm a detective with Louisville Metro. Murdered your father?"

"Hang on a minute," I said. I knew I must be on some heavy drugs because I could feel my brain beating too slow on the uptake. "Can we wait to discuss this someplace else where we won't have other people listening? And could you guys raise my bed so I can talk to you easier? And how about a bit of water?"

Coffey pushed a button on the side of my bed and moved me to a sitting position while Samantha left to ask for water from one of the nurses which gave me time to think. What I thought was that I was toast.

When Samantha returned with the water, she also brought a nurse, a matronly woman with a tuft of unruly white hair and a ready smile.

"Mr. McCain, I'm Louise and I'm your day nurse. I have to admit you're doing incredibly well, considering the circumstances."

She took my temp and made some notes on my charts. "I must say, incredibly well doesn't really cover it. You must have some great genes. With numbers like this? I think we can move you out of ICU. Let me consult with the doctor and we'll see about moving you to a private room."

Coffey started to say something and I raised a hand to stop her. "When we are in a private room I'll answer any and all questions. But not here."

Coffey wasn't happy, but she held her tongue and sat down again. Samantha continued to stand at the end of the bed.

"Joshua told me you were shot in the chest and it didn't look good. He made it sound like you wouldn't make it a full day. Guess he got it wrong. You look pretty good to me."

My heart rate shot up with the comment and I noticed Coffey glance at the machine tracking my pulse, then look at me with one eyebrow raised. Even now, Samantha made my body react in ways I could never explain.

I fought for control of my body and managed. Just.

"You come to watch me die?"

The words stung and I regretted them the instant they slipped out. She stuck her hands in her back pockets and stared at the floor. "You think I'd do that?"

"Considering you quit taking my calls I really don't know what to think. You weren't exactly happy with me the last time we spoke. Hell, who knows. I'm sorry. Blame it on the drugs they have me on."

The three of us fell silent and before long a couple of nurses came in doing nurse stuff and then a few minutes after that, they rolled me up to a room on the fifth floor, with both women tagging along.

Once they got me settled into my new digs, the nurse left and closed the door. Coffey pulled the two chairs in the room close to the bed and motioned for Samantha to sit on one. She took the other.

"Fine. I've waited until you were in a private room. Now spill it. And from the beginning. If you leave anything out this time, Vic, I'm gone. Permanently."

And I knew she meant it. I started with my brother selling his soul to Satan and the deal I made to try and save his soul, losing mine in the process. I explained Samantha's part and how my brother tried to kill thousands of children. About meeting Dominic Montoya and what it meant to be the Hand of God. I told her of how I allowed Mikey and his lapdog, Deveraux, to kill Montoya, of taking his place and then how I tracked down and killed my own brother, tossing his body down a sinkhole.

I told the story of the Watchers and why I shot Samantha, and about the Infernal Lords and how my brother managed to return from the dead, a near immortal.

I told her about Cyrus Tyler and his plans to murder the President and Vice-President and how he was blown to bits by Elizabeth Bathory, a woman several hundred years old.

And finally, I told her about the bounty put on me by Alex Dabney for $10.000.000. "In my opinion, I think someone tried to collect on the contract he put out on me. Two other guys tried it the morning Ruth Anne was kidnapped."

"And what happened to them? You kill them, too?"

"Well, yeah. I mean, it was either them or me. I decided I'd rather it be them."

When I finished, she sat there a few minutes, then turned to Samantha. "And you're telling me this is true?"

"At least the part I'm aware of. I don't know Bathory, but video showed a woman getting into the car with my father. The rest I can tell you from firsthand knowledge happened." Samantha turned to me. "You worked with an Infernal Lord? Trusted her? Are you insane?"

"Well, those are two separate questions. Turns out she was right. Samantha, your dad planned to bump off the President of the United States. If Elizabeth didn't take him out, I'd have been forced to. You know how this works. Your dad made his bed and he got buried in it. Do you realize how many people he would have killed if the bomb had gone off as planned?"

She didn't say anything. Samantha lost her mother when she was a young girl and her death, or the anger it left behind, led to her father accepting Satan's help to become more powerful. With her father's death, she lost the only family she had left. I know she loved her father. She also knew he was a real son of a bitch.

Coffey stood and went to the window and stared at the approaching sunrise. "You both sound nuts. You know that, right?"

"Yeah, pretty much. Doesn't mean it's not true. Mikey's in town and his goal is to punish me and those close to me." A thought occurred to me. "Samantha, if Mikey knew where you were, I wonder why he left you alone?"

"Look, after my surgery, Brother Joshua arranged for me to rehab at a monastery. This is the first time I've left their grounds. Mikey could never touch me there."

Coffey looked over at me. "Come again?"

"Infernal Lords, or anything else from the gates of Hell, can't step foot on church property. It's a sanctuary for those of us fighting the good fight. We don't have many perks, but that's one of them."

Coffey leaned against the window and rubbed the bridge of her nose with a couple of fingers. "You guys are nuttier than a fruit cake. You know that?"

Samantha and I looked at each other and she shrugged. She stretched her legs out and put her feet on the end of the bed a few inches from mine. I felt the old familiar feeling with her in the room. The woman rang all my bells. Yet I wondered if our ship had sailed. When it came down to it, it mattered more to me what Linda Coffey thought than Samantha Tyler.

"Listen, Linda, I know it sounds crazy. But I swear to you it's all true." Something hit me. "Where's your badge and gun? I've never seen you without both."

She let out a long sigh. "Well, whether I believe you or not, your brother managed to land me on suspension."

She told us what happened when Mikey broke into her place and left the photos and note. "That's the only thing which makes me even come close to believing your story. Damn it, I know I hit him and more than once. Your brother should be in the morgue, not driving around. Then there's you."

"What about me?"

"You were shot by a sniper. I was there. You had a wound in the front and a huge hole in your back. No way you should be sitting up and talking to us. That brother Joshua guy was right. You should be as dead as your brother, but you're not."

My mind drifted to the dream of talking to my father under the old oak tree and I felt a huge sense of loss. With every fiber of my being, I knew Linda was right: I should be dead. Wanted to be dead. I felt like the kid who wakes up to find Christmas stolen from under the tree.

"Yeah, well, what can I tell you? I guess my number wasn't up."

Samantha shook her head. "I don't think that's it."

"Oh? Why not?"

"She's right. When you shot me in the hip, it took months and months for me to recover. And here you are a few hours after being shot in the chest by a sniper sitting up in bed and talking like, at worst, you took a beating. The other reason is Joshua. If anyone would know how close you were to death, don't you think Brother Joshua would be the one? For him to be that wrong? I don't think so. I think something else happened." And she pointed up to the heavens.

I didn't respond. I couldn't shake the feeling of loss and the thought I should have died. I felt incredibly tired, but not anything near death. And the memory of the oak tree.

"Right now, I'm exhausted and I think I'd like to take a nap. But first I need to call Winston. I'm surprised he's not here. Either of you know where my phone is?"

Linda took her phone out and handed it to me. "The nurse's station will have it. I'll get it in a minute. Use mine. Winston sat with you all night. I took over for him because he said he needed to take care of something."

"How about my gun?"

"LMPD has it. You dropped it when you were hit. It's part of the investigation. My guess is it will be awhile before you have it back."

I punched in Winston's number and it rang but dumped into voicemail. I left a quick message asking him to call me and hung up. I called Kurt next.

I could tell I woke him up. "Kurt, is Winston with you? Linda said he needed to take care of something. Are you two together?"

"Big Guy, I can't tell you how glad I am to hear your voice. Dude, you're not going to believe what's happened since you went down."

He filled me in on what happened over night. "He's on his way over to their place to talk to them about what happened to Purcell and Greene. I offered to go with him, but he insisted I stay here. I'm surprised he didn't answer his phone. Maybe he ignored it because he didn't recognize the number."

"Yeah. Maybe. Call me if you see anything on your camera. If Mikey's there, we'll want to hit him hard and quickly."

I hung up and handed Linda her phone.

"Did he get a line on your brother?" she asked.

"Not yet, but maybe. We tracked one of his hired hands to a place by the river in Shively where they may be holding Ruth Anne."

I repeated to Samantha and Linda what Kurt told me. "Great. I can call Alvey and let him know and they can hit the place."

"No. You can't. If they try and bust into the basement before we have the code it can all go to Hell. But this raises a larger question: what do you plan to do about what I told you? Are you going to turn me in?"

I'd put my life in her hands. After all, I admitted to being in on the murder of the Speaker of the House of Representatives, of torching

Mikey's warehouse, and several other crimes punishable by life in prison or the death penalty, and told them all to a cop. I knew this was the main issue between the two of us. And the fact she might have me committed.

Samantha stood, her posture relaxed. But I knew better. She possessed a black belt in Tae Kwon Do and the way she watched Linda bothered me. If Linda tried to make the call, what would Samantha do?

Linda drummed her phone against her leg a few times. "If you catch your brother, do you plan to kill him?"

"Nope. I've tried that. I've got something more permanent planned for Mikey."

"More permanent than death?"

"For an Infernal Lord? You betcha."

"I want him to pay for what he did to Wallace." She was silent for a minute. "No, that's not right. I want him to suffer the way Wallace did. And I want in."

"Done. But what about me? I think you can see why I never told you about being the Hand of God. Are you going to turn me in?"

She put her phone away. "No. You're way too pretty for prison."

Samantha snorted and I did my best to look offended. She asked, "What do you have in mind for Mikey?"

"Fire and Ice."

Fire and Ice, Mikey. Fire and Ice.

CHAPTER TWENTY-SEVEN

Winston was lying on the floor of the room staring at the door, knowing Death stood on the other side. He began to whimper when the knob began to slowly turn and the door swung open. When it did, a river of blood flowed out and into the room and engulfed him. His body remained frozen and unable to move and he knew he would soon drown.

His eyes flew open and he raised his head above the level of the water and gasped for air, the memory of being forced off the road and into the river returned with the flood of cold water which rushed into the van. He hung upside down, held in place by his seatbelt. He struggled to unlatch the buckle.

When the seatbelt finally released, he fell into the water while the van continued to sink upside down. Winston knelt on what would have been the ceiling and stripped off his coat, shirt and Kevlar vest. He thought about his boots, but knew he didn't have enough time, with water now up to his waist and rising quickly.

He began to crank the window open with both hands, thankful the van was too old to have power windows. Memories of Samantha drowning in a Florida canal kept passing through his mind, not wanting the same fate to happen to him. The river poured in faster with each inch the window moved and his body began to shake from the cold. He knew he would only have a few minutes to make it to shore before hypothermia rendered him unconscious.

With the window fully open, he grabbed the underside of the dashboard and pulled himself up near the floorboard where the last bit of air remained and tried to keep the panic from overwhelming him while the van filled completely with water. When the water reached his chin he took several deep breaths. Then he pushed down until he found the window and wiggled through it and into the river.

He kicked hard and managed to break the surface where he sucked in the freezing morning air. In the distance he could see the city and the new bridge construction. He spun in the water and saw the barge was now much further upstream. No other boats were in sight. He turned to swim to shore and his body felt numb while his teeth chattered uncontrollably and his boots felt heavy.

"There he is."

On the road above the river two more trucks had joined the first and he could see a group of men looking in his direction. The river had floated him about thirty yards from where the van plunged into the water. The men all raised guns and began to fire in his direction, bullets slapping the water around him.

Winston dove below the surface of the water and swam down several feet. He only managed a few strokes when he felt a sting in his calf and another on his back. Thankfully the water slowed the bullets down enough to keep them from penetrating too far into his body, but they hurt like hell, regardless.

He used powerful strokes with the current to swim another minute or so downstream, but his energy began to leave him and he knew if he did not climb out of the river soon, they wouldn't need bullets to kill him. The river would do it for them.

He once again broke the surface of the water and found a thick copse of trees and bushes between him and the road. He made a beeline for the water's edge and pulled himself on shore. His entire body shook and he clung to a bush to keep from slipping into the water.

He heard voices on the road and they were headed his way. He needed to keep moving. Then he saw it. The Riverside Inn. If only he could make it there. He forced his legs into motion and scrambled along the edge of the river. The last ten yards the river bank rose sharply and he needed to, once again, jump into the river to make it to their dock.

Winston prayed to God for the strength and dove into the water. This time the shock of the cold water almost killed him when he went below the surface. But a few strokes later, he made it to the dock ladder and through sure force of will, made his fingers grasp the rungs and his feet to climb.

He clawed his way onto the dock and tried to stand, but his legs refused to listen and he collapsed onto his stomach. He used his arms and began to drag himself towards the door of the Riverside Inn.

He made it only a few feet when a large fat man opened the door and pointed the business end of a Remington 870 Tactical shotgun in his direction. The man wore the vest of the Tyranny Rides biker and a large red beard: Tank Bone.

Winston rolled onto his back and raised his hands into the air. "I'm Winston Reynolds. The men who killed your guys—"

He never got to finish. The trucks squealed into the parking lot with men jumping out before the trucks stopped moving, guns in hand. Tank yelled something, raised the Remington to his shoulder and began to unload on the trucks.

A red dot laser sight on the front of the shotgun made his aim deadly accurate and the man showed no fear. He advanced on the trucks and his shotgun roared. Three men fell dead before firing a shot of their own. Two more returned fire but missed and soon they joined their fellow assassins on the ground.

Other bikers poured out of the inn and cut loose, one with an AK-47. Truck window glass exploded and in a few seconds the shooting ended. All the assassins were dead.

Tank lowered the shotgun and shouted orders. "C.C, you and Seth load the bodies in the trucks and drive them to the salvage yard. Have Lionel take care of them. John, you and Willy pick up all the brass. Henry, you and the rest of the guys find some shovels and turn over the gravel where the blood is pooling."

He tossed the shotgun to one of the guys and ambled over to Winston, bent and lifted him up and over one shoulder in a fireman's carry.

"You know when you said you'd be here in five minutes, you didn't' say anything about taking a swim first. Wrong time of year, don't you think?"

Winston only grunted while he fought to hang on to consciousness. Tank carried him inside and into a back room where he dropped him on a cot next to a space heater. The biker covered him with blankets and cranked up the heat. He left the room and returned with a large glass of bourbon. He helped Winston into a sitting position and held the glass to his trembling lips while he drank. The bourbon burned, but warmed him.

Winston put his head back down on the cot and pulled the blanket up to his chin. Tank left the room and Winston drifted off. At one point he heard loud talk in the front room but then things went quiet and he drifted off again.

He didn't know how long he'd been out when Tank came back

into the room with a chair. He closed the door, turned the chair around backwards and sat down.

"I think you owe me an explanation, don't you?"

Winston nodded and sat up with the blanket wrapped around him. Before he talked he picked up the glass of bourbon and downed a few more sips.

"The commotion out in the front room? Trouble?"

Tank waved it off. "Cops. They have to come out and check but they leave us alone. We told them some strangers pulled into the lot and we took a few shots at each other then they left."

"And they believed you?"

"Hell, no. But most of the local cops don't want to mess with us. They couldn't see any evidence of a crime, so they split. Now you tell me about my boys."

Winston doubted he would believe a story about shadow monsters, so he kept it more normal. "The same guys who tried to take me out hit Kurt last night. They killed Greene and Purcell."

"And you didn't think calling me last night would be a good idea? Why wait until now? You call me last night and we could have hit the fuckers. You better have a damn good reason for waiting."

Winston told the biker about the secret underground area below the factory and the need to learn the key code to gain entry. "Once we have that, we can rescue Ruth Anne and take out the man in charge. He's the only one with the code. When he goes down there, we'll know it and then we hit them."

"And I don't get their bodies until then?"

"Tank, I'm guessing they don't keep bodies around. When we hit them we can ask."

"Fine. For now, we do it your way. But if he don't show up soon, I'll burn it to the ground, you hear me? Now what's this shit about McCain being shot? Same guys?"

"Not exactly."

"Jesus, man. How many people have you guys pissed off? You sound like one of us."

"Nah. Only one Tank Bone, baby."

The biker laughed and stood to leave.

"I'll have the guys check on you. You stay out of sight for now. You need a phone?"

Winston pulled his phone out of his pocket and turned it on. "Mine survived. I always wondered if buying a LifeProof case was a waste of money. Guess not. And Tank? Thanks."

"You don't mess with me and my boys. You come to my house and try and start somethin', we're going to make you pay. Time to saddle up and ride off to war. I'm calling everyone in. And believe me, war is somethin' we're good at."

He shut the door behind him and Winston sipped a bit more bourbon, warming his body from the inside out. Then he checked messages and saw he'd missed several calls. While he listened to the voicemails, he thought about Tank's words. War. If he only knew.

CHAPTER TWENTY-EIGHT

Black Ice drove around the hospital parking lot, disappointed McCain survived the night. Not only survived, but was making a miraculous recovery. His sources told him they moved him out of ICU and into a room on the fifth floor. There were no vantage points high enough for him to even consider another long range shot. To finish him off today would require an up close and personal. Making a run at McCain, while in his hospital bed, might be an option. He would need to scope out the situation first before making any decisions.

He found an empty spot in a side lot and parked. While he made his way to the hospital entrance he tried to rationalize away his sense of foreboding. Obviously what he thought to have been a kill shot missed the mark. Even if he had yet to die, McCain must be in a weakened state and would be an easy mark.

All rational thoughts. All likely true. Yet, it still did not change the fact McCain never should have survived the shooting. In all his years as an assassin, no other similar situation came to mind and it bothered him. The urge to pack up and leave and let someone else take out the Hand of God continued to grow, despite the hit it would be to his pride.

When the doors parted and he stepped inside the hospital he came to a decision. If he did not kill McCain by the end of the day, he would leave. Passing on ten million dollars would be hard, but he did not need the money. He had secured his retirement years before by investing his contract money wisely. Over the years he came to trust his intuition and perhaps his subconscious clued in to something he had otherwise missed.

He rode an elevator to the fourth floor first, checking out the layout of the hospital. The floor design followed a square with a bisecting hallway allowing nurses to access either side of the floor easily with a nurse's station on one side.

"Excuse me, Father?"

He stopped at the door of the room where the voice called to him. An elderly woman sat in a recliner wrapped in a blanket, an oxygen tank next to her. He stepped inside and knelt by her side, taking her frail hands in his. She stared at the collar around his neck. For this reconnaissance mission he had on a priest's shirt and collar. No one ever questioned why a priest would be walking the halls of a hospital.

"Will you pray for me, Father?"

Black Ice smiled and they both closed their eyes and he said words he did not believe but hoped would comfort the woman. When he finished, she thanked him and he stood and left the room, his unease growing with every step. When he came to town he did so as Death. He never thought about the afterlife, and what was next for each person when they died. He certainly never thought about it from a personal standpoint.

He punched the elevator button and while he waited for it to arrive, he made an effort to clear his mind and used a brief meditation technique to try and find some inner balance. When the doors opened he felt better. He stepped onto the elevator and pressed the number one button. Before the elevator doors closed completely a hand knifed between them and forced them open.

A man got on with him, smiled, and went to press the same button. Seeing it lit up he put his hands in his jacket pockets and started whistling. Black Ice returned the smile, but his alarm bells began to go off. He smelled something not quite right, like the smell of meat left out a bit too long in the sun.

The man smiled at him again and winked. Standing only a bit over five feet tall, it was hard to picture him as a threat, but something about the man rubbed him the wrong way.

The elevator reached the first floor and the doors parted. Black Ice retraced his path and left the hospital, the man behind him by a few paces. He didn't take a direct path to his car and, instead, circled the hospital. A dumpster and tree sat near the edge of a children's playground. He ducked behind the dumpster and slid the long hunting knife from the concealed sheath strapped to his ankle, turned and waited.

The man made no attempt at stealth and continued to whistle. When the stranger rounded the dumpster he saw the knife and pulled up short. Spreading his arms to the side he said in an Australian accent,

"You call that a knife? Better make it count."

Black Ice struck with speed, the knife entering below the ribcage on the left and then up into the heart. The blow lifted the other man onto his toes. The stranger gasped, shock on his face. Then he broke into laughter.

"Oh man, the stab up the rib cage into the heart trick. Well done."

The man struck him with a swiftness Black Ice had never seen. He slapped him hard on each ear with a force that stunned his senses. He followed up the attack to the head with a punch to the rib cage. Sharp pain lanced through his body with the breaking of two ribs.

"You know, I've used you a couple of times. Nice job on the family in Montana. You were worth every penny."

Black Ice spun in the tight space and tried to sweep the smaller man's legs out from under him, but the other man leaped and avoided the move.

"You're from Senegal, right? Trained in Sudan with the Sudan People's Liberation Army. But never one of the Lost Boys. Your family has money. You do this for the thrill and enjoyment, am I right?"

The man knew too much about him. Ignoring the pain in his side, he launched a flurry of blows, but landed none of them. The stranger, with the dagger still stuck in his abdomen, blocked each one. The man did his own spin faster than humanly possible and swept him off his feet. When the assassin tried to stand, the other kicked him hard in the chest and slammed him against the stone wall of the hospital and knocked him down, unable to move.

"Not bad. You're much better than average. Right Mathiam?"

The stranger pulled the knife out of his body and tossed it a couple of times in the air, catching the hilt each time. The man should have blood soaking his shirt, but other than the hole made by the knife, nothing. The stranger lifted the lid of the dumpster and tossed the knife inside.

"What are you?"

"Now that's the most intelligent question anyone has asked me in a long time." The man pushed a button on his watch. "We're over by the playground. Bring the van around." He turned his wrist to show the assassin his watch. "Every time I talk into this thing I feel like Dick Tracy. How cool is that?"

"You're going to kill me, aren't you?"

Black Ice struggled to his feet and settled into his stance. If he was to die, it would be fighting to the last.

"Me? Never. But for shooting my brother, I think I'll rough you up a bit."

The smaller man attacked and each time he tried to block the blows and counter punch, his own blows missed by fractions of an inch, while each of the other man's hit home. Before long his counter punches faltered and he sank to his knees, battered and bruised.

"I'll tell you this much, you sure can take a beating better than that cop did. You should be very proud of yourself. As for what am I? I am beyond your comprehension. I am Belial."

He tried to respond, but the world spun and he collapsed onto his stomach, his consciousness fading. The last thought before darkness engulfed him was McCain's only brother was dead. And dead men don't bleed.

CHAPTER TWENTY-NINE

"How many times do I have to tell you, detectives, I don't know where my brother is?"

Detectives Alvey and Ventura arrived with my morning breakfast of clear foods: Jell-O, applesauce, and some oatmeal. Great. I didn't care for any of it.

"If you're connected with the death of Detective Wallace, you'll get the needle. Come clean now and we'll convince the D.A. to take the death penalty off the table."

"Wow, Ventura. Have you been watching a *Law and Order* marathon? It never works for them either. Just sayin'."

Linda and Samantha sat on the bench seat next to the window, watching. Alvey turned to Samantha and asked, "The third photo shows Michael McCain has you in his sights as well. If you have anything you can share which will help us, I can arrange for your protection until we catch him."

"You can't even protect your own people and you think you can protect me from Mikey? I think I'll take my chances on my own."

"Suit yourself. If you change your mind..." He removed one of his cards from an inner suit pocket and offered it to Samantha. She made no move to take it from him and after a couple of seconds he shrugged and put the card away and turned to leave.

"Aren't you going to tell me not to leave town, detective?" I quipped.

"Don't leave town. Let's go, Ventura."

Ventura stared at Linda. "I guess we see which side you're on, don't we?"

Linda smiled and flipped him off, making Samantha laugh. Ventura's face turned a shade of red normally seen only on Saturday morning cartoon shows. "You're going down with these assholes. I can't wait to testify at your Cause Hearing."

"I can't wait for you to testify either, Ventura. Means you'll have to put some intelligent sentences together all in a row and I want to see if you can pull it off. My money is on not."

He left, followed by the laughter of the two women. When both men were gone, Linda looked at her watch. "Time to go face the music. I've been summoned to make an appearance at headquarters in about forty-five minutes. Everyone is giving me the cold shoulder. When I went home to change and clean up before coming here you would have thought I was a leper. All I ever wanted was to be a cop and now your brother may have taken that away from me."

"I'm really sorry, Linda. This is why I kept you at a distance. I wanted to protect you from all of this. Every time I end up close to someone, bad things happen."

Samantha didn't say anything but offered up a small nod of the head. While I directed the comment to Linda, I meant it as much for her. Samantha, Linda, Winston, Kurt, Ruth Anne, the list continued to grow. Wars have casualties, but my friends were paying a heavy toll for their efforts to help me.

Linda came and sat on the edge of the bed. "I'm a big girl. I made my choices. When I tried to blow your brother's ass away, I didn't follow procedure and that's on me. Since joining the force I've had trouble playing well with others. Guess I've been on this path for some time. But the one thing I don't regret is you."

She leaned over and gave me another kiss and I loved it. Though, with Samantha only a few feet away, it felt beyond strange. She broke it off, offered Samantha a short wave of the hand and left.

She left an awkward silence in her wake. I didn't know what to say and figured this would be a good time to keep my mouth shut. Finally, Samantha asked, "Do you love her?"

Good question. I turned it over in my mind a few times. "I'm not sure, but would like to find out. Not really an answer, but it's all I got."

She offered a half-smile. "You know, one day, I might want to give her competition. But that day won't be soon. I'm still working through some things. Dad's death hit me kind of hard. Plus, I'm not sure I'll ever be able to have a normal relationship. And she's a good woman, Vic. She's tough and can handle more than you think she can."

A knock on the door saved me from having to respond. A young nurse came in with a bag with my personal effects. "Detective Coffey said you wanted your phone and other things."

"Thank you. I feel lost without my phone. It's always attached to my hip."

She set the bag on the bed next to me while she took my vitals. Blood pressure, temp and heart rate all normal. Yay me.

My phone rang in the bag. "That's great timing." I fished the phone out. Winston. "Joe's bar and grill. How can I help you?"

"Aren't you in a good mood?"

"All things considered, yeah. I am. How'd things go with Tank?"

"Well, I'm about to ruin your good mood."

Winston gave me the run down on the attack on his life and about the van ending up at the bottom of the Ohio River. "Aw man that stinks. J will be pissed about the van. Looks like I'll have to buy a new one. But you're in one piece?"

"Yeah. You won't find me going swimming any time soon, but I'll live. Tank and the gang are itching for a fight. When we give the word, they're in. And we have a few other guys on the way. I called Stiles last night and he and four guys will be arriving this morning. When we hit their hideout, we will have a small army. He also has a line on who it is who shot you. Guy named Black Ice."

"Black Ice? Never heard of him. Glad Stiles is coming to lend a hand. We might need it."

The phone beeped with another call from a number I didn't recognize. "Hey, someone else is calling in. Let me grab this and I'll call you back."

I switched over. "This is Vic."

"Well, well, well. My little brother really is feeling better. How's it hanging, bro?"

Mikey. "Why don't you come see me and I'll show you?"

"I think that's a great idea. But I have a better one. Why don't we meet somewhere else? I have a present for you and I don't think your hospital room is the place to open it."

"The last time you gave me a gift it was a book about Arabic culture. Written in Arabic. I think I'll pass on the gift."

"Come on, Vic, that was a great gift. I figured if you were going to play in the sand for the government, then you should learn more about them. But this gift is one you'll want. I mean, it hits the mark, it will knock you dead."

"Dead? I'm sure it will, coming from you."

"Brother you're a hard man to please. But I promise no one else will receive a Christmas present like this one. Who else is giving out assassins for the holidays?"

I felt my heart skip a beat. Maybe two. "What are you talking about, Mikey?"

"If you can manage to haul your ass out of bed, then how about we meet at the old Johnson house, the one down off Story Avenue and you can find out. You can bring your sidekick, Winston, if it makes you feel better. No one else."

The Johnson's house had been abandoned since the day in the early eighties when old man Johnson came home and shot and killed his entire family, then himself. A Victorian home which looked like it came straight out of a B-movie, the house went to a family member who lives out of town. When no one wanted to buy the house because of the murders, she let the house sit empty. When we were kids we would play hide and seek inside. We gave it up when one of the kids hid in the refrigerator and the door stuck. They ended up having to call the fire department to pry her out and she almost died. Our parents forbade us to ever go back inside and my father let us know the punishment would be severe if we disobeyed him.

"When?"

"The Bengals play at one against the Steelers, so why don't we say around noon? I don't want to miss the game."

"I'll be there. And, Mikey? You're a dead man walking."

He laughed. "Well, duh. Dead man walking? Were you making a joke? One more thing. You and Winston must be unarmed."

I laughed. "Yeah, right. That's not going to happen, Mikey."

"You have my word as Belial that no harm will come to you from either myself or any of my men. You'll be allowed to both enter the house and leave the grounds with no threat of harm from me or mine. I promise this as Belial, a king of Hell, to the Hand of God. You know I must keep the promise. It is the only way you may have your 'gift'".

I ground my teeth. I did know he must keep the promise. I tried to figure out how he meant to screw me if I agreed, but the promise seemed straight-forward.

"Done."

I hung up on him and called Winston. "I need you here at the hospital. How soon can you make it? Mikey called. He wants to meet."

"I'll have Tank to drop me off at my car, then a short stop by my place to change clothes. Think it's a trap?"

"I don't really give a rat's ass. If it is, I'll flip it on him. Do me a favor and drop by the mission and pick me up some clothes, too. And switch your car for the Ford. The keys are on the nightstand."

I'd had my Ford Flex modified after I bought it to hide a gun locker in the rear. The last thing I wanted to do was to take on Mikey without some serious hardware strapped to my side.

"Will do. On my way."

When I put the phone down on the bedside table, Samantha stood. "Mikey wants to meet? I'm going, too. I think you need as many people at your side as possible."

There was a time I would have told her no, it was too dangerous. Not anymore. She knew more about what Hell on Earth was like. "Thanks. I'll take the help."

I picked up my phone and texted Linda to call me when she got out of her meeting. She deserved to know the latest. I tossed the phone down onto the table and pushed the table out of the way and slid the blankets off.

"You need my help?"

"Let me see what I can do on my own first."

I swung my feet off the bed and pushed myself up. I teetered, then gained my balance. The hospital gown they had me dressed in barely covered what it needed to cover in mixed company. I guess they don't see many six foot six guys.

Samantha nodded appreciatively. "Good to see you've been staying in shape. Nice legs."

"And here I thought you loved me for my winning personality."

"Dream on, Wonder Bunny. It's all about the legs."

Women. Always bustin' my chops. I moved a few steps and felt good. Better than good, I felt damn good. Good enough to meet my brother and do some chop-bustin' of my own.

CHAPTER THIRTY

"They're going to pitch a fit when they find out you're gone."

Winston, Samantha and I rode the elevator down to the main floor. After Winston brought my clothes, the two of them created a minor distraction while I slipped out and down the hall, leaving my room beeping when I removed all the lines.

"Samantha, when you're right, you're right. They won't be happy with me, but tough."

I felt tired, like I'd run a mini-marathon, but no worse for wear otherwise. Over the summer I'd been stabbed and Elizabeth sewed up the wound. The bullet entry and exit wounds felt the way that wound did several weeks after being sewed up. The spots itched quite a bit, but caused me no real discomfort.

Winston led the way into the parking garage and we strode up the ramp to the Ford. Tank Bone sat in the front passenger seat, a shotgun between his legs. Well, sat was an understatement. Tank filled his entire side of the car.

I let Winston drive and I hopped in the back. Samantha told us to wait and she jogged further up the ramp to her car. When she jumped in on her side, she held a long case in one hand and I noticed the bulge of a gun under one arm. I knew the case contained a katana with an edge sharp enough to slice clean through a man—or an Infernal Lord—in this case, with ease.

In the gun locker hidden under the rear compartment of the Ford I had one of my own. I got mine after taking out a madman Samurai Infernal Lord named Muramasa by turning him into a crispy critter with a flame thrower. That's one of two ways to return them to Hell and that's what I did to Muramasa. I hit him with the full effect of a flame thrower. Mission accomplished. The other is to cut off their head. Samantha's katana is the perfect weapon to make that happen.

I introduced Tank and Samantha and he gave me a thumbs up. "Damn, McCain, if you'd told me you were gonna bring women like this along, I'd have signed up to help you a long time ago."

Samantha blew him a kiss. "Thanks, Tank. I bet the women all love you."

"Honey, I have to beat'em off with a stick. You get tired of this guy, you come on over and see ole Tank."

I did my best not to lose my breakfast at the thought of Samantha and Tank.

"What type of lead launcher do you have under your arm, little lady?" I said this in my best Western drawl. Samantha seemed less than impressed.

"A Walter PPK. Don't make me use it on you."

"I can see it now: Samantha, international woman of mystery. Tyler, Samantha Tyler."

She rolled her eyes. "Dear Lord. Your Sean Connery is as bad as your cowboy."

Winston chimed in, "I second that opinion."

"You know, buddy, you're supposed to be on my side, remember?"

I gave him the address and we left the hospital. My phone rang a few times, but I didn't recognize the number so I let it go to voice mail.

Tank half-turned in his seat. "What's the plan here, McCain? Winston said your brother will be there. I want a piece of his ass."

"Let me ask you something, Tank. Do you believe in the supernatural?"

"You mean like the shit on that TV show, *Supernatural*?"

"Yeah, just like that. Do you believe in ghosts, demons and the like?"

He scratched his beard. "Well, I've seen some strange crap over the years. Don't say I rightly do or don't. Why?"

"Because that's what my brother is. Let me tell you a little story, Tank."

And I told him about how I killed Mikey and how he rose from the dead, thanks to Satan. "So when we hit him, he won't be like other people. And he may have other things on his side like him."

He looked first to Winston and then to Samantha. "You two believe this bullshit?"

They both said they did. "They've both seen it up close and

personal. You're about to do the same. I'm telling you this so that when the strange stuff happens, you won't hesitate. You can't hesitate."

Tank grinned and it's not the kind of thing used on the faint of heart. "McCain, I never hesitate. Hell, if your brother turns out all freaky then I'll stomp his freaky ass."

"It's why I called you, Tank. Bad to the bone."

"Damn straight."

We made small talk the rest of the trip. Well, mostly Tank made small talk while pouring on the charm to Samantha. I felt a pang of jealousy, even though I had no right to feel that way.

I leaned in close to Winston. "See the large hedgerow up on the left? The house is on the other side of the hedge. Take the next driveway."

Tank let out a low whistle. "Holy shit. That's the Adam's Family house."

"The Adams's family house was in Los Angeles, Tank. But yeah, they look alike."

The Johnson family built the house in the mid eighteen-hundreds. A two story house with a gothic tower rising another level, it sat in the middle of five acres of land. Small trees and wild grass filled most of the area around the house, but strangely enough, not the house itself.

Despite the years, the house still stood in much the same condition as it did the night of the murders. What amazed me is the roof remained intact. The windows had been boarded up on the main floor, but not the second floor or tower windows.

I knew the house was just that: a house. But the feeling of malevolence hit you like a jack hammer when you stared at it for a few minutes. I remembered watching the Amityville Horror when I was a kid and being unable to sleep for days afterwards. This house gave me the same heebie-jeebies.

Winston eased the Ford up the driveway and we kept our eyes open for an ambush, but the entire place looked deserted. He stopped the car short of the house and turned off the engine. Ours was the only car in sight.

"Here's the plan. He said only Winston and I go in and we have to be unarmed. I want you two to wait by the car, heavily armed. If we yell, come running, guns blazing. And Tank, we have to actually call for help. You can't pretend you heard me yell and then come running in."

"Spoil sport."

"You know you're an idiot, right?" Samantha asked.

"Yeah. Pretty much. But when an Infernal Lord gives their promise, of all the weird things, they must keep the promise. I think the two of us will be all right when it comes to Mikey. The rub comes from what else is in the house besides them." I glanced over at Winston. "You ready?"

"Old man, I stay ready. Think you can keep up?"

We got out and approached the front door while Samantha and Tank got out and stood behind their doors. "You know I'm only a few years older than you, right?"

"I do respect my elders. On a more serious note, what do you think he has planned?"

"Hell if I know. Knowing Mikey, something big."

"Remember when you told me you would love to make my uncle's favorite supervillain come to life to use against Mikey? I called him and he should have a package for me some time later today."

"Excellent. Wish we had it right now, but such is life."

We stopped and listened at the front door. Nothing. I motioned for Winston to stand to one side. I took the other, turned the knob and shoved the door open.

The door swung into a foyer dusty from long years of neglect and burgundy wallpaper hung in strips on the walls. A long hallway stretched off to the other end of the house, a stairway going up about halfway down its length and ending in what may have been a kitchen.

Hanging from the hallway ceiling was a huge piece of poster board with "Bad Guys This Way" written in red with an arrow pointing to a room on the left.

Winston laughed. "Subtle, don't you think?"

"Like a jack hammer."

The house smelled of mold and decay. I stepped over the threshold, with Winston behind me. To my right was a sitting room, the fireplace long since dormant with a rat's nest where the fire grate used to be.

We made our way into the room and looked inside. Two large windows framed a large stone fireplace. Thick black curtains made of what might have been velvet covered the windows. The only stick of furniture left in the room was a chair placed in front of the fireplace and in it, a guy I recognized. The guy from outside Molly Malone's. Mikey stood behind him with two hired goons holding automatic weapons.

"Wow. You guys made it. Vic, you look—" He paused for a

second, his eyes narrowing. "Well, well, well. Winston Reynolds, you old dog you."

Winston and I glanced at each other. "What the hell are you talking about Mikey?" I asked.

"Brother, did Winston tell you I offered to save your life but he wouldn't meet the price?"

"Yeah, Mikey. He told me. Said you wanted his soul in the bargain. He did the right thing in turning your ass down."

"But it seems he *did* make a bargain with someone else."

Winston shook his head. "No I didn't. You're one lying prick, Mikey."

"He didn't let you remember, did he? Oh, that's priceless. Victor, you've been touched by the Divine. Didn't you wonder how you recovered so quickly? How you managed to cheat death? I sure as hell did. I can see the aura around you. Here I wanted you to live so I could continue to make you suffer and Uriel has given me an early Christmas present. Super."

Winston's brows knitted together. "You know, Vic. I don't know how I know this, but he's right. I think he's telling the truth."

I thought of the dream with my father, of hearing a trumpet and of not being allowed to go with him. Had I really been called back? Had I been that close to Heaven? I felt an ache at the core of my being, but I didn't have time for self-revelations.

"You know what, Mikey? I don't really give a crap. You brought us here. Who's the guy in the chair?"

"First, the hired help needs to make sure you're not packing."

He gestured and the two goons crossed the room and patted us down, being none too gentle about it.

When the guy searched between my legs, I said, "Listen, if you want a date, you can always pick up the phone and call."

Not even a snicker in response. Some people just don't have a sense of humor. When they didn't find anything, they returned to stand next to Mikey, guns still held at the ready.

"Worried we might blow your ass away, Mikey?"

He waved Winston's comments away. "You know guns aren't much good against me anymore. No, I wanted to make sure it's a fair fight. Vic, meet Black Ice, your Christmas present."

"We've met. I loved your coat, by the way."

The man tilted his head in my direction. "Thanks. It was a gift from my wife. She's got better taste than I do."

His arms and chest were duct taped to the chair. He'd been worked over a bit but his eyes followed everything in the room at once.

Mikey gestured at the man. "I found him wandering the hospital this morning. I think he planned to finish the job he started when he shot you." Mikey punched him playfully and added, "Not your fault. The only reason my brother is still here is an angel came down from Heaven and laid hands on him."

The man raised an eyebrow, but said nothing. If he was scared he didn't show it. I saw him test the limits of the tape job. A flex of an arm muscle here, a calf muscle there.

"You were going to shoot me when you passed me in the street in front of Molly's, weren't you?"

"Yes, but your police friend interrupted. Too many variables trying to shoot you and her. And then she almost clipped me last night when I shot you. She's good. She's very good."

"Well, yeah. Better than average."

Mikey pulled a knife from his pocket. "If you two are finished, I'd like to move this a long a bit." He began to cut the tape away from his body. "Here's the way it's going to work. When I cut him free, then it's down to the three of you. We won't intervene. Black Ice against the Hand of God and the trusty sidekick. And, Vic, you should know he's like Jackie Chan, but bigger. And stronger. And not nearly as nice."

When he finished cutting away the tape, the other man stood and I noticed he favored his right side a bit. He no longer wore the coat, dressed in a black shirt with a priest's collar, pants and shoes. Long and lean, the man gave off the ready to kill vibe of a big cat.

Mikey and the goons circled around us. When they got to the hallway, he shouted, "Begin" and left the room.

And we did.

CHAPTER THIRTY-ONE

Winston and I moved several feet apart to make Black Ice fight two fronts at once. The other man pivoted, his balance perfect. The main thing to keep in mind when fighting someone trained in a deadly martial art is don't. In most cases if you take on someone with better training, you're going to end up with your ass handed to you in a sling.

But if you have no other choice then you want one of two things to happen: a confined space or to put your opponent on the ground. The room we were in bordered on huge. This meant, unless we got the man into a corner, confinement wouldn't be much of an option and this meant, I needed to go with option number two.

Winston broke into his own martial arts stance. I knew he'd been training for years and held several black belts and stood a better chance to fight another martial artist. Me? I preferred dirty street fighting. Winston attacked and the two men traded blows, each trying to land a deadly strike.

Winston landed a blow to the man's ribcage and he grimaced in pain, but didn't slow down and launched into a counter-attack. When Mikey and his boys took him down, they must have busted a few ribs. The assassin moved, doing his best to keep Winston between the two of us negating having to fight two of us at once.

This led me to do what he didn't expect. I feinted a move to go around Winston's left side and the assassin used several quick steps to reposition himself, keeping Winston between us. But that put the fireplace to his back. When he started to move I dropped low, grabbed Winston around the waist and tossed him into the other man.

The surprise move caught the assassin off guard and knocked him off balance for only a second, but that's all I needed. I bull rushed both men, hitting them like a tackling sled. I got what I wanted when all three of us smashed the chair into kindling and hit the ground at the foot of the fireplace.

Black Ice picked up part of a chair leg and struck Winston in the temple, which stunned him. But it did nothing to remove his weight and his right arm became trapped under Winston's body. I kept my legs spread and to the side, negating his leverage by using every bit of my two hundred and eighty pounds to keep him pinned. He did his best to snake his left arm up and around my neck, forcing me to use my shoulder to keep him from succeeding. I've done enough training to know letting this happen would be bad news for me. Damn this guy was quick.

But before he got his hold, I struck down hard with a head butt, using the crown of my head to try and drive his nose into the ground. He turned his head and I connected with the side of his face. Blood poured from a gash to his eyebrow and I hit him again, and again with another head butt while we grappled on the ground.

He managed to wiggle a bit from under Winston and used his free hand to gouge at my eyes. I scooted forward a bit and tried to turn my head sideways. When I did, I looked up into the fireplace. The handle for the chimney flue, made of cast iron, hung loose from the rest of the chimney. I reached up and grabbed the handle and ripped it clear.

The change in my position gave Black Ice a shot at my throat. He punched hard with a knuckled fist in an attempt to crush my windpipe. He missed, but not by much and pain erupted in my neck.

I reversed my grip on the flue handle and drove it down with every bit of strength I possessed. The sharp edge plunged into his left eye, through his skull and embedded in the floor. Black Ice spasmed, his body went limp, and his other eye opened wide, staring up at the ceiling.

I sat up and rubbed the side of my neck while Winston did the same with his head. One on one, neither of us stood a real chance of defeating the assassin. Together it was still a close match.

"Throwing me? That was your plan?"

I stood up and offered him a hand which he accepted. "It worked didn't it?"

We both looked at the man who tried to put a bullet in my heart, his blood spreading across the wooden floor. I searched my heart trying to find some small measure of regret, but found none. You live by the sword, you die by the chimney flue. I'm sure someone famous said those words at some point.

"Why don't you go get Samantha and Tank, while I search the body?"

"Roger that."

I went through the dead man's pockets, but found only car keys. No real surprise. I heard Winston open the front door and yell for Samantha and Tank. And then I heard the front door slam shut.

I stood and shouted Winston's name but got no response. I started to yell again when a woman's scream cut me off. It came from somewhere else inside the house. I rushed from the room and heard the booming report of a shotgun upstairs, then I heard someone running across the floor, more screams and another shotgun blast.

From up the steps came the crying of a small child. In between the sobs she said, "Help me. Please help me. He's going to kill me."

I felt a cold settle inside me which had nothing to do with the temperature outside. Something wasn't right.

"Whoever is upstairs, throw down your weapon and come down now and you won't be hurt." It was a bluff considering I didn't have a gun with me, but worth the try. No answer. Only the child's cries. I paused, waiting for Winston and the gang to bust through the door with guns locked and loaded. But nothing. I swore and ran quickly to the front door. When I tried to turn the knob, it wouldn't move. I searched for a lock, but there was none. I went to the window next to the door and tossed the curtains to the side. I kicked hard at the boards which covered the window but they didn't budge. I slammed the boards hard with a shoulder and only managed to bruise my shoulder.

I heard another shotgun blast upstairs. The girl. I ran to the stairs and charged up them two at a time, watching for the shooter. I kept low when I reached the top step and peaked around the banister, but found the hallway empty. A door to my left led to a bathroom which was also empty, save for the rusted out tub and plumbing. I tore a metal towel rack off the wall to at least give me something to use as a weapon. I pictured the news headline now: **Man takes on shotgun with towel rack. Shotgun wins.** No shit, Sherlock.

Down the hallway there were two doors to my left and one to my right at the end of the hall. I moved with the word "quiet" in mind. The floorboards up here were not surviving the neglect of decades like the lower floor and they creaked under my bulk. Some of the slats were missing and showed the floor below.

Before I reached the first door a young girl who looked around eight years old bolted from the last room on the left into the room across the hall. She wore a nightgown covered in pictures of Winnie the Pooh and stringy blonde hair bounced around her shoulders while she ran.

I darted after her, the towel rack rod held high while I ran by the other two rooms. I caught movement in the first and dove for the floor. The shotgun boomed and the plaster on the wall above my head blew to pieces. I rolled and then dove into the room right behind the girl and forced the door shut. The faded wallpaper depicted a circus or county fair scene with small children playing. A child's chest of drawers and a bed were the only pieces of furniture in the room. I hauled the chest over in front of the door, angling it to wedge the top edge under the door knob. Not much, but it would have to do. A small window allowed in a feeble amount of sunlight on a room bare of furniture. A closet door stood cracked open and I approached carefully.

"Hello? Little girl? I'm here to help."

"You never should have come here."

The voice, both soft and sad, came from the darkness.

"I didn't have a choice, Little One. Why don't you come out so we can get out of here?"

"We are never leaving here. Ever."

I felt my throat go dry. Definitely something wrong.

"Yes we can. And we can right now. You have to trust me."

Her voice lowered, changed in tone, deeper than an eight year old should sound. "No we can't. You killed the bad man. His blood woke my father. He's not going to let us leave."

Holy crap. Father. Family being shot. "Uh, what's your name?"

"Emily. You can come hide with me in here."

The closet door moved a few more inches, the interior cloaked in darkness. The girl remained out of view and the reptilian part of my brain shouted at me not to come any closer.

"Emily, what's your last name?"

A small laugh. "You know my name, Victor. Daddy's going to come for us. He's very angry."

Bloody hell. I backed away from the closet and put my back to the far wall. When I did, something large in the hallway slammed against the bedroom door. The chest of drawers held, but barely, the top splintering down the middle.

I jumped to the window and tried to force it up, but years of weathering left it jammed shut. I ran to the bed with plans to remove the baseboard and throw it through the window to give me an avenue of escape, but when I shoved the mattress to the side, a mass of tiny spiders spilled out from underneath and all over my hands and arms.

I fell and landed on my ass, then scuttled on my hands and feet away from the bed. I slapped at the spiders, trying to brush them off, but they swarmed under the sleeve of my coat and shirt and crawled up my arms.

I started yelling for my friends. Where were they? I tore off my coat and stripped off my shirt looking for the spiders, but they were gone. They were gone from the bed, too. What the hell? I felt dizzy and fought to gain control of my fear.

The thing in the hallway slammed into the door again and the chest of drawers began to split apart. Another good blow and it would give way.

"You can come in here with me, Victor. We can be together forever."

A small hand made of bones and tattered skin which hung from her fingers, beckoned to me from the darkness of the closet. With a growl I stepped to the closet and kicked it shut.

"Go to Hell."

The shotgun let loose in the hallway and a basketball-sized hole appeared in the bedroom door. A skeletal hand reached into the room and tried to push the dresser out of the way. The girl in the closet began to scream and it made my skin crawl every bit as much as the spiders.

I wrapped my bomber jacket around both hands, said a quick prayer and then ran and dove through the window. The window pane shattered and the jacket kept it from cutting my hands, but did nothing for the rest of me. I felt the glass slice into my shoulders and stomach, with one long sliver going all the way through my arm when I landed on the roof.

I bounced once and let go of my jacket with the thought of trying to stop my fall, but only managed to barely catch the gutter and flipped off the roof. I twisted in mid-air and pulled my hands in to my chest, landing hard on my back, all the air forced from my body.

There are days I really hate my job.

Winston and Samantha, who stood on the porch, ran to me. Tank stood in the yard, the Remington to his shoulder while he scanned for something to shoot. I saw his eyes go wide and then he cut loose at the bedroom window with all seven shells his gun held.

He pulled several more shells out of his pocket and began to reload. "Did you see that? What the hell was that?"

I managed to make it to a sitting position and held out my arm. Winston took hold of my wrist and with one quick movement, pulled out the sliver of glass and tossed it into the yard. I stifled a scream and got to my feet.

"Where's your shirt? What happened in there? We tried to go in, but the door wouldn't open." Samantha shook the glass out of my jacket and draped it around my shoulders.

"If I had to guess? Ghosts. I think the Johnson family is back. As for my shirt, I'm trying a new look." I felt too embarrassed to tell her about the spiders.

She pointed. "Jesus, is that a child?"

The little girl stood framed in the window of the Gothic tower. The front of her gown showed a large gaping hole in it and her chest had tiny spiders crawling in and around the wound. Two empty sockets stared down from where her eyes should have been, but I knew she was staring at me.

"Not a kid you want to have anything to do with. Winston, bring me the flamethrower from the Ford. We don't have much time."

He jogged to the car and returned with the flamethrower. "Want me to do this? You're a bit banged up."

I took the gear from him and slipped the harness over my shoulders. "Thanks, but they tried to kill me. I'll be the one to return the favor."

I opened the pressure valve on the propane tank and pulled the two triggers. A large plume of flame shot out and covered the front of the house, the old wood catching instantly. I walked from one side of the house to the other and hosed it down with fire.

I stopped when the house became fully engulfed in flames. I popped the harness, dropped the tanks from my shoulders and walked to stow the gear in the car.

"We better hustle out of here. Between the gunshots and the fire, I think we will have company soon."

We piled into the car and Winston got us the hell out of Dodge. I reached into the back and snagged the first aid kit and handed it to Samantha. She got the kit open and started to wrap up my arm while I kept eyes on the house. The girl still stood in the window and I watched until the roof collapsed and she disappeared in the flames. I read once that ghosts were attached to the place where they died. If that's true, then burning the house down should remove the problem.

It seemed a proper metaphor for my life. Burning the house down was something I'm good at. Too good.

CHAPTER THIRTY-TWO

Winston's phone beeped with a text message. He glanced first at his phone, then at me in the rearview mirror. "Stiles and crew have landed. Where should I tell them to meet us?"

I turned my arm over and inspected Samantha's patch job. "Well, now that I'm no longer bleeding all over everything, why don't we head over to Tank's and have a pow-wow."

He nodded and at the next red light, and sent them a quick note with the address and then one to Kurt to join us. We didn't talk much on the trip to the Riverside Inn. I spent most of the time thinking of Samantha's touch when she worked on my arm.

I loved watching her. If you told me all I would be allowed to do for the entire day is watch her do nothing, I'd be okay with it. The woman sent my body into overdrive, no doubt about it.

But if I was honest, we always seemed to end up in one crisis or another. I didn't know if things would be different with Linda, but I wanted the chance to find out. Still...

When we arrived at the biker hangout we found the parking lot packed. I got my emergency clothes bag from the car and we went inside. They'd put a large sign on the door "Closed for private party."

There were a couple dozen Tyranny Rides members at the tables watching football on the big screens. Guns in various stages of cleaning were scattered in front of some of them as they prepared to go to war.

Tank showed me to a room and I got cleaned up and changed clothes. I took a long look in the mirror and wondered at the man staring back at me and I didn't like what I saw. There were the beginnings of dark circles under my eyes and it made me think of Emily Johnson standing in the window of the burning house. The great American philosopher, Indiana Jones, famously said, "It's not the years, it's the mileage" and my body had been wracking them up in bunches. I'm in my early thirties but before long I would qualify for an AARP card if judged by looks.

My body showed a growing collection of scars. A nasty scar puckered my left abdomen, compliments of a knife wound which should have killed me in Tennessee. The spot where Black Ice put a bullet in me showed a pink scar much like a small starfish. The Archangel healthcare plan worked miracles it seems. Now I had cuts from a broken window and a hole in my left arm with an ache which showed no signs of fading and my back felt stiff as the proverbial board after falling off the roof.

A weekend where I'd been shot, reborn, fought in a life or death struggle with the man who shot me, shot at again by a ghost and brain screwed by phantasmal spiders made for a large amount of stress and more lines on my face. Add in Samantha Tyler and Linda Coffey and it made me worry how much more abuse my body and system could withstand.

I took a couple of Hydrocodone pills Tank gave me. I hate taking pain meds because it can dull your reaction times, but I didn't have much choice. I could ill afford to spend time thinking about how much I hurt. My focus needed to stay on Mikey.

I turned on the cold water in the sink and splashed some on my face in an attempt to snap out of it. My phone rang and I toweled off my face and glanced at the screen. Linda. No rest for the weary.

"Where are you? They pulled me out of my meeting saying you've left the hospital and they're beyond upset. They thought they had you cornered for a bit. Why did you leave?"

"Are you asking as a cop or are you asking as the hot chick?"

"Very funny. Considering I'm not currently a cop, it's a moot issue. I've been suspended, with pay, but they made it very clear they plan to try and bust me out. My union rep says we can fight it, but it won't be easy. I broke a lot of rules, Vic, but screw'em. Right now, I want to be where you are. You need me to watch your back."

"Well, it would be nice if you watched more than my back. I'll tell you about this morning when you get here."

"I plan on it. Tell your ex to keep her hands off you. Where are you?"

I told her and we hung up. All of a sudden my stomach growled. The hospital breakfast didn't do much to hold me over and I went out to join the rest of the gang.

Tank, Winston and Samantha held court at a booth in the corner by the pool table while they ate lunch. Tank was in the middle of telling Samantha how he and I met. I sat down next to Winston and then waved the bartender over.

"So, Tank, what do you recommend for eatin'?"

"You want the Tank burger and onion rings. Best damn burger you'll ever eat."

"Works for me."

Winston got a call and stepped away from the table. A moment later he motioned me over. "You know that little surprise we talked about for Mikey? My uncle has it ready. I'll head over and pick it up."

"Sweet." I slapped him on the back and he left.

I joined the table and we spent the time waiting for my lunch and talking about the haunted house. Tank pointed a meaty finger in my direction and around a mouthful of burger said, "I'm telling you, McCain, the thing I saw in the window you jumped out of looked like that guy on the *Goosebumps* TV show. I nearly pissed my pants."

"Well, guess I'm glad I never got a look at him."

A biker by the door announced, "We got company."

We went and gazed out the front window and watched two black Cadillac Escalades come to a stop in the parking lot. Stiles and four other men piled out, the four men with large duffels.

"These guys are with us."

I walked out and greeted the mercs. Stiles, a man in his forties, still sported the Marine buzz he wore during his military days. A frickin' Jar Head. The other men with him all carried a similar look and bearing. No doubt they were ex-military as well.

Stiles and I met the first time in an old train tunnel below the streets of Philadelphia right before he turned me over to a sadistic torture master. Thanks to Elizabeth and Mirsada, a fellow Hand of God from Europe, he didn't hurt me too bad. Once all the dust settled following the death of Cy Tyler, Stiles came over to the side of the angels and gave me the names and location of two wickedly evil people who needed eliminating. Whether he stays there is open for debate.

I offered my hand and a "Semper Fi."

"Semper Fi." Stiles and I shook hands and he made the introductions.

"I brought my Alpha Team." He pointed to each man. "Ethan, Blake, Kwame and Brandon. They've been briefed on who and what we are after."

I pointed to the duffels. "Seems you came prepared. I'm

guessing you didn't fly commercial?"

"Hell no. Private all the way, baby. And with enough hardware to take down a small nation."

I lead the new arrivals inside and made yet more introductions. The Alpha Team found their own table and ordered lunch. I got a kick out of watching the bikers and the mercs eye each other.

When I introduced Stiles to Samantha, she greeted him coldly. "Weren't you the one my father hired to keep him alive?"

"True that. And I can't tell you how sorry I am for your loss. In full candor, I'm the one who pushed the button which set off the bomb. He gave me the instructions on what to do and I followed them to the letter. I was unaware of what transpired in the minutes prior to detonation. I highly recommended we stay together until it was over, but he wanted to keep me out of the spotlight. If I'd been there Bathory never makes it into the car. Infernal Lords have their own agendas and your father died because he didn't keep that in mind. What can I say, shit happens."

The muscles in her jaw flexed a few times and her eyes shot daggers in his direction, but he gave no reaction. He'd painted the situation exactly the way it went down, even owning up to pulling the trigger, so to speak.

He turned to me. "So what's our play?"

I started to reply but stopped when Kurt's Mustang skidded into the parking lot, the car with his two biker guards right behind him. Before it came to a complete stop every biker and all the mercs drew their weapons.

I yelled for everyone to stand down. Kurt fell out of his car on a dead run, his laptop lid up and in his hands. He tore through the door, oblivious to all the guns pointed at him.

"Vic, we got him. He went through the secret door three minutes ago and I got the code. I got the code!"

I directed Kurt to a chair. "Man, have a seat and try to control yourself. You're starting to hyperventilate."

He sat down and shouted for someone to bring him a Diet Dr. Pepper and then motioned for us to watch his screen.

"See, here's Mikey coming into the room, he punches in the code and the door slides open. He steps inside, turns to face the door and pushes a button and the door slides shut again. Dude, he's on an elevator."

"And we have no clue what's down there?" Stiles asked.

Kurt shuddered. "Maybe more of those shadow things.

"Night Shades? Shadow creatures with long nasty talons?"

"Yeah, man. They killed two of Tank's guys."

"They can be nasty, but one flash-bang and they're toast."

I stared at the screen. "Kurt, play it again." I watched my brother type in the code, Samantha looked over my shoulder.

"0-8-2-4-1-5. August 8, 2015? If it is, I wonder what the significance is?"

"Bloody hell. That's the day I killed Muramasa. Your dad sent him out to kill Elizabeth, Mirsada and me. Must be the day he got promoted to Infernal Lord."

"Mirsada? How many women have you been with since we split?"

I felt my cheeks burn red. "She's another Hand of God. Strictly work-related. I promise."

"Is she beautiful?"

I laughed. "You have no..."

I stopped when I saw the look on her face. "She's okay. Nothing to brag about."

Kurt snickered. "What are you talking about? She's smokin' hot."

With friends like these, who needs enemies?

"How about we turn our thoughts to attacking Mikey? Hmm?"

We spent the next half hour arguing over who would be in charge of the attack force. Tank didn't like taking orders from anyone, let alone military types like Stiles and the Alpha Team.

I ended up having to step between the two men when they came nose to nose over some choice comments from Tank calling Marines fairies and Stiles responding that this Marine fairy would kick his donut eating ass.

"Boys. Enough. You both work for me on this, remember? Save your energy for what we find at the bottom of that elevator. Tank, your guys are some of the toughest in the business, it's why I came to you. But these guys have training in this kind of thing." To Stiles I said, "We will have each of your guys be in charge of a squad of bikers. You and Tank play nice and split them up."

I instructed Kurt to pull up a map of the distillery. "We won't hit him until Winston is back, but in the meantime I'd like to have four groups monitoring these streets in case he leaves before we arrive there. Stiles, you know how to run a moving surveillance on a target, so you set it up."

One of the bikers at the door shouted, "We got an unmarked pulling in. Hide the hardware."

I glanced out the window. "Don't sweat it, she's with me, too."

"What the hell, McCain? You invited a cop? Are you fucking nuts?" Tank's beard hair bristled with anger.

"Everyone keeps asking me that. The answer is, 'yes'. But today she's one of us."

I held the door open and Linda kissed me before stepping inside. I'm not used to public displays of affection and might never be used to the experience. But no reason I can't enjoy it until I do.

She walked inside, put her hands on her hips and said, "You assholes better have a permit for all the guns I know you have in here and if I find illegal drugs, I'll personally arrest your ass right now."

An angry mumble went through the bikers and the Alpha Team looked to Stiles. After a few seconds went by, Linda laughed. "Lighten up, guys. Jesus, you all are tighter than a bull's ass during fly season."

She'd changed into black jeans, boots, and wore a black jacket over a dark colored AC/DC T-shirt. She shed the jacket and grabbed a pool stick.

Tank leered at her and snagged another stick. "Damn, McCain. You sure do hang out with some bad-ass women."

She pulled some money out of her pocket and slapped a twenty on the table. "Come on, Slim. Put your money up or put the stick down."

Tank laughed in a way most people would find threatening and a bit scary. Coffey only winked at him. He slipped a twenty out of a wallet and laid it on top of hers while she racked the balls.

Samantha moved up next to me. "I have to admit, I like her."

I tried to find some kind of subtext in her tone, but it wasn't there. "Yeah, me too."

"Don't shoot this one."

She placed a hand on my arm and then went to fetch another beer. I watched her for a bit, then returned my attention to the pool game.

It's not often you receive dating advice which involved not shooting another human being. Necessary in my case. And how sad a statement is that?

My phone dinged with a text from Winston which said he was on his way. I let out a sigh and scanned the room. How many of these people would still be alive when the sun came up in the morning?

Only one way to find out. Time to saddle up and try to make

Mikey atone for the evil he'd been spreading like a cancer. I made a promise to the spirit of Ashley Truman and I planned to keep it. I added a grudging promise to Wallace, wherever he currently resided, to do the same for him.

I planned to prove to Mikey there were worse things than death. And I was one of them.

CHAPTER THIRTY-THREE

Stiles and the Alpha Team left to set up surveillance on the distillery. Kurt rode shotgun with Stiles and they were followed by a half dozen bikers. He gave me an encoded satellite phone to allow the two of us to communicate and not have Big Brother listen in on our conversation.

Thirty minutes later Winston rolled up in his Jeep. Samantha, Linda, Tank and I went out to greet him. Samantha and Winston shared a long hug.

"Good to see you, girl. It's been too damn long."

"I know. Thanks for helping to take care of him. He needs all the help he can get."

"Standing right here. Right here, remember?"

Tank and Winston traded fist bumps, then Tank turned to me. "Great. He's here. No more waiting. I want a piece of your brother and I want it now."

I raised my hands in surrender. "Saddle up, big boy. Just be careful what you wish for."

The biker flipped me off and went to talk to his troops and mumbled the whole way. It made me laugh seeing Evil Santa mad.

When all the bikers gathered outside, I called for their attention. "We're going up against some dangerous people and things. I emphasize 'things.' You're likely going to see some things you have never seen before in your life. I explained this to Tank and now I'm going to tell you. If you hesitate? You will likely die. If you have trouble pulling the trigger? You will die. If you try and run? You will die. See a pattern here?"

Some of the men laughed and waved me off. A large portion of them didn't. These were hard men and violence came second nature to them. With Mikey, violence was the one thing which might keep them alive.

"Tank, you, Linda and Samantha can ride with me."

"If it's all the same, I'll ride with Winston," Samantha said. "We've done this before. It'll be like old times."

I nodded and didn't point out the last time they rode together he ended up shot and she ended up being held captive by Mikey, but why bring up the past at a time like this? I felt a twinge of jealousy too, but brushed it off.

Winston led the caravan and the rest of us fell in behind him.

I pressed the quick call button on the satellite phone and Stiles answered on the first ring. "What's the situation?"

"We've been in place and monitoring the building with long-range glasses. We've seen no evidence of guards, either on the roof or patrolling. If they think we're coming, they don't seem worried about it."

"Most likely because they're all underground. They won't know we have the code to the elevator."

"Yeah, about that. If that's the only way down, then we will have a tactical disadvantage. Nothing like riding down to your death."

"We'll work something out when we check out the situation in person. Let's concentrate on making it to the shaft first."

We formed up in the parking lot of a rubber manufacturing plant down the block from the distillery, the plant was closed and the lot empty on a late Sunday afternoon. Stiles took the lead.

"Kwame, you and Ethan will lead the assault through the front of the building. Blake, you and Brandon will hit them from the rear. Be prepared to use some flash grenades on the Night Shades if they are there." He took a quick headcount. "We have twenty-four bikers which will make it easy. Split into four groups of five, with each group of five pairing up with one of the Alpha Team members. The other four will move to the positions where they can watch the building from all four points in case they have a bolt hole. If they do, then follow them, don't engage. For the rest of us, we don't know what we'll find down below, but this arrangement will give us some flexibility while maintaining some semblance of cohesion."

The men did as they were asked and our strike force stood ready.

"Victor, Winston, Kurt, Samantha, Linda and I will make up a unit. I doubt we'll have the element of surprise and they'll likely know we are coming. Hard to hide this many guys. When we hit them, do it fast and hard. Aggression wins. Let's move to our positions. We move on my command."

Stiles and the Alpha Team now wore black combat coveralls with pockets full of weapons and ammo they would need for the coming battle. Each one also carried a katana strapped to his back in quick pull sheaths. They knew how to take down an Infernal Lord. They also wore night vision goggles around their necks. The bikers wore their Tyranny Rides jackets and had a hodgepodge of weapons tucked in belts or in holsters. While not as formidable a look as the mercs, they weren't far short.

We went to the cars and the group split, half going to the front of the building, half to the back. When we got into the car, Linda asked, "You know this is a cluster-fuck waiting to happen, right? The military boys might be able to maintain discipline, but not a chance the bikers do if bullets start flying."

"You got a better idea? Mikey always has well-armed goons around him. We need manpower. If Ruth Anne is still alive, then we have to go get her. I'm open to suggestions."

She didn't have any and we pulled into the front parking lot of the distillery. We got out, guns in hand and pointed at the roof and the building, but no one took a shot at us. I ran to the rear of the Ford, lifted the door and opened my weapons locker. The Scooby Gang joined me and I handed out com links and night vision goggles to each of them, along with a few flash grenades of our own. I slipped on my flak jacket, grabbed my MP5 and several magazines. I tossed Kurt the bag Winston picked up at his uncle's and he slung it over one shoulder along with our equipment bag.

"Kurt, you and the bags stay near me. Anyone need a flak jacket?"

When no one spoke up, I pulled out the flamethrower and with practiced ease switched out the canisters. When I finished, I shut and locked the car and handed the flame thrower to Winston.

Linda's eyes nearly bulged out of their sockets. "Jesus, Vic. You got more firepower in your car than most cities in this state."

"Like I told you. We're at war with an evil which don't play nice. You never want to find yourself in a shooting war with a Satanist when you're the one on the short end of the destructive toys."

We were as ready as we would ever be. I signaled Stiles and he punched his own com link with his guys and shouted, "Go!"

We hit the front door and found it locked. Kwame slapped a package the size of a deck of cards on the lock and pushed a button. A few seconds later a small blast destroyed the lock and we poured inside. We found ourselves in a circular reception area with a beautiful oak bar following the contours of one side, and a row of comfortable couches and chairs on the other. A round receptionist's area took up the middle of the circle with an archway on the opposite side of the room from where we stood.

A large photo of an elderly man in a gray down jacket and Scottish cap hung from the ceiling above the receptionist area, the only other face besides ours in the room.

Stiles motioned to the left and Kwame quickly searched the area behind the bar, but found no one. I led the way to the archway and through. From studying the layout of the building provided by Kurt, I knew the offices and the secret room were through several connecting doors to a hallway on the left side of the building.

I banged through another set of doors and then headed left, my MP5 up and ready, but finding no resistance. The whole place was unnaturally quiet. I found the long hallway and motioned for Kwame and his group to take the lead.

We cleared each office on the way, again finding no one. Half way down the hallway we heard the sound of two grenades going off. Stiles asked for an update through his com and got a reply they were taking out the Night Shades. The far door opened and the rear entry team started into the hallway.

Stiles and I stopped outside the office with the secret door. I saw the broken mirror on the far wall where Kurt shot the Scotch bottle. "I don't like this."

The merc nodded in agreement. "When he came in and found his sentry dead and the damage in this room, they knew we had found this place, but Kurt's seen no one leave since he went down. Think it's a matter of they don't think we can make it below?"

"Hell if I know. Could be we're more confined here and we're easier targets when we come down the elevator. Time to go down and ask him. Guns up and ready."

I stepped into the room and walked over to the third bottle of Scotch and yanked it down. The door to the room swung out to reveal the alcove, also empty. I felt the hair stand up on my neck. None of this felt right. It felt like Mikey wanted us down below. I always think things can be a trap, but this time I knew I was right.

I stepped to the keypad and typed in the same code Mikey used and the door slid to the side. An elevator large enough to hold ten or so people stood waiting. I put my foot on the threshold to force the door to stay open while I glanced inside.

The button panel only showed two buttons one on top of the other and neither marked. It didn't take a rocket scientist to figure out there were only two stops. Up or down. Lighting for the elevator came from light bars around the top. In one corner, a black camera stared back at me. I offered the camera a great view of my middle finger.

"Kurt, toss me the black paint."

He fumbled around in the equipment bag and then tossed me the can. I gave it a few shakes and then hit the camera, covering the lens with a thick layer. When I finished I tossed it back to Kurt. I waved Stiles over and pointed at the ceiling.

"They were kind enough to give us a maintenance hatch. We're only going to shuttle a handful of guys down at a time. Here's what I have in mind."

I lined out my plan and he didn't have any objections. Stiles called over Ethan and Blake, told them what he wanted and then put words into action. Blake stepped into the elevator and boosted Ethan into the air and he carefully lifted the maintenance hatch, pulling himself up. He then offered a hand to the other merc and they both disappeared from view. After a few seconds Ethan stuck his head through the opening.

"There's room up here for two more people. If you push the button and climb up, we can make this work."

Stiles slapped me on the back. "What do you say, McCain, ready for a trip to Hell?"

"Every day of my life, man. Every day of my life."

CHAPTER THIRTY-FOUR

We worked out an invasion plan should we live long enough to give people the signal to come down using our com links. Blake dropped into the elevator and Stiles and I climbed up. We decided it would be easier for the more nimble Blake to push and dash. He hit the button and jumped. We caught him and hauled him up and we rode the metal box down. We dropped for several seconds which meant nothing to me. Depending on elevator speeds we may have traveled twenty feet or forty. Who the hell knows?

We didn't have to wait long to see if there was a welcoming committee. The doors opened and a stream of lead peppered the elevator. Stiles and I tossed two flash-bangs through the opening, then averted our eyes. Two heart beats later the grenades went off and Ethan and Blake dropped into the elevator with a speed only the well-trained military elite can pull off.

One went left, the other right, their weapons on full auto, then Stiles and I landed behind them. We both stayed in the elevator holding the door open and scanned for targets.

Before us stretched a long corridor cut from limestone rock. About twenty feet high and around twice that wide, it reminded me of the Mega Caverns on the other side of town. Those caverns make up the largest building in Kentucky, all underground. They also have zip lines, a mountain bike course, and this time of year, they allow people to drive their own cars through the caverns to see a special Christmas light tour. It's a fun place. Everything this cavern was not.

Several rent-a-thugs sprawled on the ground dead next to a golf cart, now looking more like Swiss cheese from the efforts of Ethan and Blake. Lights hung on each side of the corridor and below them the walls had been painted. It reminded me of the paintings of Edvard Munch, the guy who did *The Scream*. The few that were visible from where I stood depicted scenes of torture or debauchery, particularly human sacrifice. Kind of like a Baptist preacher's worst nightmares come to life.

Further down the corridor there were other tunnels branching off from the left and the right. The Mega Caverns were mined from the 1930s until the 1970s. I'd never heard of any other mining being done, especially this close to the river.

I pressed my com button, but got no response. No surprise considering we were below at least twenty feet of rock. I asked Stiles, "You hearing anything on com?"

"Negative."

"Figures. You ride to the surface and start shuffling the gang down here. These two and I will hold down the fort until you make it back. Tell Kurt we seem to have another Mega Cavern down here and see what he can find out about it."

"You got it. Stay alive until I get back. I'd hate to miss the fun."

Mercs. I allowed the elevator doors to close and I quick-stepped it over to the other two. "Listen, if you think you see one of those paintings start moving, don't stare at it."

When you tell most people something like that, they look at you funny. In this case the two men merely nodded and kept their focus on the tunnel. I'd run into a thing called a blood painting and it almost caused my death. I felt a shudder go through my body at the thought. I guess hanging with Stiles they were used to things which go bump in the night.

Before long the elevator dinged and Stiles returned with the other two mercs, Winston, Kurt, Linda, Samantha and Tank.

Tank sported the Remington with a sidesaddle full of shells. One look at the man and you knew he had one thing on his mind: shooting bad guys.

I started to move forward down the tunnel when Kwame put his hand out to stop me. "In all due respect, Mr. McCain, let me and the team lead the way. You're the man in charge and the one we can least afford to have shot. It's why we're here, sir."

A man in his late twenties or early thirties, he spoke with the air of command. And when you're right, you're right. "Fine with me, but then I want you to wait until you have your squad of bikers with you."

"Yes sir. We will set up a defensive position until another load of bikers make it down. Then we will move out and establish a forward position. Being in this spot with the entire contingent would not be a wise move as it makes for an easy target."

His comments made me want to start strutting and bragging about my job with Black Ops in the Middle East, but I resisted. One, because he was right. And two it had been more than seven years since I led a seek and destroy mission. Every man finds it hard to admit he's older and can't always to the things he used to do.

"Okay. You da man."

Kurt closed his laptop and placed it on the bullet-ridden golf cart. With no signal, his laptop turned into a paperweight.

"Kurt, did you have enough time to find out anything about this place?"

"Dude, there's no record of any mining on this side of town. Ever. And the Mega Cavern is only one hundred acres. No chance it's connected to here. I got no clue."

Samantha and Linda walked over and stared up at the closest wall painting. A figure with the head of a bull sat on a throne, while people stood around the base and offered up human sacrifices. I joined them and pointed to the writing above the artwork. "That looks like Hebrew to me."

"Yes," Samantha agreed. "It's the story of Moloch."

"Since when do you read Hebrew?"

"Hang eight months with a bunch of fanatical monks and you learn all kinds of stuff."

"Any idea who he is or was?" Linda asked.

"Yeah," Winston responded, "He was a bad MoFo. They used to offer up child sacrifices. In Leviticus God says, 'And thou shalt not let any of thy seeds pass through the fire to Moloch.' The Canaanites used to burn children alive in sacrifice to Moloch. It was a form of idolatry which ticked God off big time."

Kurt nearly broke into tears. "All the paintings we can see throughout the cave have this guy in them. Garey told me they planned to sacrifice Ruth Anne. We have to find her, Vic. We have to find her now."

"Kurt, that's why we're here. We're going to bring her back to you."

I watched Kwame reach the tunnel on the left and disappear with his contingent of bikers, while Brandon did the same on the right. The other two mercs took up positions with their guys at the corner of each side passage while keeping their focus on what may yet come down the tunnel.

I waved Stiles and Winston over for a quick meeting of the minds. "So he has us right where he wants us, down here on his turf. Time to find out what my brother has in mind."

"Any chance they slipped out a back door and left us down here chasing shadows?" Stiles asked.

I started to answer but stopped when all the lights went out at once plunging the tunnel into complete and utter darkness. I put my night goggles into place and turned them on, the tunnel reappearing in different shades of greens. The goggles came equipped with infrared illuminators allowing them to function in complete darkness. Some of the bikers shouted in fear when it happened and fumbled for a flashlight or used apps on their phones.

"As for your question. I don't think so."

The sound of gunfire erupted from a side tunnel and a minute later a red light lit up the darkness from where Kwame and his men disappeared.

Stiles hissed. "Red flare. Means it's bad. Let's go."

He took off at a jog and as I fell in behind him, my energy went into overdrive. Linda ran on one side of me, Samantha the other, with Winston, Kurt and Tank right behind us.

And so, it begins.

CHAPTER THIRTY-FIVE

Kwame Abiodun served his twenty for Uncle Sam, then got out, happy to still be alive and in relatively good health. He met Brad Stiles through a mutual acquaintance and when the job offer came along, he didn't hesitate. The money would go a long way to supplement his military pension and he still loved being in the game.

Though he never thought he would find himself traveling several stories underground leading a squad of roughneck bikers on a hunt for what passed as a modern day vampire. Another plus for his current employer: never a dull moment.

Looking ahead, the side tunnel ended in two huge metal double doors. He held up a closed fist and his group of bikers came to a halt about fifty yards short. One of the bikers, a tall bald man packing an AK-47, leaned over his shoulder and wrinkled his nose.

"What's that smell? Smells like roadkill down here."

Kwame had been thinking the same thing and scanned the tunnel for the source of the smell, but the tunnel was empty, except for the metal doors. Whatever the source, it must lie on the other side. There were no cameras visible, but knew it didn't mean they weren't there. The computer hacker employed by McCain proved that point.

"Listen up. Here's what we're going to do—"

He never got to finish his instructions as the lights in the tunnel winked out and the doors swung open at the same time. He managed to pull his goggles into place and in time to see a horde of men rush them. The stench from these men made him gag and he nearly reversed his last meal. He managed to keep it down, but two of the bikers lost the battle.

The men rushing them wore clothes that hung in tatters on their bodies and many wore no shoes. In the green of the night vision goggles their eyes were solid black, their skin a pale white. The eyes reminded him of the dark elves in one of the *Thor* movies.

He brought his Colt AR-15 to his shoulder and cut a swath through the front ranks, the bald biker yanked out a Maglite from his jean pocket and flipped it on and fired his AK-47 one handed.

Several of the charging gang went down when a round hit a knee or blew off part of a leg, but another two dozen ran towards them, the bullets seeming to have no effect on them at all. The men held clubs, baseball bats and hatchets.

Kwame shouted, "Fall back!" His magazine empty, he ejected it and let it drop to the floor and slapped another into place, all while he ran. Two bikers turned tail and ran with him The bald biker remained frozen in place. The two throwing up their dinner also never moved.

Kwame knew if he stayed to try and save them, he would be overrun. He heard the AK go silent and glanced behind him in time to see one man bury a hatchet in baldy's skull, nearly splitting it in two, while another crushed a biker's head with a swing worthy of Babe Ruth. They bore the third biker to the ground and Kwame lost sight of him beneath a flurry of flying fists and weapons.

Kwame skidded to a stop, yanked a grenade from his belt, pulled the pin and tossed it into the middle of the mob. He turned and ran and covered his ears. When the grenade exploded in the confined space the sound was deafening. After the dust settled he had reduced their numbers by a third. The rest kept coming. He paused long enough to pick off several more attackers, aiming low at legs and knees, before taking off at a full sprint. He passed the first biker who ran with a small keychain flashlight to see the way. He was almost to the next biker when the man fell in front of him. Kwame leaped over the man and was nearly clear when the biker reached out and grabbed his ankle and yanked him to the ground.

"Don't leave us," the man cried.

Kwame kicked him hard in the face and the man let go of his ankle, but too late for him to make it to his feet before the crowd of men were on them. He bought a few seconds emptying the Colt into the heads of his closest attackers and made it to his knees when a man clipped him on the arm with a club and he lost his grip on his weapon. They were all making noises as if they were trying to talk but could not form any words. Up close the stench of decay nearly made him pass out.

Kwame knew he only had a few seconds left and yanked a flare gun from his belt and fired off a round down the tunnel to warn the others. He dropped the flare gun and pulled out the katana. He never trained with a sword but knew the sharp end did all the damage and managed to hack off several arms and one head before sheer numbers overwhelmed him. He screamed when one of the men removed his left foot with a blow from his hatchet, cutting all the way through the bone at the ankle. Others hit him with their fists or with their weapons and the last thing he saw before death claimed him was the logo of a Louisville Slugger bat covered in blood—with his blood.

*****

"Holy crap, what they hell are they and when was the last time they had a bath?"

A group of men, smelling like a dead animal decaying on the side of the highway on a bright sunny day, were beating and hacking three men to death. One of the victims wore the black coveralls of the mercs and I knew Kwame wouldn't be making it out.

It didn't take them long to clue in to our presence and they began to run down the tunnel towards us. Stiles and I unloaded on them with the machine guns, but hitting them in the body didn't even slow them down. Impervious to bullets? Pale skin? Black eyes? Ugh. Undead.

I yelled, "Winston, bring the fire."

Winston stepped in front of us, cranked open the propane tank and squeezed the two triggers. Flame filled the width of the tunnel and consumed the group of undead, their bodies going up like a field party bonfire.

I turned to the people behind me. "Forget the guns. Anyone with a sword or bladed weapon. That's how we bring them down."

When Winston eased up on the flame, only a handful of undead remained standing. Stiles, Ethan and Samantha charged the undead and made short work of them, slicing off their heads. I'd seen Samantha use her sword before, but she'd been practicing. Her moves were fluid, beautiful and deadly. Stiles and Ethan looked like they were chopping trees with axes compared to her. There were several other undead on the ground with missing body parts who were still moving, but were easily dispatched.

When they were all dead, again, I scouted out the rest of tunnel. I was forced to cover my nose with the sleeve of my jacket and breathe in only through my mouth. The tunnel ended with two metal doors leading to a large room. Thin mattresses and cots filled the space. I guessed this was where they bunked down until needed.

I re-joined my team. They were standing around the dead body of Kwame, now unrecognizable. The ferocity with which they attacked was almost out of this world.

"New katana?" I asked Samantha.

"Yes. It's a gift from the monks. It's special."

"I bet. Looks sharp enough." I turned to Stiles and Tank. "I'm sorry about your men. There were just too many of them. Stiles, I thought only Infernal Lords got another chance at life after they died. And then, only twelve at a time. What the hell was this?"

"I honestly don't know. I know Cy had been checking into necromancy but all he'd been doing is research. Someone's taken this well past the research stage."

Kurt snapped his fingers. "The bodies they tossed down the shaft. They must have been preserved somehow and they found a way to animate them."

Samantha said, "Moloch. When I worked in the office for my dad, I had plenty of time to read about this kind of thing. Back then I thought they were nuts. According to the Church, some demons possess the power to raise the dead. If they've found a way to bring back Moloch, he may be doing this. Considering all the paintings of Moloch in the main tunnel, I think it's likely."

Great. A demon.

"We need to help the other units. Double time, folks."

*****

We re-traced our steps and found the main tunnel still empty and the other side tunnel eerily quiet, with no sounds of fighting. This tunnel curved sharply to the left and out of view.

We made our way cautiously with Winston and me leading the way. He whispered, "Man, I used up a lot of the tank with them other undead. If we hit many more zombies, I'm gonna run out pretty quickly."

"Then you hold off unless it's absolutely necessary. And we don't know for sure they're zombies."

I felt my heart rate going at full speed. There's something about zombies that creep me out. I never watched the *Walking Dead* and can honestly say I've never seen any of the George Romero movies either. When you're dead, you're supposed to stay that way. Infernal Lords are different in that if someone didn't tell you they were returned from the dead, you would have no clue. Hell, I spent nights in bed with Elizabeth and she seemed like any other hot chick. But the ones we just fought, were nothing like Elizabeth.

I could see the end of the tunnel and on the floor by the far wall it appeared there was a hole in the ground. A single body was lying in front of it, wearing black combat coveralls of an Alpha Team member. There was no one else in the tunnel, all gone, except one.

"Stiles, Ethan and Winston, you're with me," I said. "The rest of you wait here."

When we got closer to the hole in the ground, the stench increased. I was close enough for a good look at the body to see there was something wrong about it.

"Winston, you go wide to the right. If anything pops out of that hole, you hit it with everything left in the tank. Ethan, you go wide to the left and try and find an angle to cover us. Stiles, you and I close the distance."

The merc and I eased closer to the body, taking baby steps, our weapons up and ready to go. We made it to the man on the ground and now knew why I thought he looked weird.

Blake was lying on his back with every inch of visible skin covered in blisters and boils. His face and hands were swollen in a way which made me think he'd been boiled from the inside out.

Stiles cursed a blue streak. "He looks like the victim of a chemical attack. I saw some of this when we were doing some black op work in Iraq when Saddam was still in power. He used gas against the Kurds and I ended up in a hospital where they brought a lot of the victims. But I don't smell any residual gas. We would smell something."

Demons. I pointed at the hole in the ground with my chin and he nodded in return. We carefully stepped over the body of the slain merc and approached the hole. About twenty feet in diameter it formed a rough circle. The stench flowed up and out of the shaft and I once again did all the breathing through my mouth. When I looked over the edge the hole dropped out of site, leaving me unable to see the bottom.

Stiles tapped my shoulder with his weapon and pointed at the ceiling and walls on the far side of the shaft. In the green of my night vision goggles, a dark colored liquid dripped from the ceiling and oozed down the walls. I pushed the night goggles onto the top of my head and removed the small flashlight from my pocket. When I shined it around, everything was covered in blood, with a little brain matter mixed in for added horror.

The first image which came to mind was of the Incredible Hulk grabbing people by the legs and then smashing them into the walls. I turned off the light and pulled my goggles down again.

"Do you think they're down there?" he asked.

"I don't see how they're not. If you want, I can toss down a rope and lower you down for a look."

"That's all right. I'm good."

We both knew the men were dead. We waved for everyone to move out. Once we got to the main entrance I did a quick head count. Of the thirty people who came down only twelve remained. One of the bikers ran to the elevator and pushed the up button, but nothing happened. The biker pushed the button several more times, his finger like a piston, but nothing happened. The elevator was turned off.

"Ah, man. We're going to die down here," he wailed.

Tank spun around and placed his shotgun against the man's chest. "I tell you what, Hank. You say another word and I think I'll shoot you myself. You hear me?"

"Anyone got any bars at all on their phone?" Linda asked.

No one did. "Then I think this is a pretty simple decision. We move forward. It's clear this is what Michael McCain wanted, to draw us, or at least, some of us, down here. Now that we are, I plan to put the son of a bitch in the ground."

"You know," I said, "that's my mother you're talking about."

"Oh. Sorry. I didn't mean it that way."

I slapped her on the butt. "No worries. Let's go mess with my brother.

CHAPTER THIRTY-SIX

Out of the five bikers left, three of them refused to move away from the elevator, no matter how many times Tank threatened to kill them. There were scarier things down here than Tank Bone. And I didn't blame them one bit and told Tank so.

Still didn't make him happy. He muttered, "Damn pussies" for like the tenth time since we left them behind. Evil Santa was not in a good mood. We walked in twos, Stiles and I in the front, followed by Linda and Winston, Samantha and Tank, Kurt and a biker named Tom with Ethan and a biker named Rupert bringing up the rear. Tank wore the night vision glasses which had belonged to Kwame, after he cleaned off all the gore. The ones who didn't bring a katana now also carried a baseball bat or hatchet.

We passed painting after painting of Moloch and I felt like they were watching us. Stupid, I know, but it bugged me. I stopped the group, went to Kurt and rummaged in the gear bag until I found the black paint. I shook the can a few times, removed the cap and turned the closest Moloch image into a man wearing a black hat, mustache and two large devil horns.

Before I finished, a huge bellow of something large and pissed off came from far down the tunnel. Everyone froze, including me.

"Think that was a coincidence?" Linda asked.

I shrugged and went to the painting on the opposite wall and spray painted the words, 'Your mamma' across his face. Once again, the bellow of something large and angry greeted my graffiti. "What the hell?"

Winston pointed to my handy work. "Moloch considered himself a God and forced people to worship him. These paintings may be a form of worship. Defiling them might be pissing him off."

"Well, screw him if he can't take a joke." I tossed Kurt the can of paint. "Kurt, spray something on the walls as we walk."

The tunnel began to slope down for a bit and then it evened out. We caught a whiff of the undead a few minutes before we met them. I saw a large room up ahead with a row of the undead blocking our path. They didn't charge this time, but waited. They carried the same weapons as the other group and smelled just as bad.

Behind them my night goggles picked up a large light signature which flickered. I pressed a button to switch my goggles to thermal. The undead radiated no heat, but behind them the flickering light revealed a large fire.

When we got about forty yards out, the undead backed up and retreated into the room as if inviting us to join them. I scanned the floor and ceiling, looking for some type of hidden traps, but I didn't detect any. Whatever Mikey planned was now in the room ahead of us.

Stiles asked, "How do you want to handle this, McCain?"

"Pretty standard: we hit the room, kill anything that moves. Anything but Mikey. He's mine. I have a little surprise for my brother."

He wanted to ask more, but didn't. He stretched his neck from side to side, working out the kinks. "Then let's do this."

I turned and looked at Linda and wondered what was going through her mind. Did she regret coming down here with me? Maybe she wished she'd never heard the name, 'McCain'.

She caught my gaze and said, "Come on, Vic. Get moving. *Rudolph* is on tonight and I haven't missed it since I was a little girl. We need to wrap this up."

Or not. The comment made me really laugh out loud. I might die in the next few minutes, but at least I would die with friends. I let the MP5 dangle from the strap around my neck and made sure two grenades were in each of my coat pockets.

From somewhere in the room my brother shouted, "She's right, Vic. I've been waiting. Come on in and join me."

I glanced around at everyone else. "Shall we?"

I stepped to the edge of the room and viewed a scene which might have been straight out of Dante's *Inferno*. The room was about a hundred feet across and wide. The ceiling rose almost five stories high. A large pit in the middle of the floor held a roaring fire. With plenty of light, I pulled the night vision goggles off and let them hang around my neck.

On the far wall, Mikey and his crew had built a large throne and in the glow of the fire, I saw it was made of brass. On the throne sat a man who was at least seven feet tall and might weigh more than four hundred pounds, and all of it looked like muscle. Well, he was mostly a man. All but his head, which looked like the head of a Texas Longhorn. His eyes were larger than the average human's and dark red.

I got the same weird feeling looking at him as I did when I saw one of the Watchers. The creature sitting on the throne was another fallen angel. Lovely. But he was not possessing someone else's body to move around—like one of the Watchers—this guy sat on the thrown in his own body, and I knew his name. After all, I'd spray painted his picture a few minutes before. Moloch. In one hand he held a long club. His nails were the type to make a grizzly bear jealous.

Mikey stood next to the throne, a huge Cheshire cat grin splitting his face. He wore some type of ceremonial garb decked out all in red with a long flowing red cassock and vestments covered in symbols I didn't recognize, but pentagrams figured prominently. On his head sat a towering hat similar to the one the Pope wears and around his neck was a bright gold crucifix, hanging in an upside down position. He held a long staff with the emblem of the sun adorning the top.

On both sides of the pit stood a group of undead, around twenty each. And in the middle of each group huddled three women, each of them naked and covered in dirt and filth. I did a quick scan and didn't see anyone who resembled Ruth Anne.

Between us and them stood the undead welcome committee who once stood across the entrance, ten all told.

From behind me I heard Linda let out a low moan. "Victor, the fire."

I concentrated on the flames and felt my anger explode. The charred remains of several bodies littered the pit. They'd been sacrificing people to the demon Moloch and I remembered Winston saying they did so with the sacrifice still being alive. I met my brother's gaze and he nodded slowly.

"Where's Ruth Anne, you prick?" Kurt screamed the question.

"Oh, your lady love? Don't worry, Kurt. We were saving her for last."

Mikey struck his staff on the ground three times and from behind the throne two of the undead appeared. Between the two of them they held Ruth Anne up by her arms. She was naked and her body had been painted red and covered in the same symbols which adorned Mikey's cassock. Her eyes rolled back in her head, either from shock or drugs, but she was alive.

Stiles stood next to me and leaned in close and I said in a whisper, "The girl is one of us. On my mark, you shoot the guy on the right. I'll go for the one on the left."

"Done."

"Hey, Mikey, what's with all the undead? Can't find any real friends so you gotta make your own?"

"Do you like them? Seeing how God made man in his image, I thought I'd give it a try. I learned about Ives and all the bodies dumped down here and I figured why not? Imagine my surprise when I found out Ives and company had been excavating down here. Old man Ives wanted to compete in the limestone business but gave it up after a few years."

I gestured at Moloch. "And big, tall and ugly here, you found him down here, too?"

"Nah, I found a group of worshipers who were trying to bring the big fella back to power and I merely helped out. Do you know how many people I had to kill to make this happen? Hundreds and hundreds. We built the throne, decorated the place in paintings of him and then started the sacrifices. With a little help from the Lord of Light, here he is. For every sacrifice we make, he raises an undead to do my bidding. And when we are ready, I'll set him and my followers loose on the world. Can you imagine? Zombies in the streets? A new god reborn? How cool is that?"

"Mikey, Moloch is not a god, only another fallen angel who got his ass whipped and tossed to the curb."

Moloch stood and I swear I could see smoke coming from his nose. Mikey held out his staff in front of the fallen angel. "Calm down there, Moloch. He's only trying to get a rise out of you."

"Not a rise, Moloch. I'm going to rip out your heart and throw it on the fire myself. Promise."

The fallen angel roared and his eyes darkened, the red going near crimson. Nothing like pissing off one of the Divine. I returned my attention to my brother and then started to laugh. I don't know what he expected, but laughter was clearly not it. The smile vanished and even from this distance, I noticed his cheeks turning bright red.

"You think this is funny, brother?" he snarled.

"Mikey, you look like a kid dressed up for Halloween trick or treating wearing some of his mom's old dresses. Man, you look like a dork, know what I mean? Hell, that hat is almost as big as you are."

"Don't you dare talk to me like that, do you hear me?" Spit flew from his mouth when he yelled.

"Or you'll do what? Make me stop? Mikey, you've always been a little shit and you're still a little shit. I can't even believe you're a McCain. When I leave here, I'm going to ask mom to tell the truth. You had to be adopted. There's nothing of mom or dad in you. Nothing. And that's what you are, Mikey, nothing."

Mikey might have warned Moloch about me only trying to yank his chain, but seemed incapable of heeding his own words. Mikey whirled around and screamed at Moloch, "Kill them! Kill them all!"

"Now?" Stiles asked.

"Now."

We raised our weapons at the same time and fired. The shot wasn't an easy one, considering the distance and the flames, but the heads of the two undead holding up Ruth Anne exploded and the three of them dropped to the ground. And then all hell broke loose.

The undead welcoming committee charged and the battle was on. Stiles and I quickly shot three each, with Ethan and Linda tapping the other four.

We split into two groups, half going right and the rest of us left. The flamethrower would have made quick work of most of the undead but with the women mixed among them, Winston didn't dare pull the trigger. Time for old fashioned methods.

One of the larger undead, dressed in hospital scrubs and with a dark black beard, swung a large hatchet in an overhead bid to split my skull. I stepped to the side and felt the blade whistle by my ear and brought my own bat around in a double handed swing which hit the mark. When we were kids we used to take the fall pumpkins in the backyard and smash them with bats. This felt the same way. I caved in the back of the man's head with a wet thud and he went down.

Others were engaged in their own battles. Moloch strode through the fire like I would a pool of water on a collision course to engage me. Tank Bone stepped between us and unloaded the shotgun into Moloch's face. The demon's head snapped back with each impact, but suffered no damage. With another roar, the fallen angel swung his club and caught Tank in the side, knocking Evil Santa a good ten feet in the air before he landed in a heap.

Mikey laughed. "You can't hurt him with normal weapons. Time to die, Mr. Bond."

Linda shot another half dozen undead in the head while watching my back. Kurt managed to take out two while he zigged and zagged between several others as he made it to Ruth Anne's side. Two of the undead snagged one of the bikers, a small diminutive man, and threw him screaming into the fire pit.

I caught a glimpse of Mikey as he ran behind the throne and started after him when I heard Samantha shout, "Moloch!"

Samantha stood in a circle of dead bodies, her clothes and katana covered in blood. She had taken out a good ten undead all on her own. The fallen angel stopped and faced her.

"That's right. Think you can do better than these guys?" She pointed to the undead at her feet with her sword. "I bet you're easier to kill than they were."

Moloch roared and raised his club high and charged. Samantha, with her red hair glowing in the firelight, stood straight and tall, her sword held loosely at her side, and waited for the blow.

Moloch raised the club high over his head and brought it down in what would be a crushing blow. I felt my heart catch and shouted, "No!"

But it was too late.

CHAPTER THIRTY-SEVEN

Moloch's club smashed the ground hard enough to make a small crater in the limestone, spider web cracks radiating out in all directions. But he missed Samantha. She waited until Moloch committed to his attack, then tumbled towards the massive fallen angel and behind him. In one fluid motion she sliced her katana across the demon's hamstring.

This time Moloch roared, but with pain. His leg began to crumple and he tried to hit Samantha with a backhand swipe with the club. Again, she tumbled under the blow, her sword slicing the other hamstring, bringing Moloch to his knees.

She rose and pivoted with a blow to take off his head. Only this time, she didn't count on the speed of the demon and he grabbed her wrist and twisted. I heard her wrist snap and she dropped the katana. Samantha gritted her teeth, but didn't cry out and started to pound him with her hand.

Moloch laughed and twisted harder. Well, he laughed until I hurled myself into him. I'm not a small guy but tackling the fallen angel felt like I'd run into a brick wall. The two of us went over in a heap and he let go of Samantha. I tried to roll away but he yanked me to him and got a hand around my throat. He pulled my face close to his and started to squeeze. I felt my skin begin to blister at his touch and I tried gouging his eyes to make him let go, but it didn't affect him.

He sat on my chest and continued to squeeze. I knew I was going to die, right then and there, with a ticked off demon choking the life out of me. I tried to use my lower body to flip him off, but it didn't work. Much like when I held Black Ice down with my body, Moloch did the same to me.

He sat on my chest and my eyesight blurred and I began to lose consciousness when I heard someone say, "Get off my boyfriend."

Linda drove Samantha's Katana through the back of Moloch's skull and out the other side, the blade tip stopping a few inches short of my nose. Lucky, that.

The demon's body tensed and then the grip on my throat loosened and he fell on top of me. With every bit of energy I had left in my body, I shoved him off me and gasped for air. My neck throbbed with pain and a light touch of my fingers told me the skin had blistered.

I staggered to my feet with Linda's help and we went to Samantha. She sat with her wrist cradled in her other hand and we helped her up.

"I'm okay," she said. "Don't worry about me. Finish this."

She nodded with her chin towards Mikey. He stood next to the throne, in shock. "No. That can't happen. You can't hurt him with normal weapons. Only..." His eyes went wide. "The monks."

Samantha gave Mikey her own Cheshire cat grin. "That's right, Mikey. The monks. They made a special katana for me, out of silver. Then they blessed it. It's a holy weapon. Perfect for fighting things from Hell. Perfect for you."

"You don't say?" I asked. I went to the demon, placed my boot against the skull and yanked out Samantha's sword. I started around the fire pit after Mikey and he turned to run away but skidded to a stop when Winston advanced from behind the throne with the flamethrower pointed in his direction.

He turned to run in the other direction, but froze when he saw Kurt had pointed a large hose at him which ran to a canister under his arm. LN in bold letters were printed on the side of the canister.

"Fire and ice, Mikey. Fire and ice." I said. "In case you don't know what LN is, that's liquid nitrogen. Flash freezes human skin on contact. Take another step and you'll experience one or the other."

The battle was over. Stiles and Ethan had dispatched the last of the undead and were tending to Tank. I could see the big man was at least breathing. The remaining biker leaned with his back to the wall and was lighting a cigarette with hands which shook so badly he almost didn't get it lit.

"Victor, please, you can't send me back to Hell. I beg you. I'll do anything you say. I swear it."

I went to Kurt and traded him the holy katana for the tank and hose. I glanced down at Ruth Anne and said a quick prayer that she was still alive.

"Here's the deal, Mikey. I don't want to kill you. I really don't.

If I do, then all I get for my efforts is another Infernal Lord to kill. No, I don't want to kill you, bro."

Mikey placed a hand over his heart. "Thank you, Victor. Bless you."

"Oh, don't thank me yet."

I turned the nozzle and liquid nitrogen sprayed from the hose, covering Mikey from the waist down. When the liquid nitrogen hit his skin it began to freeze solid. A vapor cloud formed around him and Winston moved out of the way.

Mikey started yelling, "No, no, no." Over and over. My brother resembled a popsicle left in the freezer for too long, with frost covering a large portion of his body. He stared at me in horror with the dawning realization of what I had planned.

I turned off the flow of liquid and sat the canister down. I stretched out my hand for the Katana, but Kurt wouldn't give it to me.

"No way, Vic. I want to do this."

Kurt advanced on Mikey and stood there staring at him. I thought he would say something, but didn't. He swung the katana hitting Mikey in the hip. From his midsection down, Mikey blew apart in tiny fragments, with his torso landing on the ground.

A normal human being would be dead already. Mikey, being an Infernal Lord, still lived. Given enough time, he would regenerate the missing body parts. I didn't plan to give him the time.

Mikey tried to drag himself away with his arms. This time I insisted Kurt give me the katana. With two quick strokes, I separated both arms at the shoulder. Mikey howled in rage.

I emptied out the duffel of the spare canister and some other gear, got the roll of duct tape and tore off a piece. Then I placed it across Mikey's mouth to shut him up.

I placed Mikey, what was left of him, into the duffel and zipped it up. The two mercs managed to help Tank to his feet, no easy task in its own right, and they hobbled with him in our direction. Kurt knelt next to Ruth Anne and held her tight.

"She's been drugged," the hacker said. "But I think she's okay."

The other women had never moved. Also drugged. Samantha and Linda went to each one to check on them. Winston pointed to behind the throne. "There's another elevator behind here and it's working. We can take it up."

"Liquid nitrogen? Whose idea was that?" Stiles asked.

Winston raised his hand. "My uncle and I got to talking one

night about our favorite supervillains and which of their weapons would work in the real world. Unc likes Mr. Freeze, the one played by Arnold Schwarzenegger and we got to talking about all you need is a canister of liquid nitrogen and a hose. It's self-pressurizing so all you have to do is point and spray."

"What are you going to do with your brother?"

"Not sure yet, but I've got some ideas."

"As long as you put him where he can never be found, you're good."

"Count on it."

*****

Several hours after the final battle, all the dead were thrown into the fire pit including Moloch and Mikey's arms. Black smoke rose to the ceiling and out ventilation shafts to God knows where. With the help of the three chicken bikers, we transported all the women to the surface and into the distillery. With the secret door closed, the security tapes erased and all our cars moved out, Stiles made an anonymous call to the authorities and in minutes the place was crawling with cops.

We watched it all go down from an office building across the street where the other elevator emptied out. This one was owned by Mikey but never furnished.

Tank stood next to me at the window and watched another girl being loaded into an ambulance. "We saw some weird shit tonight, McCain. And I'm not going to lie, I was one scared son of a bitch. But we did some good, too, didn't we?"

"Yeah, Tank. We did some good. And thanks."

"For what?"

"For stepping between me and a demon. You never even hesitated. That says something about you and I appreciate it."

He offered me a hand and I took it. "Seeing as how I think I've got a couple of broken ribs, I think I need to find a hospital. And I've got to decide what to tell all the families who won't have guys coming home tonight."

"You'll think of something. You're Tank Bone."

"Don't forget it, either." Before walking out the door, he said, "If you ever need more help, you call me."

I nodded and he left. Stiles and Ethan offered their own goodbyes. "I'll tell you one thing, McCain, you sure make life interesting."

"No, it's not. What about the men you lost? Any families?"

"Nah, all single. Dedicated to the life of a mercenary. The company carries life insurance on each of them. We'll come up with a story about dying on a black op mission in some backwater country and pay out to whomever they have listed. Happens in our line of work."

"Mine, too. Thanks for coming out. You didn't have to and I won't forget it."

They left and only Linda and Samantha remained. I'd sent Winston to take Kurt and Ruth Anne home and to pick up something we needed to finish up Mikey.

I knew her wrist was incredibly painful, but she didn't complain. Like my neck, in addition to the broken bone her skin suffered second degree like burns. She'd refused my efforts for her to leave with Winston and go to the hospital. Instead, she spent her time watching the duffel bag. From time to time Mikey would thrash about and then he'd lay still. There was no chance of him suffocating, since Infernal Lords didn't need air, but she wanted to make sure he didn't go anywhere.

Linda replaced Tank and stood with me at the window. I slipped an arm around her waist and held her close. She rested her head on my shoulder then looked at my neck.

"That has to hurt."

"As long as I don't try and turn my head, it's not bad. Listen, thanks for saving my life down there. I'd be in a lot worse shape if you hadn't skewered Moloch like a shish kabob. And sorry you missed *Rudolph*."

"No worries. I DVRed it "

She kissed me and it felt fantastic. "You know, down there, when you killed Moloch, you said, 'Get off my boyfriend.' Does that mean you're keeping me around?"

"Yes, it does. You're a lot more fun than the last guy I dated. He liked to take walks on the beach and drink Pina Coladas."

"No battling zombies and killing demons?"

"Not even once."

"And what if it costs you your career?"

She didn't respond right way. She half-smiled and said, "Lord's will be done. Right?"

"You got it sister."

A half hour later Winston was back and he pushed a dolly with a metal foot locker. I picked up the duffel and dropped Mikey-boy inside and closed the lid.

Samantha asked, "What now?"

"Now, Winston, Linda and I are going to his uncle's house and we're going to weld this thing shut. But first, we are dropping you off at the hospital. That wrist needs to be set and the burns attended to."

"And after that, what do you plan to do with Mikey?"

I told her and she laughed. "You are one sick puppy, do you know that?"

"Yes. Yes I am."

Epilogue

"Damn it, Victor, watch your step."

I'd never been on a boat on the Ohio River, let alone a barge. Lights from the construction crew lit up the water and I gazed across at the towers being constructed for a new East End bridge.

I pulled the dolly behind me as I hauled the metal foot locker onto the barge. Dick Roberts and I had known each other since grade school when I made sure the bullies left him alone. We were both at the University of Kentucky at the same time where he majored in civil engineering and I in history. Now he worked for one of the companies building the two new bridges in Louisville: one downtown and one in the Eastern part of the county. I called him for a favor and he reluctantly agreed to help me.

"Sorry, Dick. I don't spend much time on boats."

It was three a.m. and we were the only ones on the barge. The next crew came on at six a.m. and Dick was nervous someone would see us.

"You swear to me there's nothing in this box that will get me in trouble? I tell you, Vic, if it was anyone else, the answer would have been a quick no."

"Look, Dick, the box is full of things U of K. Kind of like the guy who buried a UK shirt when they built the Yum Center."

The Yum Center is where the University of Louisville plays all their college basketball games. I'd told Dick I wanted to do the same thing here and slipped him a thousand dollars to let me do it. And the box was filled with all things UK. Mikey graduated from there four years before I did.

"Fine, I want this over with. Right here is the latest pylon. They poured the footer earlier tonight and they'll finished it in the morning."

He grabbed one end of the box and I the other and we lifted it and tossed it over the edge. I heard a wet plop. By the time the next day was over, Mikey would be buried under tons of concrete in a box with no room to regenerate his limbs. Mikey would stay there until someone tore down the bridge and let him out. And I now had one less Infernal Lord who needed killing.

We made our way off the barge and I handed Dick the hard hat he made me wear while on the site. We shook hands and that was all she wrote. I got into my car and drove back to River Road and to the Riverside Inn.

Inside I joined Tank Bone, Linda and Winston. The four of us would take turns watching the pylon construction through a telescope until the concrete was poured. I wasn't taking any chances.

Tank went to the bar and fixed me a double Fireball Whiskey. I thanked him and downed a large portion of the drink in one pull.

"My thanks."

"No problem. What's next for you, McCain?"

"Man, I think I need a vacation. My old Army unit is having a reunion after the holidays in Gulf Shores, Alabama and I think I'll join them."

Evil Santa laughed. "You? On vacation? I don't see it."

"Everyone needs some down time," I shrugged. "What's the worst that can happen?"

Acknowledgements

Writing a successful series is a collaborative effort. Thanks to my personal Scooby-gang: Wendell Farrar, Donna Krieg Monroe, Dean Monroe, Brad Stiles, and Tom McNeil. And, of course, Bob Fulks, without whom this book would never have been written.

Thanks to Starbucks Store # 2464 in Prospect, Kentucky who changed buildings to try and lose me, but I keep showing up.

Thanks to my wife, Karin, who did the major edits on this novel. She loves my writing but asks me constantly why my grammar can't be as polished as Tom Wallace. Who can?

Cover artist Karri Klawiter sees to it when people judge my book by its cover, they love it..

Thanks to all the wonderful authors and publishers I've gotten to know over the past three years. Your support is invaluable.

And as always, thank you, Dear Reader, for spreading the word about Victor McCain. None of this would be possible without you. Thank you!

About the Author

Tony Acree is an award winning publisher and the author of the Amazon bestselling novels, *The Hand of God*, *The Watchers,* and *The Speaker*. He lives in Goshen, Kentucky, with his wife and twin daughters. Visit his website at Tonyacree.com. You can find him on Twitter and Facebook. Email him at Tonyacree@gmail.com

And In 2016
Another Victor McCain Thriller:

The Unit

CPSIA information can be obtained
at www.ICGtesting.com
Printed in the USA
FFHW01n0609090818
47667593-51281FF